"Two years ago Sheriff Moreno called."

Ian's gaze was fixed on the wall behind her left ear. As if he was there, but wasn't there. He continued, "Asked if I'd noticed Daisy was getting forgetful. He'd found her car, still idling, stuck in a desert wash ten miles outside of town." He shifted, cleared his throat. "I hadn't seen her for a while. I should have figured it out, not Vince."

A twinge of remorse nagged at her. She'd done this. She'd made this guy worry more than he already did. He didn't deserve it, any more than she did.

But the touchy-feely confidences had to stop. Because if they didn't, then she'd have to reciprocate, tell him something deep, dark, revealing. And if she started, where would she end?

"Okay, I get the gist. Prodigal son is racked with guilt, throws away a promising career to care for his mother. Very commendable. More than I'd do in the same situation."

"I don't want sympathy. You asked what happened—I told you."

"Good. I'm not the sympathetic type."

He crossed his arms. "That's probably what makes you so successful, Ms. Davis. Personally, I'd hate to make a living off other people's misfortunes."

"Yeah? Well, I didn't create the system. I'm just damn good at what I do."

Dear Reader,

The imagination is a weird and wonderful thing. Ian and Vi's story began with a small article I read in a newsmagazine about Alzheimer's service dogs. Soon my daydreams produced Annabelle, a dedicated, loving service dog. My mind wouldn't rest until I gave Annabelle a challenging assignment and a family to go with it.

Annabelle's people aren't perfect. Ian, Vi and Daisy struggle and make mistakes. They laugh, they cry, they love. They are the family of my nightmares or my fondest dreams, depending on the day.

I feel very fortunate to share their story with you, especially as my first Harlequin Superromance novel. *The Road to Echo Point* will always have a special place in my heart. I hope it touches your heart, as well.

Yours truly,

Carrie Weaver

P.S. Echo Point exists only in my mind. Please excuse any liberties I took with the geography of Arizona and the Superstition Mountains.

The Road to Echo Point
Carrie Weaver

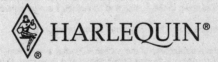

HARLEQUIN®

TORONTO • NEW YORK • LONDON
AMSTERDAM • PARIS • SYDNEY • HAMBURG
STOCKHOLM • ATHENS • TOKYO • MILAN • MADRID
PRAGUE • WARSAW • BUDAPEST • AUCKLAND

ISBN 0-373-71173-5

THE ROAD TO ECHO POINT

Visit us at www.eHarlequin.com

Printed in U.S.A.

ACKNOWLEDGMENT:

I would like to thank Pat Putnam
of Okada Specialty Guide Dogs for speaking with me
about Alzheimer's service dogs. Pat was gracious in sharing
her extensive knowledge and enthusiasm with me.

For more information on Alzheimer's service dogs:
Okada Specialty Guide Dogs
7509 E. Saviors Path
Floral City, FL 34436
www.okadadogs.com

DEDICATION:

For Luke and Michael, who have always believed
in my dreams. I love you bunches.

PROLOGUE

IT WAS A SHOCK, the effect of gravel on rubber. One minute tires gripped the road, bouncing over raised ribs of clay, the next they slid sideways.

Dust billowed, Vi's pulse pounded, short puffs of air kept her going. It was like a scene investigation gone bad. The result of excessive speed on a dirt road. What a laugh. Except it was anything but funny.

She made it around the corner, somehow keeping the car on the road.

No trees. Thank God.

Her pulse rate dropped, her breathing eased. The company car wouldn't end up a twisted wreck, along with her career.

"Good going, Davis," she muttered under her breath. Instinct had her foot pumping the brake. The car started to obey.

A brown blur appeared near her right front fender.

The sound was sickening. It was dense and dull, the thud of live flesh meeting unforgiving metal.

Her ankle ached as she jammed on the brake. The car listed to a stop.

More dust. Everywhere tan plumes of the stuff rose around the car, like a dirty version of dry ice.

That was when the shaking started, from the throb

in her ankle, snaking its way up her thighs. In seconds, her hands contracted on the steering wheel.

What had she done?

She had to get out. Had to go look.

Somehow Vi managed to make her hands cooperate and grasp the door handle. Her knees buckled as she got out.

This wasn't like her. Not anymore. She was strong and in charge. But she had never been on the wrong side of a loaded shotgun, until today.

She hadn't believed old Mr. Johnson would really shoot her. But one niggling doubt was enough to make her relive another place and time. A time when the threat was more real, though fists were the weapon of choice. A time when safety was a gift to be treasured. And survival was the name of the game.

Mr. Johnson and his rusty old shotgun had been enough to rattle her, big time. Enough to send her speeding down a dirt road, trying to outrun her past.

And now this.

Grasping the door for support, she squinted to block out the late afternoon rays. She didn't see anything unusual past the expanse of white hood. Nothing.

Her chest stung as she sucked in more air. She willed the trembling to stop.

One step at a time. That's all it would take. Like one day at a time.

How ironic that the twelve-step mantra came back to haunt her now. Wouldn't her dad be proud? The way he was still able to control her life, so many years and miles away.

Anger stiffened her spine. She'd use it, just like so

many times before. Just like when she'd left home and never looked back.

Placing one foot in front of the other, Vi refused to lean on the car. She didn't need to lean on anything or anyone.

She rounded the fender and stared at the lump. It was bad. Brown eyes glazed in pain, begging her, blaming her.

But it wasn't as bad as it could have been. It could have been the first catastrophic injury claim she'd handled all over again. Where a toddler darted out in front of a car and ended up a quadriplegic.

Vi shook her head to erase the images of the file photographs she carried around in her head. She was on edge and she knew it. Forcing herself to take a deep breath, she assessed the situation.

"Only a dog," she whispered. But she couldn't dismiss it that easily.

She'd had a dog once. Chubby and playful and a bundle of energy. Until *he* came home…

This wounded animal whined, snapping her back to the here and now. She crouched next to it. Her hand shook as she reached out to stroke the silky head. The other one had been beyond her help…maybe this one would be different.

Her hand hovered just inches away from the fur. Her fingers itched to caress, to comfort.

But the memories wouldn't let her. She tried to push them away, back to that little corner of her mind where the unspeakable stuff lived.

The animal whimpered. She let her fingertips graze its forehead. The whimpers stopped, the grip on her stomach relaxed.

Blinking away tears, she whispered, "Sorry, fella."

A loud crash of underbrush came from the opposite side of the road. Her heart hammered. Stupid, stupid Vi. She'd let down her guard. But not for long.

She turned to face the loud, crashing beast.

A man broke through the scrub brush, legs pumping, Arizona Cardinals football shirt stretched tight across his heaving chest. Meaty arms swung in time with his sprint. And his eyes. There was a desperation to him—a man with nothing left to lose.

She'd seen that look. So many years ago, right before—

"What the hell have you done?"

Run.

Vi turned toward the dog, hesitated. The animal struggled to its feet. Three legs supported it. This dog would live, unlike the one in her memory. The one her father had killed in a fit of rage.

Stones skittered behind her.

Vi spun around. The man was almost on her.

Instinct had her muscles moving before any conscious thought. Blood hummed in her ears as she jumped to her feet. Her pumps slid on the gravel for a terrifying second before she dug in her toes for traction. Panic propelled her toward the car.

Door locks, ignition, reverse, gas. This time, she used the gravel to her advantage, sliding into a tight U-turn.

A look in the rearview mirror didn't show her a thing. Just a big cloud of dust and her wide brown eyes, pupils the size of nickels.

CHAPTER ONE

"YOU'VE GOT TO BE KIDDING," Vi sputtered.

Surely the man wasn't serious? He looked more like a cowboy than an officer of the court. All western, what she could see of him, from the cotton shirt with the mother-of-pearl snaps to the bola tie at his scrawny, weathered neck.

Trying to regain her composure, Vi glanced around the Echo Point courtroom. The imitation-wood paneled walls were decorated with the usual framed copies of the Arizona and U.S. constitutions. Old black-and-white photos of copper mines and cattle ranches reflected the history of the small town.

Scattered through the photos were color lithographs of dogs. Sporting dogs. Dogs with limp birds in their mouths, dogs pointing at unseen prey. And one color, eight-by-ten of a muscular yellow dog at the side of a man clutching a rifle. Thick black plastic framed the man's glasses, a turquoise '68 Ford Camper Special stood proudly in the background. All clues that this was one of Judge Tanner's favorite photos from his younger days.

Vi swallowed the lump in her throat. She'd heard horror stories about skewed rural justice.

Judge Tanner looked over the rims of his reading glasses. "I don't kid when it comes to adjudicating a case. Just because my robe's at the cleaners, doesn't mean this is a bunch of funny business. I take my rulings very seriously. Says here, you left the scene of an accident. Hit-'n-run.''

"I didn't mean to imply I take the proceedings lightly. It's just that…well, I *did* stop."

"You didn't stay to render aid or give insurance information. Hit-and-run. I can revoke your license."

Vi bit her lip before a succinct curse could slip out. He had every right, and she had nobody to blame but herself. A hit-and-run violation, combined with a few past speeding infractions, could mean a suspended license.

Dread turned her into a one-woman perspiration factory. The lining of her blazer stuck to her back, moisture trickled in places she'd rather not think about.

She gulped. "I could lose my job…."

"Should have thought of that before."

"I wasn't thinking—"

"No. You weren't. You weren't considering that a child could just as easily have been in that road."

The thought of maiming a child scared her as much now as at the scene. Maybe more. "I didn't mean to hurt anyone. It was an accident. Just a dog…"

Vi glanced at the photos on the wall. "That didn't come out the way I meant it."

"I certainly hope not."

Stepping closer, she murmured, "I—I'm not sure what happened to me. I've been under a lot of stress, my appointment was, uh, unusual. And when the guy with the dog charged at me, I guess I snapped."

That was as much of the truth as she intended to reveal. There was no way she would describe the flashback, or the man she'd really thought was charging at her. The judge would have her in a straitjacket and *pronto.*

"I admit I made a mistake. I take full responsibility. The dog is recovering. I've offered to pay the vet bill…make things right."

The judge addressed the dog's owner, slumped in the front row. "Ian, will paying the vet bill make things right?"

"No. Not even close."

Vi could feel her cheeks flush. "That's not being reasonable."

"*Life* isn't reasonable," the man named Ian commented.

She turned to get a better look at him. What she saw confused her. He could have been a WWF wrestler on a downhill slide. Stubble covered his chin, dark circles ringed his eyes. Exhaustion was etched in the lines around his mouth. And yet, the judge seemed to value his opinion. Maybe her knee-jerk reaction on that dirt road had been rash, but the man still intended to ruin her life.

She swiped her tongue across her dry, cracked lips. "Look, I'm sorry. Really, really sorry. But you can't hold me responsible for the fact that the dog wasn't leashed. And you've got to understand. I was afraid for my life."

Judge Tanner leaned forward. "A. There's no leash law in the county area outside Echo Point. B. It's your responsibility as a driver to be prepared for the unexpected. C. While Arizona is a comparative negligence state, that applies only to civil litigation, not criminal. You can't parcel out the blame. And finally D. Ian wouldn't hurt a woman.''

Vi gulped. The judge might not look like the sharpest knife in the drawer, but he apparently was no slouch in the law department. Appealing to his sympathy was her best bet. ''I didn't know that…um…Ian was harmless. He *looked* dangerous. Put yourself in my place. A woman, alone, out in the middle of nowhere…suddenly a large, angry man comes running at me, yelling.''

The judge opened a slim manila folder and adjusted his glasses. ''Ah, yes. Claims Manager it says here. Don't imagine you intimidate too easily. Tell me about this 'unusual' appointment of yours. Who'd you meet? For what purpose?''

He was right. She normally *didn't* intimidate easily. At least not anymore. She prayed that it had been the unique set of circumstances and not an indication she was losing all the ground she'd gained in the past ten years. She couldn't go back to being that scared girl who jumped at her own shadow. The girl who thought black eyes and bruises were an everyday event. That all daddies drank themselves into a rage.

Drawing on her strength, her training, she tried to appeal to the judge's professionalism. ''Sir, I drove up from Phoenix to settle an auto injury claim with an elderly gentleman named Bob Johnson. He's going in for surgery next week, and we wanted to get his accident claim settled first.'' She leaned forward. ''As I'm sure you are aware, if he dies before settling his claim, his relatives will no longer be entitled to compensation for pain and suffering.''

''So, out of the goodness of your heart, you came

all the way up here to make sure old Bob's grand-children get a chunk of change, even if he croaks on the operating table?''

"Well, yes, in a manner of speaking.''

It sounded so cold. In her circle, it was considered more a mission of mercy. Besides, she *liked* old Mr. Johnson. That's why she'd hung on to his file after her promotion from adjuster to unit supervisor.

"I'm surprised old Bob didn't fill your behind full of buckshot," the judge said.

"But he did, I mean, he tried. He chased me off with a rusty old rifle. The stuff sprayed all over the tree next to me. So, you see, I was rattled.''

A smile twitched at the corners of the old man's thin lips, then vanished. "Be that as it may, it's not an excuse for making a poor decision. Since you see the results of accidents every day, I'm sure you can understand how serious this is.''

"Yes, sir. But—''

"With your speeding tickets and this latest stunt, you deserve to lose your license....'' The judge brought up his reading glasses, glancing through a thin file. "Violet.''

Violet. The little girl cowering in a corner, trying to make herself disappear.

Another trip down memory lane. It was almost as bad as going home, something she never intended to do again.

"Please, call me Vi.''

"Well, Vi, we have a decision here...''

"I'd appreciate any leeway you could give...sir.''

Judge Tanner leaned back in his leather chair and steepled his hands. "Maybe we can find a solution.

Hit-and-run means you lose your license. But, there could be another way.''

"Speed too fast for conditions,'' she supplied. A mere point or two on her license. Her insurance rates would skyrocket, but she'd save her job.

The judge's eyes narrowed. "I don't need you to tell me how to do my job. From the looks of your traffic violations, you always drive with your foot in the carburetor. Seems to me you could use some cooling off time. I'll give you a break. Community service, restitution.''

Relief washed over her. A couple weekends at the local soup kitchen, maybe picking up trash in the town square. How bad could it be?

"Yes, community service. I'd appreciate the second chance, sir.''

She ignored the perspiration pooling at the waistband of her skirt. "I do feel bad about Mr....ah, about his dog.'' She gestured vaguely in the madman's direction. "I'd be happy to replace it for him.''

"So ruled. Community service, replacement of the dog.'' The gavel echoed through the small courtroom. "I'll give you a day to collect your things and move in.''

The judge glanced toward the front row. "You've got a spare room, don't you Ian?''

"Uh-huh,'' the big guy grunted.

"Move in?'' Vi squeaked.

"Sure. You can't watch over Daisy properly unless you stay the night.''

She choked back a laugh. "You mean I'm supposed to watch over a *dog?*''

"No, ma'am. You'll replace the dog. Take her

place.'' Judge Tanner turned to the man. "Now, Ian, how long did Doc Woodworth say Annabelle'd be laid up?''

"A month. Six weeks if there're complications.''

"Who is Annabelle and what does she have to do with this?'' she demanded.

"Annabelle is the dog you practically killed. She's an important member of my family and a certified service dog.''

The mountain of a man spoke to her directly for the first time since he'd come charging out of the brush.

"Wha...? There was no vest on that dog—''

"She was off duty. We weren't out in public. Even a dog needs R&R, *especially* a service dog. Fetch is her stress-buster.''

"What about my job? I've got responsibilities, a good shot at District Claims Manager.''

The judge waved his hand as if to shoo a pesky fly, telling her exactly what he thought of her job. "You should've thought of that before you went speeding down a dirt road. You've got till four tomorrow afternoon to show up at Daisy's place. Ian'll give you directions.''

"But that's not fair.'' Vi stormed the bench, her heels clicking emphatically. "You can't do that. I'll get an attorney.''

"Attorney'd be a waste of time and money.'' He gestured toward the man. "Ian, I'll have Sheriff Moreno stop by for a report now and then. That'll give old Joe a chance to chat with Daisy and make sure Ms. Lead Foot here keeps her end of the deal.''

"Thanks, Ralph. I'm about beat.''

"Think you can hold out till tomorrow?" His prune face relaxed into a sympathetic smile.

The man swiped a hand across his face. "I've done it before. I'll do it now."

Fumbling through a daily planner, he found a blank page and ripped it out. He scribbled furiously, then handed the sheet to her. "See you at four tomorrow."

"Wait a minute. Who's Daisy? And why the heck do you need me?"

"Daisy's my mother. Annabelle's her service dog. You'll keep an eye on Mom at night while I sleep."

Vi shook her head. She was having a hard time relating a service dog to a woman who needed to be watched while she was asleep. Seizures maybe? She'd read about dogs trained to sense the onset of human seizures.

"Oh, and bring some comfortable clothes." He eyed her up and down. His lips curled into a smirk as he took in every detail of her gray silk suit. "You won't be needing those."

He gestured in her general direction. By *those,* she assumed he meant designer clothes, or maybe it was her three-inch heels.

"I need to know what I'm getting into. Why exactly does your mother need a service dog?"

"Alzheimer's. She has Alzheimer's."

Vi CAREFULLY NEGOTIATED the curve, keeping her speed down to a crawl. Impatience had got her into this mess, thinking on her feet would get her out.

Mentally reviewing her options, Vi figured her week's vacation would keep the rumble of discontent at Transglobal Insurance down to a dull roar. After that, they'd start talking leave of absence, a death knell to her goals.

She patted the laptop next to her. A large box of files rested on the back seat. Black leather was hell on the thighs during the scorching summer, but it sure looked good. The Mustang was her pride and joy. New, sleek and powerful. Not bad for a girl from East L.A.

Peering ahead, she saw where the scrub brush parted for a bit and a rutted path jogged off to the right. That had to be it. It was the only private drive for miles. She followed the narrow dirt road for several hundred yards and parked on a circular drive.

Letting out a low whistle, she admired the view. It was an adobe—low, squat and brown. Perfectly framed by the backdrop of lush, undisturbed desert, the Superstition Mountains rising in the distance. It looked like a small piece of heaven.

Vi got out of the car and approached the veranda, her gaze lighting on new and wonderful discoveries. Wild flowers in big terra-cotta pots. Two antique branding irons, crossed like swords, anchored to the wall.

She laid a palm against the adobe, absorbing the warmth of reflected fall sunshine, admiring the coarse texture. The weathered mud brick looked like it had been there for years. And would probably last for many, many more. It was stable, unchanging, safe.

Patrick would have loved it. He had loved all things western. Probably because of the old cowboy movies he'd watched when they were kids. Where the good guys always won, and the bad guys were easily spotted in their black hats.

Vi swallowed hard. She would *not* cry. It didn't accomplish anything. And it wasn't what Patrick would have wanted.

Laughter and joy were what he had brought to her life. And at the first sign of trouble, he'd whisk her off to their special fort and tell her jokes until she'd forgotten her fear.

God, how she missed his smile. The mischievous twinkle in his eye. The absolute goodness in his heart. The bravery he shrugged off as brotherly duty.

Vi fingered the heavy wooden door. Splinters nipped at her, but the core was solid. The bulky expanse was attached to the hand-hewn door frame with cast iron fittings. It might be old, but it looked strong enough to hold off an army. Or one really pissed-off SOB.

Yes, Patrick would have loved it.

Someday, she'd have a place like this. If she worked harder and smarter than everyone else.

Vi slipped into her favorite daydream. The one where she possessed the security only money could buy.

What would she change if the adobe house were hers? Definitely not the massive mesquite tree shading the flat roof, its gnarled black branches stretching protectively toward the house. And not the prickly pear cacti that lined the gravel drive. The ocotillo would stay, too. It looked almost like an upside-down octopus as it reached for the sky, the long, skinny stems undulating with the slightest breeze. The blooms added just the right touch of orange, breaking up all the tans and sages of the desert.

It was quiet, hushed almost. Except for the occasional call of some sort of bird, a dove maybe. What did someone do with all this quiet? No sirens, no neighbors, just quiet.

Vi shook herself out of her reverie. She didn't avoid challenges anymore, she took them head-on.

Her knuckles stung as she rapped on the striated surface of the door. Her efforts hardly made a sound. She pounded with her fist the second time and was rewarded with a dull thud.

She swore under her breath as she blew on her bruised hand.

The door swung open instantly, silently. Plenty of oil on those old fittings.

"You're here. Good."

The Ian guy stood in the doorway, his massive arms folded over his chest.

Vi took in his scruffy, stubbled jaw. She raised an eyebrow at his just-rolled-out-of-bed hair—short, dark-blond spikes here, mashed flat to his head there. And to think she'd envied guys with their wash-and-go cropped hair. Apparently, the "wash" part was critical to the whole 'do. He looked like a shower and a dab of shampoo might work wonders.

The view improved once her gaze got past the stubbled jaw. His Phoenix Coyotes hockey jersey, though badly wrinkled, outlined a very nice set of pecs, then hinted at a muscled stomach before neatly disappearing in to his jeans. No doubt about it, he was devoted to his hometown teams. The teal and purple presumably brought out the green in his eyes, but today they were just too bloodshot.

It had to be one hell of a hangover, judging from

the way his hand shook where he gripped the wrought iron door handle.

Wariness twisted her stomach. This was more than she'd bargained for. Vi let her suitcase down with a *thunk*. The laptop case remained firmly on her shoulder.

She stuck out a hand. His grip was strong, but with a tremor she could have named in seconds.

"Too much partying?" It was more of an observation than a question.

Ian scowled in response. His shoulders straightened. He had to be six-three or six-four. No wonder he'd scared the hell out of her.

"Look, lady, I don't know where you think you've landed, but there isn't too much to celebrate around here."

Vi shot him a glare. "I know a hangover when I see one."

"You do, huh? How about sleep deprivation, you familiar with that?"

She raised her chin a fraction. "I've read a bit. And my secretary has a colicky baby. She says that's why she's always late."

He looked her up and down, his gaze attacking her neatly pressed khakis, polished loafers, cotton sweater set. He shook his head. "No, you've never missed a moment's sleep. Your poor secretary."

The laptop strap bit into her shoulder. His words bit into her pride. She was a good boss, dammit. She'd come up the hard way—won a scholarship for inner city teens. She knew what it was like to struggle, to fight.

Vi took a deep breath and reminded herself that getting along with the guy might mean all the difference. "Look, we got off to a bad start. Why don't we try again? You could begin by inviting me in."

He grunted in reply, shoving away from the wall. He turned without a word, leaving her to follow like a helpless child.

She grabbed her tweed suitcase and trotted behind him. And she never trotted *behind* anyone. One or two steps ahead at the very least.

"I'd like to get unpacked right away. Get my computer set up...." Her mind was off and running, calculating how she would keep her finger on the pulse of the office, while stuck out here in the boonies. She shuddered to think that Echo Point was the closest outpost of civilization. It was a good twelve miles away.

"Yeah, we better get moving. The witching hour is almost here," he muttered.

She barely heard him. "What was that...witching hour?" she mumbled, still mulling over office politics.

VI JUMPED at the sound of an insistent knock at her door.

She shoved her socks and underwear into the top drawer of the distressed pine dresser and slammed it shut.

"Vi?" came the deep voice.

"Just a minute," she called, stowing her luggage under the bed. As she stood, she adjusted the pile of pillows, smoothed the lovely chenille bedspread. Unbleached cotton, maybe even organic. It felt heavenly, soft, under her fingers. It'd taken years to educate herself about the finer things in life. And soon, she'd be able to afford them. Even with the big chunk of her paycheck she sent to L.A. each month.

Another knock. This time louder. Desperate almost.

Hurrying to the door, she tucked a strand of hair behind her ear. She pasted on a confident smile.

"Ready…lead the way," she said as she opened the door. She was talking to a hulking back moving down the hallway. Vi jogged to catch up with him.

The Mexican tile blurred beneath her feet—the stark white walls glowing in contrast. Migraine-inducing bright. But at least it lightened up all the colonial Mexican stuff.

Just when she thought she might go blind from the glare, the hallway opened into a great room. Large, low-ceilinged, with a big screen TV in the corner. Spare, to the point of being scary. No homey pile of magazines. Just a remote and a TV magazine—

Vi frowned. Was the remote actually chained to the coffee table?

It was.

"Mom, this is Vi."

Ian nudged her forward until they reached a leather sofa. The high gloss and buttery tones promised soft calfskin. A colorful Indian blanket was draped across the back, right behind an old woman. Slender arms, soft, silvery-gold hair worn in a chin-length bob and cornflower blue eyes that sparkled.

"Vi, this is my mother, Daisy."

"Hello." She extended her hand.

The woman grasped Vi's hand in her own. Pat-pat went the ringed fingers. Her hands were cool, her scent divine. There was a grace to her movements, a regal quality in her posture. This woman hadn't slouched a day in her life.

"I'm Daisy. Welcome."

The woman stood, and her petite frame surprised Vi—her head didn't reach much higher than Vi's shoulder. Without warning, the tiny thing enfolded her in a hug.

Vi stiffened. Glancing over the golden head to the giant, she pleaded with her eyes.

Save me.

There would be no rescue from that corner. The exhaustion had cleared from Ian's face and his eyes were alight with affection.

She awkwardly patted the woman's straight back, then disengaged herself.

"Mom, Vi's going to join us for dinner."

"Who's Vi?" she asked, a frown pulling at her brow.

"I'm Vi."

"Oh, yes, yes of course, dear. But who's joining us for dinner?"

Vi turned helplessly to Ian. This threatened to become a bad game of "Who's on First?" She'd had only a brief opportunity to research Alzheimer's and didn't quite know what to expect.

"Mom, why don't you show our guest your paintings while I get dinner."

"What a lovely idea, dear." The old woman took Vi's arm and gently led her through an arch and down a long corridor.

Vi couldn't help but notice the strange wallpapering technique they'd employed. There was some sort of border on the wall, about elbow height. It looked like metallic tape. Reflective tape?

She opened her mouth to ask about it, but never got a break in the conversation. The older woman chattered as they strolled, commenting on the weather, the ballet she'd just seen, the latest scandal involving President Nixon.

Other than forgetting the current president, she seemed remarkably in charge of all her faculties. This job might just be easier than Vi had anticipated.

"Here's my studio," Daisy commented, as they reached a set of double doors at the end of the hallway. She threw open the doors to reveal a breathtaking view. There were windows from floor to ceiling along one wall, framed by the gray and purple of the Superstition Mountains in the distance. Below, a lush meadow meandered to a stand of cottonwood trees, with a few scrub oak sprinkled in. Mostly green, but with an occasional burnt orange leaf here and there. Gorgeous.

And the supplies. She'd never seen so many wonderful paints in one place, short of an art store. Her fingers itched to hold a brush, to try the pastels she'd experimented with years ago, given to her by a kind teacher. But no, the colors were all wrong. A bolder, more brilliant medium was needed. One that would bring out all the contrasts and textures.

"It's wonderful," she breathed.

"I knew you'd like it. You have artistic hands."

The gnarled hands picked up hers, tracing the length of her fingers, pressing gently on her palm, as if assessing her strength.

"Mine were very much like this once." The old

lady sighed and dropped her hand. She turned away from Vi, but couldn't hide the regret in her voice.

"Once?"

Daisy wandered toward the window, lost in thought. "Can't hold a paintbrush."

Back she came, her movements stiff, disjointed.

"Can't dance, either. Knees won't work right."

To the window and back, faster and faster.

"Everyone knows. Hold a brush properly. First lesson."

She moved to the workbench and grabbed a coffee can full of paintbrushes. "Can't do it." She stalked toward Vi. "Can't do it, can't do it, can't do it, can't do it," she chanted, louder with each refrain. Crimson splotched her wrinkled cheeks. The rest of her face was deathly pale, almost gray.

Oh, God, she's going to have a stroke.

"It's okay," Vi soothed. Her stomach knotted with helplessness. How was she supposed to handle this woman?

"Can't do it, can't do it. *Can't do it!*" She was directly in front of Vi. Droplets of saliva showered her face. The old hands clawed at her.

"Can't do it!" she shrieked. The woman turned and with surprising strength, hurled the can, brushes and all, at the window.

The glass shattered. Large jagged cracks radiated from the spot where the can had connected.

Vi panicked. What in the heck was she supposed to do?

Surely Ian had heard the commotion. Surely he'd fling open the doors and take care of this…this situation. She strained her ears, willing his heavy foot-steps.

Nothing. No sound of the cavalry coming to her rescue.

Daisy, surprisingly nimble now, raced toward the window.

Vi made a split-second decision and sprinted after her. She caught the woman from behind in a big bear hug. Daisy thrashed and screamed, batting at Vi's arms. Vi held on tightly, gasping for air. She wouldn't let go. Wouldn't let this sick woman throw herself through the glass.

The tiny figure twisted and wrenched in her arms. Every movement forced Vi's arm upward. She could strangle the old woman if she didn't let go. But Daisy could die if she *did.* It wasn't much of a choice.

CHAPTER TWO

Vi SPUN HER BODY to the left, taking Daisy with her. Enraged shrieks beat against her ears. Her arm inched higher, over the lady's chin.

Then everything went red. Vi howled with outrage. The old woman was biting her.

Teeth ground down, never releasing. No dentures here.

The door flung open. Ian's gaze swept over her and his mother.

"Help me!" Vi screamed. The jaws clenched harder. Pain shot up her arm, radiating along her shoulder. Flashes of light erupted behind her eyes. Heat rushed over her in waves, her knees threatened to buckle.

Ian strolled toward them.

Couldn't the man see she was dying?

"Hurry," she yelled.

Teeth. Pain.

"Shh," he soothed. "You calm down, she'll calm down." His tone was conversational, as if they discussed the weather.

The vice on her arm eased a fraction.

"Good." He continued to saunter toward them, his voice low.

Vi tried for a fair imitation of his Mr. Roger's cheerful croon. Through clenched teeth, she sang, "She's kill*ing* my freak*ing* arm."

"It's not your freak*ing* arm I'm worri*ed* about."

"It worries me," she barked.

The vise tightened again.

"Mom, dinner's ready." He held out his hand to the woman. "We don't want it to get cold."

Vi cautiously relaxed her grip on the woman.

The jaws unclenched.

Vi backed away, ever so slowly. She didn't dare breathe until she was out of biting distance.

"Why isn't this woman in the hospital?"

"Because hospitals won't take her. This is a chronic problem, not acute. And this is her home. She belongs here."

The tiny woman faced her. Sweat dripped down her cheek. Saliva pooled at the corner of her mouth. Her eyes had lost their sparkle, dulled by confusion.

"Who are you?" she asked.

"I'm Vi. Remember?"

"I don't know a Vi," she stated. Turning to Ian, her voice shaky, she asked, "Do I?"

He stepped over to his mother's side. "This is Vi, Mom. She's our guest for dinner."

A radiant smile broke over the woman's face. She must have been quite beautiful at one time. "Of course, dear. Our guest."

"I WON'T STAY," Vi hissed. "I'm not qualified for this."

"Sure you're qualified. You think on your feet. And you know a mean half nelson." Ian gave her a lopsided grin.

His poor attempt to distract her with humor almost worked. The fact that he had a sense of humor came as a complete surprise to Vi.

"That woman is a danger. To herself. To me. She needs professional help. Wh-what would have happened if she'd thrown herself through that window?"

His grin faded.

"She didn't. And you *were* there. You handled it. Once you understand her a little better, you'll do great."

"Look, I can't take care of a houseplant. Or pets. You've obviously overestimated my capabilities."

Ian scratched his head. "It's usually not this intense. It'll take a little time for Daisy to adjust to having you around," he said. "I'm sure you can handle it, or I wouldn't ask."

"There's got to be somebody else. How about a private nurse? Someone who specializes in this kind of thing. I'll help pay."

He brushed his hand over his face. "Don't you think I've thought of that? Nurses don't come cheap." Then he named an astronomical figure. "I can't risk using up Daisy's nest egg. She might need it...later. And I doubt you're willing to foot the bill."

Vi's heart sank as she mentally inspected her savings account. There was no way she could swing it—not if she wanted to send money to L.A. every month. And there was no question about that. It kept her conscience clean.

"I'll stay a week. That ought to be long enough for the dog to get back up to par...." It was a stab in the dark, but she had to try.

"The vet said a month at the minimum. I'm not

risking permanent damage to Annabelle, just to make life easier for you. You don't have a choice. No Daisy, no driver's license. No driver's license, no job."

There was a hard edge to his voice as he scraped mangled Tater Tots and smeared ketchup into the garbage. The remnants of microwaved hot dogs, stale buns and carrot sticks soon followed. The meal made campus food look gourmet.

"Look, I'll buy you another dog. AKC, pick of the litter, whatever it takes."

"Annabelle cost over fifteen thousand dollars. Even if you could cough up that kind of money, a dog like her takes a year and half to train."

"Fifteen *thousand* dollars?" She nodded her head in the direction of the dog basket in the corner of the kitchen, where the subject of their discussion lay, head on paws, big brown eyes following every movement, every nuance. "*That* cost fifteen thousand dollars? Boy, did you get screwed."

"*That* happens to be a member of our family. She's worth every penny and then some. Believe me, by the time your four weeks are up, you'll agree."

"You never told me why this dog is so important. I can see your mother needs help, but, well, wouldn't she be more comfortable in an institution? Where there are people trained to handle her problems?"

He crossed his arms. "*Home* is the best place for her. Annabelle has been trained to help keep her here. Wandering is a big problem."

"That's what I've read." Vi mulled over her options.

"I can do two weeks. That'll use up all my personal

and sick time, but I think I can make it work. After that you're on your own.''

"No deal. This mess is your fault. You're here till Annabelle's well enough to work. You leave and I'll have the judge issue an arrest warrant so fast it'll make your head spin.''

No counteroffer. That wasn't good. This was his turf and his rules. It went against everything in her being to do it, but she had no choice but to bid against herself.

"Three weeks.''

He folded his arms over his chest, his mouth set in a thin line. "Uh-uh. Four weeks. And that's only if Annabelle heals without complications. It could be six.''

Vi pictured her future sliding down the drain in six weeks. Jerry Jones could be well on his way to stealing her promotion.

But knowing when to concede was one of her better survival skills—she'd learned that at home a long time ago. She'd let Ian think he'd won, *this time*. "It seems I don't have a choice.''

The man nodded, accepting her apparent defeat. A crooked grin pulled at the corner of his mouth. He had dimples. What a waste.

"It'll be interesting to see who wins. You or Daisy.''

"I don't lose. Ever.''

"Uh-huh,'' he grunted, an eyebrow raised in speculation. "I'll take the shift tonight. Tomorrow while Daisy's at the center, we'll discuss her care. You better get some sleep, you'll need it.

Vi FLINCHED. Her heart pounded. Some sort of noise?

She struggled to focus. It was dark, only vague shadows of heavy furniture against pearly white walls.

Where the heck was she?

A strange bed, high off the ground, a footboard with swirls of black against misty gray. Intricate, hand-worked wrought iron.

The noise. There it was again. Pounding, yelling, more pounding.

Daisy. The old lady. What was going on?

Vi burrowed farther under the covers, muffling a curse. With the bedspread over her head, she could barely hear it. Ian had promised to take this shift.

Sure enough, a muffled, "I'm coming, Mom."

Something heavy thudded against the wall, then footsteps dragged outside her door. It was like something out of the Simpson trial. Had Kato been this scared?

She clenched a corner of the crisp muslin sheet.

More hollering. A doorknob rattled. The pounding resumed.

Vi couldn't take it anymore.

Fresh air hit her in a cool wave as she pawed her way out of her cocoon. Throwing on her robe, she slid her feet into her slippers.

The door latch was cool beneath her hand, the door opened easily, silently. She sucked in a breath, rattled by what she saw—Ian, a pair of Arizona State University maroon-and-gold sweatpants slung low on his hips and nothing else. Shirtless, he was more Greek god than hulking monster.

Ian fumbled in his pocket and took out a key. He

barely got it clear of the lock when a figure came through the doorway and bounced off his chest.

He didn't grab the figure. Instead, he stood there, arms hanging at his side, talking. Just talking.

Daisy jabbered in rapid-fire succession. Not a word made sense.

Ian inclined his head as he spoke to Daisy, his voice low, reassuring. "It's okay, Mom, I'm here. It's me. Ian. Everything's okay."

The jabbering slowed to English. "I was trapped. Somebody kidnapped me and locked me in there to die."

"No, Mom. I locked the door so you wouldn't get lost."

"I *don't* get lost." Daisy straightened, the top of her head barely reaching Ian's chest.

"Sometimes you don't remember so good."

"I remember perfectly." She smoothed her wild hair. Stabbing a finger in Vi's direction, she shrieked, "She did it. She broke into our house and locked me in my room. She stole my paintings!"

"Shhh. You remember Vi, our guest." He laid a hand on his mother's withered arm. "Come on, I'll walk you to the bathroom."

"Yes, of course," she murmured.

The two walked down the hall, hand in hand, one robust, the other tiny and confused.

Vi shook her head and shuffled back to bed, where she flip-flopped for more than an hour. What about this Alzheimer's stuff? What was it she had read? Progressive, no cure. Eventually fatal. Not a pretty picture. The old lady would die. But what happened in the meantime?

Sighing, Vi contemplated the mess she'd made. Her futile attempt to outrun the past had sent ripples through three lives, four if she counted the dog. The thought of Annabelle with her bandaged hind leg and Daisy with her irrational tantrums made Vi want to crawl under the covers and hide. She'd messed up big time and turned life upside down for everyone involved.

Was she any better than her dad? Letting her emotions get the upper hand until she lost control and did something stupid? Something that hurt another living being?

Vi shook her head. She wouldn't accept that. There was a world of difference between her and her dad. She intended to make things right for Daisy and Ian. But she wasn't a trained nurse, or even a social worker. What if she screwed up? The woman could have gone through that glass panel today. If the fall hadn't gotten her, the glass would have sliced her to shreds. This was too much for them to expect of her.

The decision wasn't easy, but it was best for everyone involved. She would leave in the morning. Call her attorney. Have him explain everything to the judge. Sell her car, if necessary, to pay for a qualified nurse....

IAN POURED HIMSELF another cup of coffee. Thank God for the senior center. Tuesdays and Thursdays were what kept him going. The first few hours were exhilarating. Freedom beckoned, with endless possibilities. What should he do first? Read? Jog? Work at the computer? Sleep maybe? At nine in the morning, the world looked rosy.

But the crash always came. Along about noon, he'd come down off his high. The responsibility would drop on his shoulders like a rack of free-weights. By two o'clock his gut started churning, tying itself in knots. Fear? Disappointment? Dread for sure. Maybe even a little guilt. He could do better. Be more patient.

Vi staggered around the corner, interrupting his thoughts. Her pink terry cloth robe was belted haphazardly, her black hair wild. She scratched her head, leaving a big cow lick behind.

He shook his head. This couldn't possibly be the same woman. He let his gaze rove from her face, down her neck, to where the nubbly fabric dipped between her breasts. The ratty old robe was an improvement over the power suits and country club casual stuff. *Breasts?*

Ian shoved his mind into reverse.

Breasts. The boardroom barracuda had breasts. Imagine that.

He shook his head, bemused.

"Morning, Vi," he drawled, his gaze seeking out more visual clues, from her shaggy pink slippers upward. Breasts meant hips and a waist. But the bulk of her robe kept everything else hidden.

He stifled a sigh of disappointment. The deprivation was getting to him. Abstinence had never been one of his strong points.

"Morning," she mumbled, shuffling past.

He winced as she slammed a cupboard door. So did she.

"Where the hell do you keep the coffee cups?"

"My, aren't we cheery this morning. Upper left."

She turned, briefly, to fix him with a bloodshot glare.

"Too much partying last night?" He hid a smile in his coffee cup. That'd get a reaction.

Vi grunted, noncommital.

Was she even conscious?

She poured herself a hefty cup of coffee and gulped down a good third of it. The woman might have nerves of steel, but her esophagus had to be cast iron. She closed her eyes and sighed with bliss.

"Cream, sugar?"

"Uh-uh."

He raised an eyebrow. Impressive.

"Sorry about all the noise last night."

She waved a hand and grunted as she shuffled past him, back the way she had come.

It was at least half an hour before she returned for her second cup. This time there was a little life in her step. And the light of battle in her eyes.

She poured another healthy cup and slurped away.

He waited. He was good at that. A fight was coming, he was sure of it. Couldn't really blame her—who would voluntarily stay here? It was different for him. This was his promise to keep, not hers.

He'd hoped things would be different. Hoped her arrival would come on a good day. When she'd fall under Daisy's charm before she realized what she was getting into. And maybe, just maybe, she'd stick with them until Annabelle could get around under her own steam.

Ian shook his head, amazed at his own gullibility. He could dream, couldn't he?

At best, she'd last a couple weeks. He needed to

make sure they got at least that. But how? He couldn't hold her by force. Maybe appeal to her humanity?

One look at her straight spine and hard gaze and he gave up on empathy. The woman didn't have much. Nope, he'd have to appeal to her sense of self-preservation.

"Where's the dog?" a gravelly voice asked. He did a double take and, sure enough, the words seemed to have come from her. Maybe her esophagus wasn't indestructible after all.

"I carried her out back. There's a fenced yard, lots of shade. It's the place where she knows she's off duty. Fresh air and sunshine'll do her good."

"The faster she heals, the better. Where's…um… Daisy?"

"Senior center. You'll learn her schedule pretty fast."

Vi crossed her arms over her chest. "I won't be here long enough to learn schedules. I'm sorry about your situation, but I'm not the right person for the job. I'll figure out another way to make this up to you."

Ian bit back an oath and reminded himself that this woman had no way of knowing just how precarious the situation was. And how few options he had. "Whether you think you're right for the job or not, you're all I've got. The only way you can 'make this up to me' is to commit to being here at least a month."

She met his gaze. "I'm leaving. Today. I don't care how much it costs—I'll hire a nurse or something. Someone who has experience with this kind of thing."

"The hell you will. You've seen what happens when someone new is introduced into Daisy's environment. We're over the worst of it, and she'll adjust to you. Nurses work in shifts. It would be constant upheaval. No way.''

"Come on, be reasonable.''

"I *am* being reasonable.'' Ian clenched his jaws and vowed not to wrap his hands around Vi's throat. "*You* need to step up to the plate and take responsibility for what you've done.''

"I've taken responsibility all right. I'm here, aren't I? I simply think there has to be an alternative to my staying here. One that will be better for everyone.''

"Believe me, there's no alternative. Even if Daisy would accept several nurses in the house, I doubt you could get them to promise to stay out here for the duration. I have no intention of subjecting my mother to constant change.''

Vi's eyes flashed with panic, then anger. "There has to be another way. I'll work something out with the judge. Something we can all live with.''

"Yeah, Ralph seemed real persuaded with your arguments the other day.''

"I'll hire an attorney.''

He checked out a speck of dirt under his fingernails. Never let 'em see you sweat. Good strategy on the football field, even better in life.

"Have you been listening to a word I've said? Still need that job of yours? Remember, no Daisy, no driver's license. No license, no job. That would be a shame.'' He made a tsk-tsking sound.

Her chin came up, her full lips compressed into a line. "A good attorney will make sure that doesn't happen.''

"So you think your lawyer'll make it all go away? Pull the proper strings?''

"That's the way the world works."

"Yeah, unfortunately you're right," he conceded. "But, see, Judge Tanner is more than just an old coot playing at law. He's part of one of the oldest ranching families in Arizona. This is kind of a…retirement job."

"Retirement job?" She nibbled on her lower lip. Nice teeth. He had her now.

"Sure. He was a Superior Court Judge till his heart attack about ten years ago. Then he decided to come home to Echo Point, where he could make the rules and play the game his way. Eccentric, I think they call it. But he's got more pull than any lawyer you could hire. And you know what? He's been Daisy's…uh, admirer for most of those ten years."

"Oh."

She pulled her robe more closely around her. It was almost disappointing to see the light of victory fade from her eyes. A good challenge always revved up his competitive juices. But not this time. The risk was too great.

"Hey, look, truth is, sometimes *I* don't want to be here. But Daisy needs me. And she needs you. I'll do whatever it takes to make her happy. Not you, your job, or anything else is going to get in the way of that. Now it's time to set a few ground rules. About your vocabulary—"

"She's your responsibility, not mine."

It was true, too true. His debt, his responsibility. All the crap he'd put his mom through—the cops dragging him home in the middle of the night, the petty theft, the scum he'd hung out with. That, on top of his dad's death.

Yeah, he owed her. Big time. And he'd promised to keep her safe, in her own home. And in one split second, this she-devil had almost destroyed the house of cards he'd built. Annabelle was the only thing standing between Daisy and a nursing home. He couldn't do it alone, much as he wanted to.

No, Vi was the only solution. Otherwise, he'd have to break a string of promises. And he didn't break promises.

"Lady, you did the crime, you do the time. You can consider her your responsibility, too. For the next month treat her as if she were your own mother."

CHAPTER THREE

VI ABSORBED Ian's statement, but couldn't comprehend it. She wasn't quite sure how normal people treated their mothers. Maria Davis Peralta had kept her sanity, Vi supposed, by cocooning herself in denial. Denial that their life was a nightmare, and half the time, denial that she had any children at all. It was easier to pretend they didn't exist. That is, until Patrick died. Then she was the grieving mother, so brokenhearted she had to divorce her husband, leave her two daughters, remarry and move to San Diego.

So when Ian instructed her to treat Daisy like her own mother, it exposed a raw nerve she refused to explore. Instead, she propped her fists on her hips and challenged, "Not only am I to keep the lady from wandering off and getting herself killed, but you want me to be all warm and fuzzy and treat her like family? You've got the wrong woman, buddy. If she were *my* mother, I'd put her some place where she could receive appropriate care."

She watched her statement sink in. Ian's eyes were shadowed for a moment. Guilt? Uncertainty? It was gone before she could identify it. Replaced by whitehot anger.

Vi backed away until her hips met the kitchen counter. No escape. She lifted her chin and waited.

But the raw frustration in his face made her squinch her eyes shut.

When the blow didn't come, she cautiously opened her eyes and saw him standing before her, defeat evident in the slump of his shoulders.

Relief washed over her. She'd stared down fear. Something she couldn't have done five years ago. He wouldn't destroy her. Couldn't make her cower. No matter how big or how strong he was.

Step by step, she forced her feet forward until she stood toe to toe with the hulk. Craning her neck, she made sure she didn't lose eye contact.

"I think I'll just call a few of my attorney friends. Find out a little about Judge Tanner," she challenged.

Green, clear and steady. Ian held her gaze. The seconds ticked by, neither of them moving.

When he leaned one elbow back against the breakfast bar, she exhaled slowly. He was giving her room to breathe. Or enough rope to hang herself.

"Go ahead." He nodded toward the phone on the kitchen counter. "I'm sure your legal beagles will get a hoot out of this one."

Vi reached for the phone, then stopped, her hand suspended midair.

She studied his expression, searching for a weakness, an inconsistency. He didn't blink, just gave her a cocky half grin.

Damn.

He set down his coffee cup, the one that proclaimed Ruggers Do It Down And Dirty, and retrieved the phone. Shoving the receiver in her hand, he said, "Here you go. Need privacy?"

"Nooo…that won't be necessary."

It *was* necessary to keep this whole fiasco as quiet as possible. He might be bluffing. But what if he weren't? It was bad enough she had been banished to this godforsaken place for a month. A month where she was seriously out of the loop. A month for that weasel in the Scottsdale office to suck up to the big boss without any competition. No, she didn't need to compound the problem by making a laughingstock of herself.

Or worse, find her butt parked at a desk in Under-writing. That's exactly where eight points on her driver's license would get her. The big boys upstairs took a dim view of impulsive behavior, especially if it opened up the company to liability. The boss would cover for her to a point. But if it became common knowledge around the legal community...

This little episode had to be erased. Like it never happened. No points on her license, no reminders.

"I—I believe you. I'll stay."

For now.

Ian eyed her suspiciously. Maybe she'd capitulated too fast.

Shrugging, she spread her hands wide. "Hey, you've got me over a barrel."

The taut line of his shoulders visibly relaxed. "I'm a pretty mellow guy. Just be good to Daisy and we'll get along fine."

"Sure. Fine." She flashed him a smile, an earnest, kid sister kind of smile. If she couldn't beat him, she'd join him. Their goals were the same, after all. Get the dog back on its feet ASAP. "And since it looks like I'll be here a while, why don't I get dressed and you can tell me exactly what I can do to help Daisy and her four-legged friend.''

He still looked at her warily, but didn't respond. Just frowned.

Then he shrugged his shoulders and said, ''We'll meet in the den in, say, about half an hour? The den is down the hall, to the right.''

Vi EASED INTO the battered old wingback chair. The torn leather armrest scratched the tender skin on the underside of her forearm. It reminded her of home. Only their furniture hadn't started out as nice as this.

She suppressed a shudder. Someone needed to tape some holes, or better yet, scrap the chair entirely.

''Okay, shoot,'' Vi prodded, notebook open, pen handy.

Ian sat behind his desk, in an equally worn leather executive chair, that one hunter green. The burgundy and green theme continued throughout the den. Floor-to-ceiling bookshelves, distressed wood of course. In the corner stood an adobe beehive fireplace, the inside smoke-blackened, but bare. Cozy.

Indian rugs, hand woven and old, judging by the muted colors and workmanship, were scattered on the floor, warming the brown ceramic tile. Here and there were a few knickknacks, something missing in the rest of the house. Hand-carved kachinas, outfitted in flamboyant turquoise and red, jockeyed for space between tan woven baskets and some sort of odd sculpture. Made out of a horseshoe and barbed wire, it looked like a cowboy twirling a lasso.

She cocked her head to the side, checking it out

from another angle. Maybe it was a cowboy doing some sort of funky dance....

Her gaze slid to the wall behind Ian's head. No more western stuff there. No, it was pure modern sports memorabilia. Photos of Randy Johnson and Jake "The Snake" Plummer and some guy in a hockey uniform. All were autographed, all personalized to Ian.

"You'll watch Daisy from 10:00 p.m. to 8:00 a.m."

She waited for him to continue.

He didn't.

"And..."

"That's it. Watch Daisy. If she so much as steps out of bed, you follow her. Help her find the bathroom if she gets lost. Wait for her, make sure she goes back to her room."

"You said she'd calm down. Now that she's used to me."

He didn't quite meet her gaze. "Yeah. She'll calm down."

"Sounds simple enough if there's no wrestling or windows involved." Vi snapped closed the notebook. "That's all the dog does?"

"Originally, Annabelle was trained to watch Daisy only at night, and come get me if she got out of bed. But she gradually extended her shift, so lately she's spent most of her time with Daisy. There are only three other certified Alzheimer's dogs in the world, so no one really knows what she can do."

It was amazing. How they could train a dog to do stuff like that. How the dog seemed to *understand* almost on a human level.

Vi was intrigued, but didn't want to give the guy

any false hopes. So she suppressed all the questions whirling around in her head and attempted to look disinterested. "Cool," she commented.

Ian raised an eyebrow.

"You'll think it's pretty damn cool, after about a week with Daisy. Last night was just a small sample. When I told you about the witching hour, it was to prepare you, not scare you. The technical term for it is 'sundowning.' A lot of people with Alzheimer's get restless when the sun goes down. At night, their sleep patterns are disturbed and they frequently roam."

"They childproof homes for kids. Can't you do something like that for her? Special locks on the doors?"

"Daisy's figured out every obstacle I can put in her way. The last time she roamed, she ended up two miles away, and it took Search and Rescue nearly six hours to find her. It was June—she was severely dehydrated and almost died."

"I didn't realize," she murmured.

"Most people don't." He sighed and rubbed a hand across his forehead. The bags under his eyes made him look like one of those sad old hound dogs that never moved from the porch. "Hell, *I* had no idea. Nobody does, until you've been there."

She almost felt sorry for the guy. Almost. There was no way she intended to get drawn into his problems. She had enough of her own.

"So I'm off duty during the day?"

He nodded slowly. "If I were you, I'd sleep. You're gonna need it."

"I'm sure I can handle it. You a sports nut or something?" She gestured toward the pictures on the wall.

"I guess you could call me that. I was a sports writer."

A writer. Interesting.

"Was?"

"Until two years ago. When Vince—I mean—Sheriff Moreno, called." His gaze was focused on the wall behind her left ear. Like he was there, but wasn't there.

"Asked if I'd noticed Daisy getting forgetful. He'd found her car, still idling, stuck in a desert wash ten miles outside of town. Said she'd seemed disoriented, didn't know where she was or how she got there."

Ian shifted, cleared his throat.

"I hadn't seen her for a while. Been on the road. I should have figured it out sooner. Not Vince."

A twinge of remorse nagged at her. She'd done this. She'd made this guy worry more than he already did. He didn't deserve it, any more than she did.

But the touchy-feely confidences had to stop. Because if they didn't, then she'd have to reciprocate, tell him something deep, dark, revealing. And if she started, where would she end? Her stomach rolled at the very thought.

"Okay, I get the gist. Prodigal son is racked with guilt, throws away a promising career to care for his mother. Very commendable. More than I'd do in the same situation."

"I don't want sympathy. You asked about the sports stuff and I told you."

"Good. I'm not the sympathetic type."

He crossed his arms and leaned back in his big leather chair. "No? That's probably what makes you so damn successful, Ms. Davis. Personally, I'd hate to make a living off other people's misfortune."

"Yeah, well I didn't create the system. I'm just damn good at what I do."

"I'm sure you are."

Vi MUMBLED obscenities around the pen clenched between her teeth. The computer screen went blank again, only to be replaced by gibberish. For the second time today.

There was a tap at her door. "Ten o'clock. Your shift."

Not already. She'd barely made a dent in the files she'd ferried in from work. There were a couple demand packets to review along with adjuster recommendations for settlement. Not to mention twenty or better status reports, case reserves and the usual interoffice B.S. to go through.

"In a minute," she lisped around the pen.

This time the rapping was louder. Hard knuckles. "Vi, ten o'clock. Get a move on."

Sighing, she removed the pen. "I'm coming already. Don't get your shorts in a wad."

Silence.

Maybe just one more file.

"Vi. *Now.*"

"Oh, all right." She threw one last look at the computer screen and left the room.

Ian gave her barely enough room to squeeze through the doorway into the hall. He waited, arms crossed, ready to escort her to her own personal hell.

Frustration made her middle finger itch, the thumb and three other fingers started to bend of their own accord. She reminded herself that obscene gestures got her nowhere. Clamping her rebellious fingers into a tight fist, she rapped on Daisy's door. "It's me, Vi. Can I come in?"

"Go away. I don't know a Vi."

This was turning into a nightly ritual. Even though Vi had been there nearly a week, Daisy could not, or would not, understand that Vi was there to help. She refused to call her by name, always referring to her in the third person, like she wasn't there. And then it was usually to accuse her of some heinous crime, such as stealing her paintings, locking her in her room or making a mess. A mess, coincidentally, that only occurred when Daisy was around.

"She'll get used to you," Ian assured her for the hundredth time, as he rapped gently on the wooden door. "Mom, Vi's coming in now. She'll keep you company, just like Annabelle did."

"Don't need company."

"Sure you do. And I betcha she'll even sing to you," he wheedled.

It was the only way Vi could get into the room. The only way the woman would accept her. Good thing she had a passable voice.

"The Daisy song?" came the muffled reply.

Vi groaned.

Not again.

"Go on," Ian urged, as he landed an elbow to her ribs.

"I'll sing you the Daisy song," she promised.

The door swung open and she was admitted to the inner sanctum. "I'll bring you a daisy a day, dear…" she sang. "I'll bring you a daisy a day."

It was a lovely old ballad, all about the endurance of love. The suitor vowed to bring his love a daisy a day. And after she died, he brought a daisy a day to her grave. The first time she'd heard Ian sing it to Daisy, goose bumps had prickled her arms. Full moon, PMS, the Celtic part of her soul, the Hispanic part of her soul, whatever the reason, the song always made her throat ache, her eyes mist.

Daisy climbed into bed as Vi sang, humming right along. Framed by the crisp white pillowcase, her face relaxed, the lines and worries smoothed away. Her smile was angelic, her eyes unfocused and dreamy.

Vi usually sang her to sleep, then tiptoed to the daybed tucked away in an alcove. But tonight Daisy didn't drift off. As Vi sang, the old woman's eyes became more focused, inquisitive almost.

"You've a beautiful voice, dear."

"Thank you."

It was the first time Daisy had acknowledged her directly, other than in wild accusations.

"Edward used to sing that song to me." She sighed, her finger doodling across the patterned chenille bedspread. "He was tall, like Ian. Made me feel so fragile, cherished."

"Oh. That's…nice."

Fragile? People only hurt you if they knew you were fragile. Cherished, now that sounded good. She'd never experienced it, but it sounded good. Safe.

"He'd watch me dance, for hours it seemed. And he'd hum that song. It was as if we were the only two people left on earth. Alone, but so close to Heaven I could almost hear the angels sing."

"Angels. Sure. You bet. What do angels sound like? Celine Dion? Alicia Keyes maybe?"

Daisy reached out and patted her hand. Her smile

was warm, her eyes sparkled. "You're teasing me, aren't you? It was an allegory, dear. To illustrate my point, about love being the closest thing to Heaven we can find here on earth."

"An allegory. Sure." What next, a discussion on the origin of the species? World politics?

"And dance. The next best thing to sex."

Vi tried to steer the conversation in a safer direction. "You danced? Professionally?"

"I danced. Still do, when the joints allow. Not professionally of course. I met Edward in New York, when I was auditioning for the ballet. It was a wonderful time. I met Edward and knew he was the one. Everything else paled in comparison. Even dancing. We were married by the justice of the peace and left New York without even finding out if I'd made the cuts. It just wasn't important anymore. Only being with Edward was."

Daisy's eyes shone. Edward must have been one helluva guy.

"How'd you give it all up? All your hopes and dreams?"

"New hopes, new dreams. Different, but better in some ways. A family, my own dance studio…"

"Did you ever regret it?"

The other woman's eyelids drooped, her smile faded. "Only once."

Vi wanted to shake her, make her explain. But Daisy's eyelids fluttered shut and she snored lightly.

THE NOISE reached Vi's ears, as if filtered through layers of cotton. It was a rattle, like a doorknob. Somewhere though the layers, she knew it was important. Something she should do about it. Burglar?

She bolted into a sitting position. The night-light in the hall illuminated the room. No burglar. White-washed stucco walls, big rustic beams holding up the ceiling. Ian's house.

She glanced around the room. Not her room. Her room didn't have colorful paintings anchored to the walls.

Daisy's room.

She turned to check Daisy's bed. Empty. How could that be? It seemed only a moment ago that the woman had drifted off to sleep after reminiscing about her dance studio.

Vi muttered an oath as she swung her legs over the side of the daybed, ignoring the dull throb in her temples. Her bare toes curled away from the cold tile, but she pushed through the discomfort. No time for slippers. The reflective tape was cool, eerie beneath her fingers, as she followed it toward the bathroom. The door was open.

Her breath came in deep, ragged breaths, her pulse pounded. No light. Where could the woman be?

She rounded the door frame to check.

There she was, slumped on the toilet seat, her chin resting on her chest.

Thank God.

"Daisy?" She touched the woman's arm, then gently shook her shoulder.

No response.

CHAPTER FOUR

"I THOUGHT I'D LOST HER."

Vi waited for the bombshell to sink in. She held her coffee cup suspended at chin level, denying herself that first luscious swallow. Hot, steamy fingers of aroma wafted upward, stinging her nose. Caffeine withdrawal seemed like a light sentence for her crime.

"Hum?"

Ian leaned against the kitchen counter, more interested in cramming a whole power bar in his mouth than her confession. He wore black nylon shorts, a white T-shirt and a gray hooded sweatshirt, his usual running uniform. The senior center bus had barely chugged down the drive, and he was ready to go.

"I said, I thought I lost her," she bit off every word, enunciating clearly. "I got up with her at midnight, one-thirty and three. No problem. But the last time…I didn't wake up. Didn't even hear her until she was out the bedroom door. I'm not a real rise-and-shine kind of person—it took me a couple minutes to get going. By the time I found her, she was asleep in the bathroom."

Ian chewed slowly. His jaw was smooth for once, his eyes alert and ready for the day. He looked years younger than the first time she'd seen him, boyish almost. Except for the frown.

"You found her. No harm done."

"But what if I don't next time? What then?"

"Look, you can do this. I wouldn't trust you with her otherwise."

"*Why* are you so sure you can trust me?"

"You're smart and determined." He hesitated for a moment. "And whether you admit it or not, you care."

Restless energy prodded her into action. She paced the kitchen floor. "No way, you've got me all wrong. My career is the most important thing in the world to me. And right now it's in danger of going down the tubes. I'm behind already and so exhausted I can't string together a coherent thought."

Ian shrugged. "You'll get used to it. Just sleep in the day."

"I can't. That's when I get my work done. I've still got a job to do, no matter what happens here." The tightness in her chest expanded to a fist-sized knot of frustration. "I've got a shot at District Claims Manager. It's big, really big."

He hesitated, chewing slowly. "Okay, so you sleep during the day, then work at night in Daisy's room. We'll set up a desk."

"You don't understand. I get tunnel vision when I'm working. The whole place could burn down and I'd never notice. Besides, Daisy'd be a wreck—the light, rustling papers, dictation. She wouldn't sleep a wink."

Ian pushed away from the counter. He loomed over her, his bulk no longer benign. "So what do you want me to do? Let you off the hook? Say okay, go back to your important job in Phoenix. We'll manage just fine. Well, you know what, we won't manage, thanks to you. And I won't let you off the hook. Nice try.''

He crumpled the wrapper and tossed it in the general direction of the trash can. ''I'm going for a run. You do whatever you want. Just don't leave.''

It was hard to believe this was the same guy who tended the old lady with such patience. There was a hard glint in his eyes and his voice vibrated with anger, as if he wanted to wrap those big hands around her throat and squeeze. Hard.

But he didn't.

Instead, he slammed out the kitchen door without a backward look. She wasn't worth the effort to strangle.

Vi set her coffee cup down on the counter and pushed it away. Then she bent over and banged her forehead against the Formica. Once, twice, three times. Not hard enough for it to hurt, but she hoped hard enough to knock some sense into her.

''What am I going to do?'' she asked the empty room. As long as the walls didn't answer, she figured she must have a shred of sanity left.

Daisy could have been lost, or seriously hurt. It had seemed simple enough. Watch Daisy sleep. She hadn't counted on getting only a couple hours of uninterrupted sleep a night. It was starting to take a toll. Her eyes were gritty, her head felt like it was stuffed with cotton.

Vi rubbed her temples as she mulled over the whole mess. She'd have to adapt, somehow. That was the key to survival. In nature, in the corporate jungle, even in this weird house. Adapt or die. But how to adapt to something she couldn't understand and couldn't predict? The old woman and her idiosyncrasies ruled the whole house, no matter what time of day. Like yesterday. Only a few glorious moments at the computer before Daisy wandered in and accused her of all sorts of nasty things. Theft, kidnapping, murder, they were all part of Vi's M.O., according to Daisy.

She would get used to it, Ian had said. Ha! Changing her sleep schedule was next to impossible. It was like an alarm went off somewhere the instant her head made contact with a pillow during the day. So much as a long blink and Daisy would wind up. It could be something as simple as a bath and World War III would erupt. Even the thick adobe walls couldn't block out the yelling, the slap-slap of escaping bare feet on tile, the thud of Ian's tread in hot pursuit. And sometimes, a dirty word or two.

Once, before she learned to lock her door, Daisy had rushed into her room. The old woman had been nearly naked, her eyes wide with fear, her breathing shallow.

Vi shook her head as she remembered the strange episode.

Daisy hadn't said a word. Just stood there, scrawny arms wrapped across her sagging, wrinkled breasts, and shook her head frantically from side to side.

Ian had followed close behind, his breathing labored, as if he'd run an eight minute mile.

"Mom…" he'd gasped.

Daisy had feinted to the left, then dodged right.

But Ian was too quick for her. He wrapped her in a big bear hug from behind.

She bit and clawed and lashed out. "Let me go," she screeched. The air crackled with her terror.

Ian let go.

She backed away from him and cowered in a corner.

It took several minutes for Ian to catch his breath. Vi waited, mute, unable to differentiate between perpetrator and victim.

Finally, he said, "It's okay, Mom. No bath today. I'll get you a nice warm washcloth to sponge yourself down with."

"I don't need a bath. Had one yesterday."

"Sure you did." His voice held more defeat than conviction. "But a warm washcloth wouldn't hurt. You know, knock down the trail dust."

"It's a trick. Just like that woman." She pointed an accusing finger in Vi's direction. "She was sent to spy on me."

"It's not a trick, Mom. I've never lied to you before, have I?"

She ruminated on that for a minute, hands on hips. Apparently she'd forgotten she was naked from the waist up. But Vi hadn't. Her gaze bounced around the room as she looked everywhere, but at Daisy. At least the other woman wore white cotton briefs.

"Nooo...you haven't lied. But she's sneaky. See, she won't even look me in the eye. And she won't tell me her name. She's hiding something."

Ian shrugged helplessly. "She has problems with new things. Remembers stuff from twenty years ago, but has a hard time with anything new."

"Can't teach an old dog new tricks," Daisy chirped.

Ian's lips twitched into a smile. "Exactly. Well, Vi, we'll just have to keep trying."

"Who's Vi?" Daisy interrupted.

Ian sighed and shook his head. "She's having a

hard time with the Vi part. Sometimes giving her a point of reference helps. Mind if I try something?''

"Go ahead.''

"Mom, this is Violet. She's named after a flower just like you.''

"Yeah, as in shrinking Violet,'' Vi muttered.

Daisy practically glowed with excitement. She gestured with her hands as she spoke. "Another flower woman. I should have known immediately. We're kindred spirits, my dear. This is so exciting.'' She floated across the room and slid her arm around Vi's waist. "I'm so glad you came, Violet dear. It will be so good to have another flower woman to keep me company.''

Vi forced herself not to cringe. If she kept very, very still, her elbow would not brush against the woman's bare breast. She sucked in a breath and managed a plastic smile.

"Violet. Yep. That's me.''

Ian gently grasped Daisy by the shoulders and drew her away. "Let's get you cleaned up and dressed and ready for your volunteer work. You can chat with Vi...ah...Violet, when you get home.''

"That would be lovely, dear.'' Daisy twisted around to wave gaily. "We'll talk later, Violet.''

And that had been the beginning of the end. She would continue to be Violet for the duration of her stay, she just knew it. Once Daisy latched on to something, she didn't let go. Maybe it was because of all the memories she'd lost. Maybe that made what she *did* remember all the more precious.

A high-pitched whine interrupted Vi's reverie, bringing her back to the present. The noise came from the corner. She swiveled on the stool to look into Annabelle's concerned brown eyes. This time they didn't trigger a flood of bad feelings. Annabelle was a big dog—what had Ian said?—a chocolate Lab mix? Really nothing at all like the terrier pup she'd had as a kid. The pup her dad had killed.

Annabelle whined again.

"I'm okay. Nothing to worry about, girl."

Who was the crazy lady now? Talking to animals.

The whine grew more persistent, ending with a half bark.

Vi got off the stool and approached the dog, slowly, carefully. She *seemed* harmless enough. Head on paws, big beseeching eyes, who could resist?

Vi knelt a few feet from the animal and stretched out her hand. The dog sniffed her fingers, then her big, pink tongue swiped across Vi's palm.

"Yech." Vi wiped her hand on her pants, but leaned a little closer.

The dog didn't move a muscle, just swished its tail slightly. Bolstered with confidence, Vi let her fingers wander over the soft, silky ears.

Annabelle's tail thumped her approval.

Warmth flared somewhere near her heart. That wasn't bad at all. She lowered herself to sit cross-legged next to the dog. Annabelle inched forward on her stomach and rested her head on Vi's lap.

The warmth expanded. It became a reassuring feeling that grew with each stroke of the dog's coat.

"You're a lovely girl, aren't you."

The pink tongue bathed her wrist.

"You know, girl, it was an accident. I didn't mean to hurt you."

The big, brown eyes gazed up at her, as if she were the most important person on earth.

"And I don't really think Daisy is as big a pain in the butt as I did at first. She just kind of freaks me out. Never knowing what she'll do. And that's a lot of responsibility. Ian says he trusts me, but he doesn't know me. I can't even keep a houseplant alive, let alone a confused old woman."

Vi stroked Annabelle's head and worked her way down her soft, silky back. She really was beautiful. Her hind leg was in a cast, but healing nicely according to the vet.

"And you know what, Annabelle? The woman insists on calling me Violet. I don't want to be Violet. Violet, as in shrinking Violet. As in, let-people-walk-all-over-her Violet. And run-and-hide Violet...."

Annabelle whined, stretching up to lick Vi's chin.

"I didn't mean to upset you. I promise I'll help you get better. That way you can have your job back, and I can have mine. Sound like a plan?"

She nodded for the dog. Of course it was a good plan. Next time she went to Phoenix for more files, she'd stop off at the library and do some research on fractures. It would right a wrong, good karma and all that. And it would get her out of this mixed-up place where up was down and night was day.

IAN STOOD IN THE DOORWAY, watching Vi and Annabelle. The woman held the dog's head in her lap, talking softly, so softly he had to lean forward to hear.

Remorse? And tenderness. And something missing, but he couldn't quite put his finger on it. Confidence. That cocky attitude.

Guilt, or the power bar, twisted his gut. It was okay to use her when he thought she was a heartless witch. But now she looked relaxed and very unwitchlike.

Her tender murmurs grated on his nerves. Ian didn't want to hear anymore. He didn't need to feel bad about disrupting her life.

He cleared his throat.

Vi's head came up. Their eyes met for a minute, before she looked away. What he'd seen there made him curse under his breath. Confusion. And fear. Beneath that tough-as-nails stuff was a woman hiding from something. A woman who didn't expect much from people. But with the dog, she'd let down her guard. Let out all that vulnerability. And dammit, he'd had to witness it.

"I was checking on Annabelle. Making sure she was okay."

"Yeah, no problem."

"Short run." She raised an eyebrow.

Ian tried to convince himself he wasn't seeing her any differently, but he was. "I don't like being gone long. Force of habit. Besides, I've got a lot to do."

He watched her pry Annabelle's head off her lap, careful not to disturb the snoring dog. She rose so smoothly the dog didn't even twitch.

"What exactly do you do?" she asked.

"Write. Kind of an action, mystery type thing."

His shoulders tensed as he waited for the look. That surprised look. Sure enough, there it was. Then she eyed him up and down, before letting her gaze stop at his face.

The silence lengthened. He let it go on and on, until he couldn't stand it anymore.

"I was an English Lit major. That was right after I quit dragging my knuckles and figured out those darn opposable thumbs."

A flush crept up her neck. She opened her mouth to speak, but he cut her off.

"Don't bother denying it. You're not the first to make that assumption."

Her flush deepened, worked its way up her face. Amazing that her smooth, olive-toned skin could get that red. A few more twists in the breeze and he'd let her off the hook.

"Of course, those assumptions come in handy at times. Like when I helped out in Daisy's dance studio. At first I was drafted against my will, but when I got a look at all those ballerinas in leotards, I learned a whole new appreciation for dance. The dumb jock thing was what kept me from being severely beaten on a daily basis. I learned to compensate."

The expression on her face was priceless, well worth the soul-baring. Her mouth dropped open, her eyes widened. "Ballet? You?"

"You got it. I was pretty good, too. Better quarterback though, much to Dad's relief."

Vi let the rest of Ian's disclosure wash over her without registering. It was the only way she could keep her sleep-deprived brain cells from overloading completely.

This guy was a real trip. He'd developed the ultimate line. Not just a hard body, he was a renaissance man—intelligent, gifted and cultured, all rolled into one package. The average woman would buy it hook, line and sinker.

"How about antiques, what do you think of those?" she quizzed.

"I can take 'em or leave 'em." He grinned, an amused half smile that lit his eyes. "I don't enjoy show tunes, either. Never patted another guy on the butt, on or off the football field. 'Good game' worked just as well."

Okay, so he was an interesting paradox and liked women. But she had one ace up her sleeve, one that couldn't be conned or forced. Chemistry.

Vi let her gaze roam, from the barrel chest to biceps nearly the size of her thigh. Sweat made a damp V on the front of his T-shirt, highlighting some impressive pecs. Slim hips, muscular thighs. Toned calves. Probably even muscular feet. But it didn't matter. Not an ounce of chemistry.

None. Zip. Zilch. *Nada.*

Now a guy in a crisp, blindingly white dress shirt, Armani suit, cuff links, that might be another matter.

She crossed her arms and smiled. "I'm sure Daisy'd be very glad to hear that. I imagine she wants grandchildren—most mothers do." It was good to be in control again. Another three weeks or less and she'd walk out of here the way she'd arrived, in control and knowing where she was headed.

"Nah, she never says. Wants me to be happy, that's all. Demanding old broad, isn't she?"

"Not unless you mind finger foods or stand down wind of her on a bad day."

"Hey, that's not fair. *You* ought to try getting her in a bathtub."

"No thanks. Not in my job description."

"No, I guess not. I didn't think it would be in mine,

either. But it's the Alzheimer's. If you'd known her before… Well, she was quite a woman.''

"I'm sure she was." Vi placed her hand on his forearm, then let it drop to her side.

The Daisy who had danced, fallen in love, painted—all of it was slipping away and there was nothing Ian could do. It must tear him up. But not her problem. If she kept reminding herself of that, she'd be okay.

"I've got some books about it. Alzheimer's. If you're interested?"

She edged toward the door. "No thanks. No time," she shot over her shoulder, making her escape. There was no way she'd admit to the exhaustive Web search she'd made. Or the compulsion she felt to learn what made Daisy tick. And she definitely would not admit to wanting to make Ian's life a little easier.

IF THE WOMAN didn't shut up, Vi was going to wrap her hands around her wrinkly little turkey neck and squeeze the living daylights out of her. It wasn't fair. The lady'd had more adventures than one person had a right to. Sitting next to her, Vi felt like a mere imitation of a woman.

She shifted in her chair, then flicked her watch to make sure it hadn't stopped. Ian had only been gone twenty minutes.

"…and that's when I said, 'Joe, you just put that thing back in your pants right now.'" Daisy cackled with ribald glee, a far cry from her usual tinkling laughter.

According to Daisy, she'd been quite the belle of

the ball around these parts. Every man within miles was smitten.

"Uh, Joe...he's Sheriff Moreno's father, isn't he? I met the sheriff yesterday when he came by to check up on me."

"Yes, he's Vince's father. And my, but Joe was a fine-looking man in his younger years. All that dark wavy hair and passionate Latin eyes. Now *he's* a man who knows how to please a woman."

Vi groaned. She'd never be able to look Sheriff Moreno in the eye again without imagining Daisy and his father together, horizontal.

"How'd Ian's dad feel about your admirers?"

Daisy's eyes lost their sparkle. She clasped her expressive hands in her lap and allowed the corners of her mouth to quiver, just for a second.

Her voice was husky now, the elegant widow was back. "Oh, no, dear. I didn't move here until after Edward died. The first year at home was hard. Keeping Ian out of trouble, getting over it all. Well, a year and a day later, I decided I'd had enough of cold winters and an even colder bed. Figured Arizona was a brand-new start. For me. For Ian."

Vi fought to stay detached, removed from the woman's grief, old but still raw. But she couldn't. It grabbed her and wouldn't let go.

"Did you think you'd die if you stayed a minute longer?" she murmured.

The old woman's eyes narrowed, searching her face. She grasped Vi's hand and gave it a hard squeeze.

"Yes. Who did you lose, dear?"

The kindness in Daisy's voice was almost her undoing. The loss was as sharp as the day Patrick had died in a car accident.

She swallowed the lump in her throat. "My brother."

"How long?"

"Twelve years."

Twelve years. Could it really have been that long? Patrick with the wide, giving smile. The strength that had sheltered her, protected her from the worst of it. The back that had taken many of her beatings.

"Painting. That's when I took up painting. Ever try it?" Daisy chirped.

"Not really. Just pastels."

"Violet dear, you may use my studio anytime. Get those feelings out on canvas. It will set you free."

"No, I couldn't...."

"Nonsense. *I* can't paint anymore. It's just going to waste. Might as well share it with another flower woman."

"I don't have time." She shifted in her chair. Every fiber in her being strained to say yes, to bury herself in that studio, until every canvas, every dab of paint was used.

"Whenever you're ready, Violet dear, it's there for you."

Violet swallowed hard. Nobody had given her such a selfless gift in a long time, something so precious and personal. Not since Patrick.

"Your interview's tomorrow?" Ian asked, tapping his fingers on the easel.

"At ten-thirty. Time enough to drive down to the valley."

"You really want it? This District Manager thing?" He sounded like it was a management position in Hades.

"It's what I've been working for." She avoided his eyes, busying herself cleaning the brushes. The painting session had been completely unproductive, but so stimulating she could hardly stand still. The medium was new, but the experimentation inspiring.

"This is the first time I've seen you do something for the pure enjoyment of it. You're a natural artist." He nodded toward the canvas.

Violet's cheeks warmed with pleasure. "It's not as good as Daisy's, but it's not bad." She watched him from the corner of her eye. "You seem pretty comfortable in the studio. Painting's probably similar in some ways to writing. Instead of manipulating paint on canvas, you manipulate words."

"I've never thought of it that way before, but that's exactly what it's like. I'm still amazed that I can create a whole other world. Probably sounds silly to you."

"Not at all. Art's that way for me. I'd forgotten how relaxing it can be. That's why I chose today to paint. I needed to relax. This promotion is too important to screw up because I've psyched myself out."

He leaned against the wooden workbench, splashed with layers of color. "I wouldn't have figured you as the type for great introspection."

"Ah, the old adjuster stereotype. Ice water in the veins, motivated by pure greed. Sadistic delight in putting innocent customers through hell." She grinned at him wickedly. "Almost as bad as the attorneys, or maybe those Neanderthal sports nuts."

"No way. Sports nuts are very kind-hearted under-neath it all."

Scraping dried paint off the brush handle, she could feel him watching her. But there was no way she would meet his eyes. No way she would tell him that maybe he was right. Maybe the way he treated his mother was more important than how he looked.

Instead, she fell back on safety. "Yeah, well it takes a lot more than a stout back and soft heart to get by in this world."

He reached out and fingered a strand of her hair, working out a blob of dried crimson paint. "Ain't that the truth. But who says I want to just get by? Don't you ever want more Violet? After you become District Manager, what then? More money, more promotions, more power? But what have you really accomplished?"

That one hit a raw nerve. One she hadn't known existed until she'd picked up Daisy's paintbrushes. Until she'd immersed herself in the joy of creating so thoroughly that space and time ceased to exist. But that wasn't a career. Creativity didn't pay the bills or keep her safe.

"I'll tell you what I've accomplished. I've bought my own house, my own car. I can come and go as I please, without permission from anyone. If I want something, I can reach out and grab it." She poked his unyielding chest with a paint-smeared index finger. "And you know what, that feels pretty darn good."

Vi ran out of breath. It sounded just a little bit desperate, even to her.

She braced her fists on her hips. "And what about you, Mr. Obedient Son, Mr. I've-got-my-life-so-together? You can lecture me all you want about life and priorities, because you're safely sidelined for the moment. At least I'm honest about what I want. I *like* being in charge, and that's something I won't give up. *Ever.*"

Ian grasped her shoulders, getting closer, too close. "Hey, calm down. I didn't know… I mean, that you felt so strongly about it. I never thought of insurance that way…you know, passionately. But I guess it's not the insurance you love, it's the being in charge part."

He absently rubbed her neck with his thumb.

She jerked away.

"What's so bad about being in charge? I haven't lied to you. What you see is what you get. Now don't you have some corn dogs to cook up or something?"

Turning away, she willed her hands to stop shaking.

"I thought maybe I could understand why it's so important to you." Ian studied her face.

Violet warmed under his scrutiny.

"I guess I was wrong."

CHAPTER FIVE

THE CAR SLID SIDEWAYS on gravel, but Vi didn't give a damn. Nothing to lose now. Eight years of working harder and smarter than everyone else. Eight years of kissing corporate butt. Hell, she'd even learned to play golf.

She sniffed, choking on her own laughter. Tears ran down her face until she could barely see the road. *This* was where it had started to go wrong. Where her life had careened out of control and her career hit the skids. All because her appointment with Bob Johnson had flipped an emotional switch and she was afraid, somehow, some way, she'd slipped into an alternate reality. Afraid she'd escaped from one crazy, old man, only to be killed by another.

The Mustang's tires spit gravel as she jammed on the brake, parking in the Smith's circular drive—right behind the sheriff's patrol car.

Great. Just great.

She unlocked the heavy door with her spare key and stomped into the foyer. Off came her pumps, skittering across the bare tile like wobbly hockey pucks. One came to rest at the shiny black shoes of Sheriff Moreno.

''Uh, hello.'' She couldn't quite meet his eyes. ''Sorry I'm late.''

"No problem, Ms. Davis. My dad's been visiting with Daisy."

A lewd cackle echoed down the hallway. Daisy's love life was something she couldn't handle right now. Or the mental images it engendered.

Vi blocked out the distractions to concentrate on the warmth and kindness in the sheriff's brown eyes. He was exactly as Daisy had described young Joe. Wavy black hair and a smile that could melt copper—and probably a few hearts, too.

He extended his hand. "Ian tells me you've been a big help. I'm real glad to hear it. The judge will be, too."

Nodding mutely, she shook his hand.

The unmistakable clink of glass on glass brought her head up in time to see Ian enter the room with three bottles of beer intertwined in his fingers. The green glass told her it was imported. Her mouth watered at the thought of a cold Heineken.

"Here, thought you might want a cold drink. You look kinda flushed."

He extended a beer to her. Nice thought. But not for her.

"I don't drink."

He didn't seem offended. Just interested. There were a thousand questions in his eyes, none of which she wanted to answer.

Vi turned to Sheriff Moreno, desperate to change the subject.

"Daisy's told me quite a bit about your father."

Damn. Not that.

"You sure you don't want one, Vi? It's alcohol-free."

She gratefully accepted the bottle he offered.

"Here, Vince, why don't you take the two lovebirds their beer?"

The sheriff grinned as he accepted the drinks. "You bet. That way they can feel like they're living dangerously."

As Vince left, Violet could sense Ian studying her face. Even though she averted her gaze, she had the feeling he could see every nuance of her day.

"Come on." He jerked his head in the direction of the couch. "Let's take a load off."

Following Ian, she watched as he made himself comfortable on the couch and waited, one eyebrow cocked. But she couldn't seem to force herself to sit down. Instead, she paced.

"It was a disaster. I looked like hell." She gestured toward her face. "Sleep deprivation hasn't been kind to me."

Ian grunted.

"But the worst part was the sludge I *used* to call a brain. No snappy repartee, no incisive wit. I couldn't even come up with a comment about the V.P.'s kids. And I'd memorized them all. Amber, Nathan—" Vi ticked the names off on her fingers "—Reece and Amanda. But in the meeting, could I remember a single name or vital statistic? Hell no. Was it Amber who played basketball, or Reece? Did Amanda ace algebra or Nathan?"

Pausing to catch a breath, she glanced at Ian.

He cleared his throat. "I'm sure it wasn't that bad—"

Vi stalked back to the couch until she stood directly in front of him. "Of course it was that bad. I didn't have anything to set me apart from the rest. I was boring. Ordinary. Merely passable, nothing more. The woman in that interview was good old shrinking Violet at her best.''

Running out of steam, she wiped away the embarrassing moisture gathering in her eyes.

''From what I've seen, you're pretty sharp, even on your worst days. What about the other stuff? Insurance stuff. How'd you do with that?''

Vi stilled. Her train of thought was lost in the realization of how few people ever asked about her personal life. ''You really want to know, don't you?''

''I wouldn't ask otherwise.'' His voice carried the same conviction reflected in his eyes.

''No...you probably wouldn't.'' A glimmer of understanding made her want to run as fast and as far away as possible. This man believed in her abilities even though he'd seen her at her worst. How could he be so sure when he barely knew her?

Vi stepped toward him. ''Why are you so interested?''

''It's important to you.'' He shrugged.

It was important to her.

How long had it been since someone cared about what was important to her? Years?

''Oh.'' Her mind went blank. She was in uncharted territory with this conversation. ''I—I pretty much flubbed the technical questions, too. I know case law and comparative negligence backward, forward and sideways. But I just blanked out. Couldn't even complete a sentence. It was the weirdest thing—like my brain was stuffed with cotton.''

''You wanna know about the cotton-stuffed brain

thing?'' Ian gestured to the other end of the couch. "Then have a seat. I'll enlighten you.''

Violet studied the couch, studied Ian. He waited.

It wasn't a come-on, she could spot those a mile away. It was a genuine offer of friendship.

She shook her head in wonder. Then she padded over to the couch and plopped down, propping her heels on the coffee table, crossing her ankles in deference to her skirt.

Scraping the hair back off her face, she chuckled, a sound rusty from disuse. "Okay, Ian. I need all the enlightenment I can get. What's the deal?''

"It's simple. Sympathy Alzheimer's.''

Sheriff Moreno's shoes echoed on the ceramic tile as he returned from Daisy's room, an older, salt-and-pepper version of him trailing behind.

"Hey, Ian. See ya later. I gotta drop Dad off at my sister's before I go on duty.''

Ian started to rise.

"We can see ourselves out." He stuck out his hand to Violet. "Glad to see you're settling in.''

The old gentleman nudged his son out of the way. He grasped both her hands in his. "I'm Joe. Daisy has told me so much about you. Thank you for being a good friend to her.''

"Um, you're welcome. Nice to meet you." Vi bit her lip before she revealed what Daisy had mentioned about *him*.

"Come on, Dad, we gotta go or I'll be late for work.''

Joe sighed and followed his son to the door.

"See ya, Joe, Vince," Ian called.

The room seemed too quiet after the door clicked shut behind them.

Vi wished they could go back to the easy conversation of a few minutes ago. Maybe it wasn't too late. "You two are pretty good friends."

"Yeah. Since high school. Even though he's a couple years younger than me. Joe lives with him, so we can kinda relate."

"You were telling me about Sympathy Alzheimer's?"

"It's something I made up. My theory is that the longer you live with an Alzheimer's patient, the more you start to act like one. Probably due to sleep deprivation. And isolation. Some days I'd give my right arm to talk to a rational adult."

"I can see where you could get to that point. The bad part is, it's starting to seem pretty normal to me."

"Exactly. That's the Sympathy Alzheimer's kicking in."

Vi felt her cheeks warm as she gave in to her curiosity. "Do you think they're romantically involved? Daisy and Joe?"

Ian grinned wryly. "I try not to think about it. Mom's always had her own ideas of morality. But she was completely devoted to my dad when he was alive. After he died and we moved to Echo Point, she, uh…blossomed."

"You think she needs a talk on safe sex?"

Raising his hands in defeat, Ian pleaded, "Please, no. Getting her into the tub is about all I can handle. I think I might be scarred for life after that conversation." He leaned back, clasping his hands behind his head. "Actually, if I felt it needed to be done, I'd do it. I'd do just about anything for her. But I tell her and Joe to keep the door open and at least one foot on the floor at all times. Factor in the arthritis and Vince confiscating Joe's Viagra prescription, and I think we're fairly safe.''

Vi found it more than a little discouraging that, even at her advanced age and declining mental abilities, Daisy had a fuller love life than Violet had ever had. Usually her career was ample compensation, but today it just didn't seem to count. If not her job, then what? Lots of cats and a seat on the Home Owners Association Board?

She shuddered at the thought. Though Annabelle seemed pretty okay, she wasn't in a rush to go out and get an animal of her own. Too much responsibility. And as for the board, she'd never encountered a larger group of self-serving, lamebrained, control freaks.

What would Daisy tell the old busybodies? Probably seduce the men and empower the women. Gray power and all that. She could just see the sit-in to promote a clothing optional subdivision.

''That bad?'' Ian asked, interrupting her musings.

''What?''

''You had kind of a funny look on your face. And you've been in an odd mood since you got home.''

''Funny, odd. I can see the next adjective coming. Crazy. This place'll do it to you.''

''Actually, my next adjective was nice. It's nice to see you laugh. You've got a great smile.''

Vi shifted uncomfortably and glanced around the room. ''Shouldn't you be checking on Daisy? Making sure she hasn't smuggled another man in her room, or that old Joe didn't leave her some weed.''

"She usually takes a good nap after Joe, or anyone, visits. It's not sex and it's not drugs, so I figure it takes a lot of energy for her to pretend nothing's changed. She loves to visit though. The old days were good. Crystal clear. It's just now that's so darn confusing."

"It must be hard. Watching. Knowing you can't do anything."

Ian's eyes clouded. "Really hard. But I can make now as good as possible, make things easy for her. She's in her own home, and she has a schedule to rely on. She's happy, most days."

"Yeah, but routine for a free spirit like Daisy... It's probably something she's fought against all her life."

"Sure. But now it makes her feel secure."

"The way I've read kids need routine," Vi commented.

"Exactly." He looked at his watch. "Now, if my calculations are correct, we have time to get a couple steaks on the barbecue before she wakes up. Then, the last five minutes, we'll throw on a hot dog for her. Carrot sticks, French fries, and we've got ourselves a meal."

"You mean it? Silverware even?"

"Yeah, and if you're a real good girl, I might show you where I hide the knives."

"Oooh. You smooth-talker. Most men offer the world, but you, you offer sharp cutlery."

He winked at her. "Hey, baby, once you've walked on the wild side with me, you'll never go back."

That's what she was afraid of. This mixed-up world of his was starting to feel like a real home.

DAISY SPARKLED. That was the only way to describe it. Her skin glowed, her eyes seemed lit from within.

Her graceful hands gestured to underscore her point. No wonder the old guys were smitten.

"And I told Joe all about Violet, my friend. Another flower woman." She patted her hair with one hand and gestured with a carrot stick in the other. "But I warned the old goat not to get any ideas."

She grinned wickedly and winked at Violet. "But you know what the dear man said? Said I was more woman than any man could handle."

"I'm sure you are," Violet murmured. The steak was delicious, though the knife and fork felt almost foreign in her hands. Like the first time she'd tried chopsticks.

She could feel Ian watching her intently across the table. It was almost as if he could sense the questions moving in, sapping her self-confidence. For a while, she'd felt she had a place here with Ian and Daisy. A safety net against disappointment. But that was only an illusion. Two more weeks, and she'd be gone, back to her condo. Ian would continue here with his mother. And Daisy, God alone knew what would happen to her.

"Steak okay?" Ian asked.

"Wha…? Oh, yes, it's delicious."

Ian leaned forward. "Are you still upset about your interview?"

"No." She didn't meet his eyes. She wasn't used to admitting weakness. Besides, it was easier to concentrate on her food than on the concern in his voice.

"I should've taken your shift last night. Maybe you could explain to them or… Well, I'm sorry."

Violet carefully laid down the knife and fork, as if

the world might fall apart if they weren't perfectly aligned, evenly spaced. It was hard to look him in the eye.

"Ian, it's not your fault I was a walking zombie. I chose work over sleep and it backfired."

"But—"

"Look, I'm a big girl. There'll be other promotions." Vi wasn't sure why it was so important to put on a brave face, but it was. Like maybe Ian already had too much on his plate without feeling guilty about her mistakes.

"Vi, you can say what you want, but I know this is a huge opportunity. I've read up on Transglobal. They're scrambling to move women and minorities into upper management. That discrimination suit hit 'em hard."

It surprised her that he'd taken the time to find out about her company when he barely had time to himself as it was.

"It's not your problem. Really. I might even interview with other companies," she lied.

"You could get a job in just about any type of business with your management skills. Maybe even something in Echo Point."

Violet leaned forward. It was important that he understand. "I'm good with accident claims. No two cases are ever exactly the same. I understand the rules and how the game is played."

"But do you *like* it?" Daisy's question took Vi by surprise. She'd almost forgotten the woman was there—except for the way she quietly watched Vi's interchange with Ian, her head moving back and forth as if she were viewing a tennis match.

Vi opened her mouth to respond, but the words didn't come out. Did she like it? She'd never thought about it.

"On a scale of one to ten?" Ian helped.

"Welll…"

The "one" jobs were pretty easy to define. Slinging burgers, cleaning toilets, telemarketing—she'd done them all. But the tens, those were a little harder. What would her dream job be like? Certainly not dealing with maverick adjusters and pasty-faced upper management. Or pissed-off customers and irate agents.

"Six," she blurted. But it had to be more than that. There was the money, the respect, the challenge of no two days exactly alike. But no, six pretty much covered it.

"Violet dear, life is too short for a six. Jobs, men, homes. If it's a six, it's a waste of time. The tens are what make life worth living." Daisy's eyes gleamed as she warmed to her subject. "You dream and plan and pursue those tens for all you're worth and never give up."

Violet shifted in her chair. *Easy for her to say.*

"I *have* to support myself, build a secure future. Nobody else is going to do it for me. I don't regret the choices I've made."

"Then I'll just have to enlighten you, dear. You're satisfied with a six because you've never experienced a ten. We'll start tomorrow morning. Eight o'clock sharp. Meet me in the courtyard and bring the paints, easel, all those things…." Daisy waved her hand in the air. "We'll improve those expectations of yours."

"But…I have work to do."

"Insurance work." Daisy sniffed and raised her

chin. "Not nearly creative enough for a flower woman."

From across the table Ian murmured, sotto voce, "Better just do it. Give her an hour. Otherwise she'll hound you all day."

No kidding. For a woman with a seriously defective memory, Daisy could latch on to an idea and never let go. Too bad she couldn't remember that the phone didn't belong in the garbage.

"Okay, Daisy. One hour, that's it."

"Yes, dear, one hour." She nodded, a satisfied smile tickling the corners of her mouth.

IAN TIPTOED to the French doors and peered through lace curtains, viewing the courtyard. It was almost nine o'clock and Violet's one hour of enlightenment was about up. He scanned the sunny square at the center of the courtyard, expecting to find them by the easel. It was abandoned, nobody in sight.

He opened the door and stepped out on the veranda. That's when he heard it—Daisy's carefree laugh, then another feminine laugh, a little huskier. His eyes slowly focused on a shaded corner under the mesquite tree.

There, in the cool shade, he found them. Up to their bare ankles in vivid color. Violet leaned over to listen to Daisy, then threw her head back and laughed. It was a beautiful sound, earthy and honest, melding with Daisy's higher pitch to create the most uplifting harmony he had ever heard.

A slight breeze, warm with Indian summer, rustled the hem of Daisy's ethereal cotton skirt. She held the hem bunched around her thighs to keep it from dragging in the paint. And her face—God, he hadn't seen that kind of joy since she'd thrown down the paintbrushes in disgust. It was some sort of catharsis for her, her artistic dabbling. And apparently it didn't matter what application she used, by brush or feet, it still seemed to free her.

Her joy was reflected in Violet's wide smile. His breath caught in his throat. Maybe because this was the first time he'd seen Violet with her defenses completely down. A gust of wind blew her hair in her face, frustrating his view. So he let his gaze wander to her bare shoulders, kissed golden by the sunshine. Her tank top was tie-dyed with all the colors of the rainbow, tucked into the waistband of cutoff jeans. Fluffy shreds of stone-washed cotton danced with her every move, caressing her sculpted brown thighs. She looked like she belonged at Woodstock, with flowers in her hair and a peace sign painted on one cheek.

He stood and watched, transfixed.

Household paint trays lay around the edges of the old sheet. Every once in a while, one of the women would dunk her feet in a bucket of water, tromp on an old beach towel, then dance through a new color. Onto the sheet it went, applied with verve. Somehow, the exhilaration radiating from the two beauties reflected itself on the canvas, where Daisy's yellow predominated, turning different shades of orange as it blended with Violet's red.

Ian wandered over to them, drawn by their magic.

Annabelle's tail thumped a greeting as he approached. The dog was curled up at the base of the tree, where she had an unobstructed view. Lifting her head, she pulled back her lips in a happy grin. A happy Daisy made for a happy Annabelle.

Ian stopped midstride, a tuneless whistle dying on his lips. His heart lifted. Maybe Annabelle wasn't the only one using Daisy as the bellwether for happiness. Most days were good, now that she'd grown accustomed to Violet. But what about when the good days became fewer and fewer? When there wasn't even a spark of Daisy's spirit left in the shell of her body? It was something he didn't think about. The dark thought belonged hidden in a distant corner of his mind where it couldn't jinx what they *did* have left.

And today was an excellent day. He intended to enjoy it to the fullest.

He resumed the tuneless whistle and strolled over to their impromptu art exhibit.

"A masterpiece in progress," he said, watching Violet, wondering if she would raise her guard again. Her smile faltered, but didn't fade completely. Her amber eyes glowed with something he couldn't identify.

"Daisy and I decided to try something new. I told her about an article I'd read about Farrah Fawcett applying paint with her body. Of course, Daisy was all for that idea, but I suggested we try our feet."

"Mmmm. Interesting concept."

It didn't take much imagination to replace the psychedelic T-shirt and shorts Violet wore with a layer of paint and nothing more. Her body would be lithe and strong. Lush breasts, slender hips and long, long legs.

"Mind if I watch?" he asked.

Violet's smile slipped another notch, but she shrugged her shoulders.

"Of course, dear. Kick off your shoes and join us," Daisy invited.

He shook his head. "No way. You didn't teach me to drive and you won't teach me to paint. Best way to keep peace in the family."

"Oh, Thessalonian. Are you still holding that pulled groin muscle against me? I taught you to warm up properly."

"Thessalonian?" Violet sputtered. "Groin muscle?" Her eyes widened and fastened on the area in question.

He crossed his arms over his chest and willed her eyes upward. "Ian is short for Thessalonian."

"Yes, dear, it's biblical," Daisy explained. "It means 'son of light.' And he was, from the moment he entered this world."

Violet absorbed Daisy's revelation as she glanced from mother to son and back to Daisy again. It was a horrible thing to name a boy, but done with such absolute love, who could blame her? Maybe shrinking Violet wouldn't have been so bad if someone had held her and loved her and told her how special it made her. Maybe then she could have carried the name with confidence. But what about Ian? Obviously he didn't broadcast his given name.

"Thessalonian," she rolled the name around on her tongue. It was brutal. Beautiful, melodic and absolutely brutal.

Ian's eyes narrowed, and his chin came up in a belligerent challenge.

Violet squelched a nervous chuckle. What to say? Holding her tongue had never come easily, but maybe now was a good time to start.

"Now you know why I bulked up and joined the football team." He raised an eyebrow, his mouth twisted in a grimace.

Daisy seemed perfectly oblivious to his embarrassment, probably as deeply embedded and as old as nursery rhymes.

"Son of light," Violet murmured. "A name given with love. You're a lucky man, Thessalonian."

He tilted his head to the side in acknowledgment. Stepping forward, he wiped a smear of paint off her cheek with his thumb. "And Violet. A flower and a deep, bold color. How appropriate."

It sounded pretty good that way. Like a survivor, not a victim.

Violet waited for him to move away. To take back the warmth of his approval. But he didn't. Instead, he rubbed her cheek with his thumb. The paint was long gone, along with a couple layers of skin. But it was nice. Too nice.

She cleared her throat and stepped back. "The, uh, paint's drying."

A glance at her red feet confirmed that the paint was, indeed, drying. Cracks radiated along her toes and they were stiff when she tried to wiggle them.

But the water was cool as she stepped into the bucket. She turned to see what Ian was doing. Nothing. Absolutely nothing. Except watching her.

A lively gust brought goose bumps to her bare arms. Violet wiped her feet on the beach towel and searched for her sandals.

"You're not quitting already are you?" Ian asked.

Violet glanced at Daisy, expecting her to be engrossed in her painting. She was very intense about her art, and actually quite talented, with an instinctive grasp of color and balance. But she stood there, at the edge of the sheet, absently sweeping her yellow toes back and forth, making a half-circle design amid a thick blob of red. Her gaze was thoughtful as she looked at Ian, then Violet.

"I've accomplished what I set out to," Daisy stated. "I showed Violet the ten." With that, she turned on her heel and headed for the house, leaving a trail of small yellow footprints in her wake.

Neither moved. Violet mulled over Daisy's remark. The morning had definitely been a ten. The paint, the laughter, the sheer joy of creating, it couldn't be beat. But she didn't think that was what Daisy had in mind.

CHAPTER SIX

IAN PLACED a skillet on the stove while he watched Vi enter through the French doors. She met his gaze then looked away. Color rose in her cheeks.

"Everything okay?" he asked.

"Um. Yes. Paints are all cleaned up."

He gestured with a spatula toward the kitchen table. "Have a seat. Thought I'd whip up an early lunch— grilled cheese and tomato soup, my specialty. How many sandwiches do you want?"

"One's fine." Vi perched on a chair at the kitchen table.

Ian flicked open the cabinet above the stove. Running the flat of his hand along the shelf, he located the stashed stove knobs and placed them on the appropriate posts. "Daisy proofing," he explained.

"Where *is* Daisy?"

"She headed for her bedroom. Probably taking a catnap."

Vi nodded, chewing on her thumbnail.

"Ian?"

"Huh?"

"I had fun today."

"Looked like Daisy had fun, too."

"This isn't turning out the way I expected." She

cleared her throat. "I...I didn't expect to enjoy myself."

Ian turned. He didn't like the doubt he saw shadowing her eyes. And something else. Guilt?

"And that's a bad thing because...?"

"Because I have a plan. Goals. I'm at a really crucial point in my career and if I get sidetracked...I could lose it all."

Ian pondered her statement. "Don't you think that's kind of extreme? There's got to be a balance."

"I can't afford balance. Look at my interview. I was tired and distracted and I blew it. I need to focus on my goals. Not on painting, or tens or...anything else."

"You're dead wrong, Vi. Goals without balance are pretty much just obsessions."

"Okay, so I'm obsessed with my career." She raised her chin. "There are worse compulsions."

"Yeah...you're right there. But the end result is pretty much the same."

"How can you say that? How can you compare something positive like working hard and achieving my dreams with something destructive...like alcohol or drugs?"

A whiff of browning bread gave Ian time to formulate what he wanted to say while he flipped the sandwiches and adjusted the heat under the soup.

He chose his words carefully. "I've seen my share of alcoholics and substance abusers. There was a time when I wondered if I'd gotten close to that line myself. Drugs, alcohol, work, they all can be used to bury problems."

Her eyes flashed with indignation. "There is no way you can compare my career with getting drunk. Believe me, I know. I lived with an alcoholic for eighteen years. My dad's a drunk.''

Vi's revelation didn't come as a big surprise to Ian. Her dogged determination was just the tip of the iceberg. There was so much more going on under the surface, he was sure of it.

"That's why you don't drink.''

She averted her face. "I don't want to talk about it. I shouldn't have even started this discussion but—''

"You needed someone to talk to. There's no crime in that.''

"I didn't *need* to talk to anyone. If I did, there are other people I'd choose besides you.''

Yeah, who?

Ian bit his tongue to keep from flinging the question back at her. She hadn't received a single personal phone call that he knew of since she'd been there. She never mentioned friends or a boyfriend. And the comment about her father had been the first time she'd referred to family.

"Forget I said that, Ian. I shouldn't take it out on you because I'm on edge about my job.'' Her grudging tone practically negated the apology.

Ian grunted and returned to his cooking duties.

"Ian?''

"Huh?''

"I've been meaning to ask—how long have you been hiding the stove knobs?''

"About six months. It's a long story, but basically Daisy can't be trusted with them.''

"I've got a few minutes. Tell me the story? Please?'' Her voice was low, husky.

Ian turned. The compassion in her eyes embarrassed

him almost as much as it surprised him. "One cake, broil, two hours. That's the gist of it."

"Was anyone hurt?"

Shaking his head, Ian said, "I was in my office and didn't smell a thing. Fortunately Annabelle alerted me. I was able to put out the fire pretty quickly. Then Annabelle took me to my mom—she was sound asleep in her room."

"You could have both been killed."

Ian nodded. "Now you see why it's important for me to hide stuff like that. The knives, too. Just in case she gets a wild idea and decides she wants to make a stir fry."

"Ahhh, now I understand. And here I thought you were just overly fond of finger-foods."

"Not hardly." Ian turned off the stove, removed the knobs and returned them to their hiding place. He served up the sandwiches—the soup went in bowls for him and Vi, a coffee mug for Daisy.

"Mom," he hollered. "Lunch."

He got them each a soda from the fridge.

"Mom, your sandwich's getting cold."

"I'll go get her," Violet offered.

"Thanks."

When Vi hadn't returned five minutes later, Ian wiped his mouth with a paper napkin and went to look for her.

Daisy's room was empty. He heard muted feminine voices coming from the direction of the bathroom.

"Daisy? Violet?"

Violet stuck her head out the bathroom door. "Just a little accident. We've got it under control."

"This isn't your shift. You don't have to do this. Go get yourself some lunch and I'll take care of it."

"No. I've got it." Her voice was taut.

Ian studied Violet's face. Her eyes were damp, as if she'd brushed away tears. She fixed him with a bright smile, but it wobbled at the corners. What the hell was going on in there?

Placing a palm against the door, he pushed. She had her foot against the door, but it didn't hold. He shoved again. Enough to budge Violet. Enough to see inside. Enough to smell the problem even before he saw the mess.

And saw Daisy standing miserably in the middle of the bathroom, her chin tucked toward her chest, her skirt hiked up around her hips.

Ian clamped a hand over his mouth, willing his lunch to stay down. It never got easier, no matter how many times it happened.

"Did you take her to the bathroom after coffee?" It wasn't even a question, really. The evidence was right there.

"I'm sorry, Ian. I forgot…the painting, and we were having such a good time." Violet gestured helplessly. "I just…forgot."

Daisy turned her head away from them, but not before he saw the shame in her eyes. Anger twisted his gut, made his pulse whoosh in his ears. It wasn't fair. Not to any of them.

"You forgot."

His fists felt like cramped, dead things, clenched at the end of his stiff arms. He wanted to hit something, to make something pay for what had happened to them.

Violet moved back, her eyes wide, her pupils huge. She acted as if she were afraid of him. Afraid of being hurt.

The fight went out of him, his hands falling loosely against his thighs. His shoulders sagged, he exhaled slowly, letting it all go.

He reached out to touch her hair. It looked soft, shiny, so full of life. She flinched and turned away. But not before he saw the sad acceptance in her eyes. Not only did she think he would hit her, it wasn't something new.

She'd been hit before, beaten, to the point where she had almost lost her spirit. Almost. But somehow, that great screw-you, I'll-make-my-own-way attitude of hers had survived, refined by fire. She had survived it and come out the other side, strong and independent. But brittle, so brittle she couldn't bend, couldn't veer off course.

He let his hand drop to his side without stroking her hair or reassuring her. She didn't want his reassurance. She didn't trust him.

"Go," he whispered.

"No." Violet raised her head. The doubt was gone. Her chin lifted to that familiar stubborn angle, but her lips curved into a gentle half smile she'd never shown him. He knew he was seeing how she must have once been, before all the hurts, before all the defenses.

"No." She grasped his hand. "We'll do it together."

THE COMPUTER SCREEN blurred, a jumble of blue with white squiggles. It could be a file, or a prime-time sitcom for all Violet knew. None of it registered.

It had been horrible. A task for Florence Nightengale or at the very least the Brady Bunch mom. She'd scrubbed her hands nearly raw, then her forearms and finally settled on a head-to-toe shower.

But it was Daisy who really got to her. The shame, the confusion. Gone was the bohemian free spirit. Gone was the lusty lady of the senior set. Reduced to a small, pitiful shell of shame and confusion.

And it had been all Vi's fault. If she had only remembered the one simple instruction. Take Daisy to the bathroom after her coffee. Simple. No problem. For anyone except her. Captivated by paint and freedom and Daisy's approval, she had forgotten. She'd let herself go, had forgotten responsibilities and ramifications. Lived for the moment, looked for the ten, just like Daisy said. And had let her down.

Nothing had prepared her for this. Not even living with an alcoholic—hate had gotten her through that one. Certainly not handling accident claims, though she dealt with highly emotional people. But it was usually from the impersonal safety of a phone line, or behind a desk. Sympathy, but not necessarily empathy. No touching involved. No firsthand experience with the hardships. Medical reports, police reports, recorded statements, but no gut-wrenching, you-are-there kind of thing.

Sure, she could write a report on Daisy. Give a pretty good two-dimensional account of her daily life. But it wasn't until today that it had become real.

Real people were something she avoided at all costs. Particularly real people with real problems. Which included the entire human race. It was easier that way. The only way she could survive.

Real people didn't understand that there was nothing left for her to give. They expected things she apparently was unable to deliver—like controlling her temper, avoiding animals in the road, remembering simple instructions about Daisy's schedule.

The blinking cursor taunted her. Liar. Liar. Liar. Okay, so she didn't *want* to be saddled with caring, didn't want to take the chance. It was understandable, if not very nice.

And at first, it had been enough. But now everything had changed. A warm body to keep Daisy from wandering off wasn't enough. She needed to safeguard the woman's dignity and she wasn't sure she was up to the challenge.

Two weeks down, two to go.

The white blur pulsated amid the blue. Two. Two. Two.

Coffee. It could only help.

Violet shuffled down the hallway, letting her nose guide her to the ambrosia that awaited in the kitchen. It was nearly ten o'clock. She'd waited until Daisy left for the center. Didn't want to see her this morning. It had been bad enough last night, her shift, when she couldn't avoid her any longer. She'd wanted to say she was sorry, do something to take it all back. But she couldn't. The only thing she could do was regret the dull film of shame dimming the brilliance that was Daisy. It hurt. Hurt in a way that she hadn't experienced in a long time. And now that the pain was pouring in, she didn't quite know how to get it to stop.

Tiptoeing into the kitchen, she was relieved to see it was empty. Ian had probably gone for a run. Or to work out in the garage where he kept his weight set.

Annabelle's tail thumped a greeting. She didn't lift her head though, as if she somehow sensed Vi's mood. Violet bent over to pat the dog on her way by.

Ian's mug, the one about rugby players, sat on the counter. It looked kind of forlorn—all alone and forgotten.

Violet opened one cupboard, and then the next. The coffee cups were playing hide-and-seek, and she was losing. A caffeine headache throbbed at her temples. Desperate times required desperate measures. She grabbed Ian's mug and poured a fresh cup, wrapping her palms around the life-giving brew. The warmth of strong coffee radiated through the thick ceramic cup, warming her hands, if not her heart. With enough caffeine, her options would become clear.

The low tone of the phone interrupted her morning worship at the java altar. She reluctantly let go of the cup long enough to pick up the receiver. Amazingly enough, it was for her. Even more amazing, she'd made it to the second round of interviews.

Ian sauntered in as she hung up. She opened her mouth. Nothing came out except a surprised squeak.

"What's going on?"

This time she found her voice. Wonder tinged her words, "That was human resources. I made it to the second round."

Her adrenaline surged as the words made it a fact and not just a daydream. Every doubt fled as the thrill of victory took hold. There was still a chance!

"Did you hear me?" she shrieked. "I get another interview!"

She danced a victory jig and threw her arms wide to embrace the whole big, beautiful world.

The blank look on Ian's face barely registered as she flung herself at him. She wrapped her arms around his neck and rocked his sturdy body from side to side.

His mouth dropped open, his eyes widened just a bit.

"I'm-gonna-get-the-job," she sang. "I'm-gonna-get-the-job." With that, she laid a celebratory kiss, right on his wonderful mouth.

Feet a-dancing, she started to soft-shoe away. But a strong arm wrapped around her shoulders and hauled her back. Ian snugged her up against his chest and held her close. Warmth seeped through her, leaving her feeling incredibly safe. Like burrowing under a mountain of blankets on a cold winter morning.

"I'm glad, Vi. I don't want to mess up your life." The way his life had been messed up. He didn't say it, but the words hung in the air anyway.

"You didn't mess up my life. I'll get the job and nothing's changed."

His arms tightened a fraction. Her hands splayed in response, surveying his muscled back. Things got all jumbled up in her mind. It was hard to think with him so close.

"Sorry, Ian. I know things will change for you and Daisy whether I'm here or not. If you need a friend, you just have to call."

Ian tilted back his head and looked at the ceiling. He didn't answer.

"Ian?"

He brought his head down, his eyes searching her face.

"Thanks, Vi. I can always use a friend."

Friends. That's what they'd been last night. Handling a bad situation together, as a team. No blame, no raised voices. Just handling it.

"I didn't mean to hurt her," she whispered.

Ian's arms loosened. He gripped her shoulders and pushed her away. The fire in his eyes made her want to run.

"*You* didn't hurt her, Violet. The damn disease did. Alzheimer's." His voice was tight and low, vibrating with hate. Hate for something he couldn't see, couldn't touch, could only give a name to. Some invisible enemy slowly sucking the life from his mother. "You're only human. We all make mistakes."

Vi exhaled slowly. That look was gone. The good guy was back.

"What about you, Ian? You never seem to make mistakes with her. You're so organized."

"I've made more mistakes than you'll ever know. Some a long time ago. Times I put her through hell when I was growing up. Now they're different mistakes, like not having enough patience. I don't understand what's really going on inside her head. All I can do is react, make an educated guess. And love her."

It was hard to imagine Ian as anything but a devoted son. "You *do* love her. That's obvious."

"Yeah, but is she safe? I do my best. You do your best. But mistakes'll happen. I worry that maybe I won't know when it's time…you know, time for her to go to one of those places. What if I wait too long? What if she hurts herself?"

The doubt in his voice made her want to wrap her arms around him and give him that safe haven he'd given her. A hug. From a friend. But she didn't. Instead, she tried to use words. "You'll know. Because you know her better than anyone. And you know what it would do to her spirit…one of those places. That vital, alive part would just wither…'' Her voice cracked. She couldn't even think about it.

Ian's strong fingers cupped her face, raised her chin. ''Hey, don't worry about it. That's why I got Annabelle. Another set of ears and eyes. So I can keep Mom at home.''

Violet drew in a deep breath. If he could be brave, so could she. ''Okay. So how do I make it up to her? Last night, I mean. She was so sad, so humiliated….''

''You hurt for her—it means you care. Daisy can sense that. She probably won't even remember what happened last night when she gets home today. You can't take on her pain. It'll destroy you. I know.''

Violet wiped a stray tear from her cheek. He did know. She'd seen it in his eyes.

''There should be something more I can do. I *won't* forget next time,'' she promised. ''No matter how great the painting is.''

She reached up, her hand unsteady. Gently, she stroked the smile line next to his mouth.

''Ian?''

''Huh?''

''Promise me. Someday you'll tell me. About 'all the hell' you put her through when you were a kid?''

''Maybe someday.'' He brushed her hair back from her face, then moved away a few steps. ''When's your interview?''

''Tomorrow. At ten.''

''Go get prepared. I'll keep Daisy out of your hair when she gets home and take your shift tonight. You'll be in top form tomorrow morning. The boss' kids names, punitive damages, all that stuff'll just roll off your tongue.''

Violet shrugged. Her happy dance was a distant memory as she tried to turn her attention where it ought to be, her future. Instead, her thoughts kept returning to Ian and Daisy and how unfair this whole situation was.

''Thanks. But when will you sleep?''

''Don't worry about me. I'll catch a catnap before Daisy gets home. You can spell me tomorrow when you get back.''

Take it. Give yourself a fighting chance.

Violet had taken care of herself for so long, the instinct to protect her interests was automatic.

They need you. It's too much for him.

This was a new urge, to protect someone else.

Ian traced lazy circles on her collarbone with his thumbs. Leaning his forehead against hers, he said, ''Go. So you can show 'em what you've got.''

VIOLET EASED around the corner, the car under complete control. No skidding, no flying rocks, no hurt dogs. Pride hummed inside her, like some electric force with a life of its own.

She'd nailed the darn interview. Tort law, punitive damages, bad faith, current case law. You name it, she knew it.

And she'd remembered that it was Amber who was the math whiz and Nathan who played Pop Warner football. And even that the vice president's mother-in-law was in a nursing home. Three points for the girl from L.A.

The job was hers. She could feel it. The energy had

rippled through the conference room, from gray head to gray head, as they nodded in agreement. Definitely qualified. Female. And Hispanic, not very, but just enough. Two points for human resources. They would get back to her by Friday, but they didn't really need to bother. It was hers.

She was confident that, in three weeks, she would travel to Ohio for the month-long management school, where the big boys introduced the newbies to life on the other side of the glass ceiling. And, of course, it meant more money. Much, much more money. Maybe finally move Dad to an assisted-living apartment? Maybe just forget about the old guy and buy a real, honest-to-goodness house, with a yard and a pool and her very own dog. The possibilities were endless.

The Mustang coasted to a sedate stop in front of Ian's house. She leaped up the steps, anxious to share her news with him. And Daisy, too.

Then her steps slowed. Daisy wouldn't be happy for her. She would be disappointed, convinced Violet had sold out, settled for a six instead of a ten.

Violet squared her shoulders. What did the confused old woman know anyway? It was a strong choice, a bold choice. Shrinking Violet couldn't do it, but Vi sure as hell would. Two more weeks of Violet, then it was hello Vi.

Two and a half weeks. It didn't seem like the life sentence it once had. No, it seemed…short. Only two and a half weeks to make sure Annabelle was healed, Daisy back on track, and Ian, well…make things as easy on Ian as possible. Because he really was a good guy most of the time. He had more responsibility than one person should have to shoulder, doggie assistant or no doggie assistant.

Violet shook her head. She'd been standing on the front porch, her hand on the doorknob, not moving. Just thinking. She twisted the knob, but no good. Her key. She rummaged around in her purse. Lipstick, pen, tampon, loose change. Nothing.

She had no choice but to pound on the sturdy door like a desperate salesman at the last house on the block.

Had it really been only little more than two weeks ago, when she'd pounded on this same door? It hardly seemed possible. Friends. Ian and Daisy were friends. Something she hadn't had since she was a kid, when she'd learned that friends and laughter and chattering stopped at the front door of the house where shouting, slamming doors and slamming fists reigned.

Shrinking Violet. Too scared to bring friends home. Too afraid to let anyone close. Afraid of breaking up the family, what little there was of it.

So in college, shrinking Violet had become Vi. Confident, set on success, straight to the top, I-don't-need-anyone Vi. And she'd never looked back. Until now.

All the talk of tens and dreams was messing with her head. She straightened her spine and tried to recapture the heady nectar of victory. The heck with them. Nobody would take this away from her. Nobody.

She snagged the emergency key from above the door frame, unlocked the door and went inside. Nobody waited to see how her interview had gone. No Ian offering a cold one, no Daisy making appropriate noises of how a desk job was so beneath her.

Violet's shoulders slumped, her victorious smile faded. Why had she thought they would care?

"Ian," she called.

Silence.

"Daisy…"

Silence.

Violet tramped down the hallway, her heels echoing on the tile.

Daisy's door stood ajar. No Daisy.

Ian's door stood ajar. No Ian.

She stood in the doorway to his room. It was spare like hers, in the Sante Fe tradition. But there was a warmth to it, the rough-hewn ceiling beams stained a rustic brown. An intricate wrought iron headboard, probably handmade and very, very old. Natural cotton bedspread and shams. Rustic wood furniture and a colorful rag rug to warm his bare feet as they hit the floor in the morning.

Bare feet, bare chest. Did he sleep in the nude? Probably—he'd been raised by a free spirit.

It conjured pictures of what he might look like first thing in the morning, sleep-tousled hair, five o'clock shadow, that relaxed, wry half smile she'd come to know. Warmth tickled her insides, tugging at her memories of Patrick. It was the feeling of coming home, of reaching a place where nothing awful could touch her. A place where no matter how bad and ugly the world got, she was always safe, always protected.

She shook her head. There was no room in her life for depending on someone else to ensure her safety.

Slowly, she walked away.

Why should she care? He hadn't thought her interview was important enough to be here when she got back. Hadn't cared enough to pretend her victory was worth celebrating.

Then it hit her. What if he wanted to be here, but something had happened? Something involving Daisy?

The tap-tap of her heels kept time as she trotted around the corner, down another hallway. What if Daisy had hurt herself and Ian'd taken her to the hospital? Or worse yet, Daisy'd done something crazy that had gotten *both* of them hurt?

Short, burning gasps scratched her throat as she exhaled. She pounded down the hallway and rounded the corner to the kitchen. No smoke, no evidence of fire. No bloody body hacked to pieces with a steak knife.

What if Ian had fallen asleep, exhausted from taking her shift? Daisy could have slipped out the door and be halfway to Young by now.

Violet dashed down the other hallway and flung open the door to the studio. Empty, a board screwed into place where the picture window had been. Temporary repairs until the glass guy could come.

The courtyard. It was the only place left.

Her legs cramped in protest at her sprint. How did the women in the commercial manage to play basketball in dress shoes?

Violet couldn't see a trace of them through the gauzy curtains on the patio doors. She skidded to a stop and yanked open both doors. The warm autumn breeze reached in to caress her cheek, beckoning with the sweet smell of decaying leaves.

She stepped through the doorway, only to stop, silent, still. They were there, Daisy, Ian and even Annabelle. Next to a rickety card table that had seen better days.

"There she is," Ian exclaimed. He smiled in greeting, the warmth in his voice a magnetic pull.

"Violet dear," Daisy reached out a hand to her. "Congratulations."

Violet blinked away the bright sunlight playing peekaboo through the lacy canopy of the mesquite tree. Something prickled her nose, blurred her vision.

"What? How?"

"They called," Ian explained. "Must've been right after you left the interview. You got the job. Training in Cleveland starts three weeks from Monday."

That explained the small square of chocolate cake. The one with squiggly blue lines that declared, CONGRATS, diagonally across chocolate frosting.

Violet just stared. She must have looked like a complete idiot. Then Ian cleared his throat and she noticed how tentative his smile had become. She stepped closer to get a better look at the cake, shaking her head in wonder. Homemade, no doubt about it. Like she'd always wanted. A lopsided, barely readable, made-with-love cake.

"It's not much." Ian put an arm around her shoulders and squeezed. A brotherly show of affection. A friendly one. "But it's all we could throw together in such a short time. Microwaved. Relatively safe..." His voice tapered off to silence.

Violet sniffed, but the tears and the sniffles wouldn't cooperate. Both flowed freely, much to her embarrassment.

Daisy handed her a tissue, something even forgetful old women seemed to have in abundance. "Congratulations, dear. You're a ten and you deserve your dreams, wherever they lead you.''

Violet's throat got all scratchy, making it difficult to speak. ''Thank you, Daisy. It means a lot.''

She blew her nose so hard she wished it was thousand-ply tissue.

''Hey,'' Ian said as he pushed a lock of her hair behind her ear. ''What gives?''

Her eyes went funny on her as she looked up into his face—all blurry and watery. She laughed, but it caught somewhere in her throat and came out a husky chuckle.

''Nobody's ever made a cake for me before.''

''Nobody? No birthdays?''

''None.''

It seemed like such a silly little thing. Much too silly to make a big deal about. But it mattered.

''Oh, Vi,'' he whispered, then enfolded her in a big bear hug, rocking her back and forth.

Her nose hit smack-dab in the middle of his pecs. She had the crazy vision of death by smothering against that large rock-solid expanse of chest. A hiccup caught in her throat, morphing into a burp.

The tears started all over again. And the sniffles. Nobody could ever accuse her of being dainty and genteel.

She resisted the urge to rub her face against Ian's chest. Surefire way to turn off a guy by using his clothing as a tissue.

''Let it all out,'' he soothed.

It was heaven to be held by a man who cared. A man who didn't try to lie about himself. Who accepted her, good, bad and gastric disturbances included. One helluva guy.

She shifted in his arms, turning her head so her cheek rested against his chest. She slid her arms around his waist and squeezed for all she was worth. He pulled her closer, his breath tickling her hair. His heart thudded evenly beneath her cheek. Rock solid. That's what he was. Rock solid.

CHAPTER SEVEN

IAN HUNG ON to the precious wisps of sleep, loathe to leave the peaceful cocoon behind. The slap-slap of bare feet intruded first, then the whoosh of water running in the bathroom. He opened one bleary eye to look at the clock. Seven-thirty.

He came fully awake in an instant. There was no way Violet was up this early and certainly not a giggling Violet. Swinging his legs over the bed, he padded over to the chest of drawers.

T-shirt, shorts and he was dressed.

Ian sprinted down the hall to Daisy's room. Empty. Just what he'd feared. Violet's room was empty, too.

Damn.

The aroma of coffee hit him as he rounded the corner to the kitchen. The scene that met him was like something from the twilight zone. He shook his head, sure he hadn't seen things right.

Nope. He'd seen it right. Violet, standing, at seven-thirty in the morning, eyes shining, skin glowing, actually humming a tune. Next to her, sitting on a stool, was Daisy. At least he assumed it was Daisy.

"What's going on?" he asked as he eyed the pink and purple squiggly things stuck in Daisy's hair.

"Today is the Harvest Party at the center," Violet explained, as she wrapped a section of Daisy's hair on a purple noodle-shaped thing. It reminded him of pool toys, only much, much smaller.

"Oh."

"Coffee's on." Violet inclined her head in the direction of the coffeemaker. "Now, makeup."

"Oh, goody." Daisy clapped her hands in delight. "It's been ages."

Vi tipped her head to the side and laid a finger along her chin, studying the older woman. "I think we'll go for neutrals. Enough color to brighten your complexion, but nothing gaudy."

"No red lipstick?" Daisy's disappointment was obvious.

"No. Too harsh. And messy if you do any kissing."

That sealed it. She was sold. "Okay, but none of that virginal pink glossy stuff." Daisy moued her disapproval.

Violet laughed.

Could this be the same creature who'd literally growled at him yesterday when he wouldn't give up his favorite coffee cup?

"What's the matter, Ian?"

"You do realize it's only seven-thirty?"

"Sure, but party preparations take time. Bus'll be here at nine." Vi didn't even glance his way as she talked. She concentrated solely on Daisy and the assorted bottles and compacts on the kitchen table. With her fingertips, she patted some sort of beige liquid all over Daisy's face.

"Nice. Tinted moisturizer makes you positively glow. Next, blush. Subtle...hmm."

Daisy sat a little straighter, soaking up all that girl stuff.

"Have you been mainlining coffee since seven?"

"Six-thirty actually. I'm not much of a morning person and I wanted to be able to give Daisy my full attention."

Ian snorted. "That's an understatement."

She wasn't listening. Neither was Daisy.

"I'll just go read the paper...."

Daisy waved a hand in the air. "Have a nice run, dear."

Ian settled on the couch with the newspaper, but couldn't finish a single article. As soon as he'd get engrossed, another hoot or giggle would erupt from the kitchen. It was like landing in the middle of a slumber party.

Finally he gave up. He tossed the newspaper on the coffee table and stretched out on the couch. It was much easier to rest his eyes and enjoy the lovely music women made when they were happy. Though he couldn't make out what they said, the voices held a joyful lilt. Excitement lifted Daisy's voice to a girlish pitch he hadn't heard in years.

Shoot, if he'd known some makeup and hair thingies would make her this happy, he would have bought her a truckload. But it wasn't the hair thingies that made her so happy. It was Violet. A kindred spirit and the love and attention represented in this early morning ritual. Daisy sensed it just as he did. Hell, Daisy'd apparently even taken a bath without a fight. That in itself was a miracle.

It made him a little uncomfortable though. The thought that, as much as he tried, he couldn't do it all for her. Annabelle had seemed like the perfect solution. And yeah, she helped. A lot. But she couldn't apply makeup and giggle about boyfriends.

Daisy would miss Violet when she left. So would he. But if he didn't think about it, it wouldn't happen. So he dozed, secure in the fact that all was well in his little corner of the world.

What seemed like a few seconds later, his whispered name brought him back. He sat up, blinked and rubbed his eyes. Before him stood his mother. Not a confused old woman, but the mother he remembered from his childhood. She wore a green party dress with a full skirt that swished and swayed when she moved. There were newish ballet flats on her feet. Her face glowed with excitement, making her look almost young again. And her hair brushed her cheeks in silken waves, reminiscent of her wedding photo.

"Mom, you look beautiful." His voice was husky. His heart squeezed at the proud angle of her chin.

"I do, don't I?" She patted her luxurious hair. "That old Joe better watch it. I might find another fella to smooch with during the slow songs."

"You'll be the belle of the ball." He stood and gave her a hug. The faintest trace of scent tickled his nose. It brought back memories of Mom all dressed up and Dad in a tuxedo, the baby-sitter tapping at the door. It had been an enchanted life. So enchanted that he hadn't realized it. Not until his thirty-fifth birthday, when he'd started to wonder if his chance of having a family might be passing him by. He had taken a hard look around him and couldn't find a single woman who would bring magic to his life the way his mother had enchanted his father.

A horn tooted out front. It was the bus from the

center. Not a horse drawn carriage, but it could have been, the way Daisy floated out the door.

He stood at the window long after the bus disappeared. This day was precious to Daisy, precious to him. He'd made the right decision to keep her home. She would have withered and died at a nursing home. Here, she still dreamed, still loved, still enjoyed. What more could he ask?

He hummed a soft tune, an echo of Violet's earlier rendition. "I'll bring you a daisy a day, dear…."

VIOLET YAWNED and stretched her arms over her head. Her bed beckoned, so much more inviting than the darn computer. But if she were going to be a District Claims Manager, she'd better act like one.

She pulled up file after file, making a short notation here, a suggestion there. Reserves were double-checked and tweaked when needed. Everything must be perfect when she left for Cleveland. Her replacement, whoever that might be, would have no cause to complain about *her* unit.

The clock ticked away so slowly she'd checked it twice to make sure it worked. Anticipation bubbled inside. Daisy would be home soon and she'd promised to dish.

What a character. All that zip and sparkle, with a solid core of love. Ian probably didn't realize how lucky he'd been to have such a family. Offbeat maybe, but filled with all the love and gentle direction a child could need.

So she'd named him Thessalonian and strong-armed him into ballet? He seemed to have survived it just fine. As a matter of fact, it was a wonder some petite little ballet dancer hadn't latched on to him. It didn't take too much imagination to see him with some younger version of his mother, his arm wrapped protectively around her, grinning that cockeyed grin of his.

His sportswriting days had surely provided plenty of groupies. But he didn't seem like the one-night stand type. He was too straightforward, too...well... too Ian. Like he had it so much more together than other guys.

The sound of a vehicle crunching to a stop pulled her away from her armchair psychology. She closed the file and clicked off her computer, if just for a while.

Daisy would surely come looking for her, wouldn't she?

Violet almost laughed aloud. She had to live vicariously through a seventy-something-year-old woman. Well, darn it, she had to take what she could get.

And she'd be damned if she'd let Ian hear all the good stuff first! She launched herself out of her swivel chair and yanked open the door. Stopping wasn't an option. Her socks lost traction and she skidded sideways, right into Ian.

"Whoa. Where's the fire?"

"I...ah...thought I heard Daisy's bus." God, she was pathetic. Fascinated by the senior set social life.

"Me, too. Kind of wanted to see her when she came through the door. She was positively gorgeous this morning."

He placed his hand under her elbow, escorting her down the hallway.

"That was a really great thing you did for her—the

makeup, the hair. Something I would have never thought of.''

She waved away his thanks on the outside, but on the inside she tucked away his approval, something to savor later.

''I used to do the same thing for my baby sister, Colleen, before she got old enough to be a brat. A little makeup and some hairstyling does wonders for a woman's ego at any age. It was no problem, really. I enjoyed it.''

''At nine maybe, but at six-thirty I bet it was a real effort. Remember, I've seen you in the morning. Thank you.'' His voice was low, husky, as if she'd done something astounding, like found a cure for Alzheimer's. Kindness wasn't totally foreign to her nature, just a little rusty. She hadn't gotten where she had by waiting for everyone else to go first.

''You're welcome. Hurry, or we won't be there when she comes in.''

Violet started to sprint, but Ian quickly caught up with her. They raced down the hallway, neck and neck. Violet landed an elbow to his ribs, and with the advantage of stocking feet, slid around the corner mere inches ahead of him.

''Hey cheater,'' he laughed. ''No sliding allowed.''

''Oh? Who made that rule? The National Sore Loser's Association?''

Violet stuck out her tongue at him.

''Don't stick it out, unless you plan to use it.'' He planted a swift openmouthed kiss as he swept by. It had to be the least satisfying French kiss in the history of mankind.

He thought he'd won the pole position right in front of the door. But he'd underestimated her.

Violet grabbed a big, beefy arm and swung him around. See a petite ballet dancer do that!

His eyes widened as she clamped her hands on his shoulders, stood on tiptoe and drew him close. "And don't promise what you're not willing to back up."

With that, she showed him what a *real* French kiss was all about. And the way he kissed her back, he didn't need much refreshing.

Just when she thought her socks might blow out, she heard a voice behind his broad back.

"Well it certainly took you two long enough. Thought I was going to have to draw you a picture."

Oh, God. What had she done? Kissed Ian, and in front of his mother no less.

She tried to lower her arms, pretend she hadn't been hanging on for dear life. But he wouldn't let her get away. He grasped her forearms and held her close to his chest. He simply rotated them as a single unit, so they could see Daisy.

And what a sight she was.

All that glorious shiny, wavy, virginal hair looked like a rat's nest. Tangled here, smooshed there, pieces of grass sticking out everywhere. It was the worst case of bed head Violet had ever seen.

The wicked sparkle in Daisy's eyes confirmed what her swollen lips suggested, that she had been well and thoroughly loved and didn't regret a minute of it.

"M-o-o-o-m," Ian wailed, "what have you done?"

"Honey, if you have to ask that, you've been deprived longer than I thought." She patted the rat's nest, wearing it like a badge of honor. "Now, if you'll excuse me, I need a nap."

She winked at them as she glided by, headed toward her room.

"Arthritis, huh? No access to Viagra, you said," Violet gloated. "You better have that safe sex discussion, and soon."

Ian grunted. His face was a study in contrasts—an eyebrow raised in grudging admiration, while his mouth thinned in disapproval at the compromising of his mother's honor.

Admiration must have won, because he wrapped his arms around Violet, twisted and lowered her into a dip. And rather gracefully, too. If it were true that a man made love like he danced, then Ian would be magnificent. All that lovely muscle tamed by grace and control. The thought sent a sizzle of anticipation up her spine.

Just as she was poised to give him another lesson in kissing, all hell broke loose. The phone rang, the doorbell pealed and Annabelle started to howl. Ian lifted her from the dip and stood like a deer in the headlights.

"You get the door. I'll get the phone in the kitchen and see what's got Annabelle upset," she suggested.

"Uh, yeah, you do that," he shouted through the din.

VIOLET MUTTERED a curse as she placed the handset back on the base.

Rounding the corner to the great room, she said, "Annabelle needed to go out. Whoever was on the phone hung up before I could get—"

"Hello, Vi." The look on Vince's face slowed her steps. She didn't know him well, but he always seemed to be good-natured. None of that city cop cynicism, just the sheriff in a small rural area, where everyone knew who the crazies were—the harmless and the not-so-harmless.

But today he was mad as hell. His face was red with fury. Was he angry with her for some reason?

Vi backed up a step and eased closer to Ian. A nameless anxiety squeezed her lungs, making it hard to draw a breath. She hadn't hyperventilated in years. *Please, God, not now.*

"Ian, what the hell are we gonna do?"

"About what?"

Vince stopped. "You mean you don't know? Mrs. Rivers from the center called. They've been kicked out."

"Who?"

"Daisy and Joe. They were missing for nearly an hour. Everyone was looking for them. They wandered back to the center, said they'd had a picnic down by the creek."

Vi released a shaky breath. Vince wasn't angry at her. He barely even seemed to realize she was in the room.

"Damn." Ian sank to the couch. His face turned pale, almost a greenish hue. "I thought they just sneaked away from the crowd, you know broom closet or something like that. A little necking, but nothing…nothing…well, dangerous."

Vi went to him, lightly touching his shoulder. "Ian, Daisy had grass in her hair. She'd been outside."

"Why weren't they watching them better?" His

voice was terse, his shoulders bunched with tension beneath her fingertips. "They only have her two days a week. Why the hell couldn't they keep track of her?"

He stood, dislodging her hand in the process. Then he paced. It seemed as if he needed some kind of outlet for the impotent rage she saw in his eyes. Her instinct was to back away from his fury. But this time she was able to force herself to stand strong. She kept the cold sweat of terror at bay and resisted the urge to make herself as inconspicuous as possible. She'd seen him angry and he'd never once been violent. He might be mad as hell, but he wouldn't hurt her. And he wouldn't punish her for offering an opinion.

"Joe kept her from wandering off. Wasn't he kind of…er…supervising her?"

Ian rounded on her and gestured wildly in the direction of Daisy's room. "Sure, this time she was with Joe. But what about next time? What if she wanders off by herself? That creek can run pretty high."

Vince laid a restraining hand on his shoulder. His anger spent, Vince's voice was low, calm, a man accustomed to handling distraught people. "Ian, now's not the time to lay blame. *If* they can be persuaded to accept them back, maybe we can put our heads together to make sure it doesn't happen again."

Ian's shoulders slumped. The fight went out of him. "I'm not sure I want her to go back." His voice was tired, defeated. Worse than the time she'd seen him in court. His eyes were blank, no spirit, no fight left.

"Man, I understand how you feel. Probably better than anybody. I don't have to deal with the Alzheimer's stuff, but I *do* know what it's like living with my dad, day after day. I'm pretty lucky to have family to spell me when the old guy starts to drive me nuts. And I have an office, a squad car I can go to. You don't. D'you think you can really make it, never getting away, never getting a break?''

Violet's heart went out to Ian. Vince's description stripped whatever remaining illusions she might have about caring for old folks, particularly family. She moved closer to Ian and touched his arm. ''Don't make any decisions now. Like Vince said, we'll put our heads together and figure something out.''

He looked down at her as if he didn't really see her. She squeezed his arm, and murmured, ''Please?''

His eyes focused on her face. He reached out to touch her face, his thumb stroking her jaw. ''What are we gonna do?''

''We're going to wait. Sleep on it.''

She turned to Vince and said, ''We'll get back to you tomorrow. No need to rush into anything.''

''Yeah, you're right. Sorry, I just kind of lost it.''

''It's okay. I understand.'' And as he was leaving, she said, ''Oh, and Vince…thank you.''

Violet focused all her attention on Ian. It tore at her heart to see the pain in his eyes, the helplessness in his expression. The man who always seemed to have all the answers was speechless.

''Why don't you go for a run. I'll watch Daisy.'' She reached up and stroked the lines bracketing his mouth.

''Thanks. You're one in a million.'' His voice was husky, but his eyes held a far-off look, as if he'd gone to a place she couldn't see.

CHAPTER EIGHT

V<small>I</small> PEEKED IN on Daisy to make sure she still slept, then headed for the kitchen. Comfort food, a must at times like these.

She rummaged through the freezer. No ice cream, a bad sign. No chocolate in the pantry, either. Ian said Daisy could ferret out chocolate no matter where he hid it, gobbling it up until it was gone. Bad for her blood sugar.

Okay, the easiest choices were gone. Chicken soup? None. The best she could do was a can of tomato. Maybe sandwiches, too. Grilled cheese was easy enough for her to handle and still check on Daisy every few minutes.

Violet stood on tiptoe and flicked open the top cupboard, just as she'd seen Ian do. She felt around, getting more desperate by the second. Finally she located the stove knobs.

Ten minutes later she had everything cooking— soup on a low simmer and sandwiches browning slowly enough for the cheese to melt through. She sniffed appreciatively. Not bad for a rookie.

One more check on Daisy reassured her that all was well.

Her heart skipped a beat when she heard the front door open. She wandered out to the living room to meet Ian. The run had done him some good. The coiled tension was gone, but defeat showed in every line of his body. This was the guy who thought anything was possible. But not today.

"I made some soup and sandwiches."

"Thanks, but I'm not hungry."

"You have to eat something. You'll think better after you eat."

He sighed heavily. "I guess you're right. Daisy still asleep?"

"Like the dead."

Bad choice of words.

"I mean like a baby."

Still bad, but at least it didn't bring the specter of death into it.

Ian grabbed a plate from the cupboard and got a sandwich. Silently, he dished out some soup.

Violet served herself.

They ate in silence. She should respect his privacy, let him think it out. But she couldn't stand not knowing what was going on in his head.

"Maybe there's someone else who will take Daisy," she commented.

"There's nowhere." His voice was rough and desperate. "Don't you think I tried everything? Echo Point is too small. I was damn lucky they have a senior center at all. They don't specialize in Alzheimer's patients, but they were willing to take her anyway. At least until the disease progresses to where she needs constant one-on-one supervision."

Violet folded her napkin and laid it on her plate. "But she's done so much better lately. Couldn't there be some sort of remission?"

"Nope. Not for her. The new drugs don't help. She has good spells, and then something happens that'll throw her for a loop—like when you first came. She's used to you now, nothing's disturbing her, so she seems pretty okay."

"So she can control it when she wants to?"

"Not even close. You've seen how hard she tries, how humiliated she is when it doesn't work. She's like anyone else, it's easier to compensate when she's not stressed."

"How long? That she remembers people…places… you?"

Ian pushed his plate away, his half-eaten sandwich a sad chunk of melted cheese and toasted bread in the middle of the stark white paper plate. "Don't know. Months, maybe even years. The not knowing is the hardest part. I just have to deal with it as it comes."

"I don't know how you do it. Me, I could deal with it if my dad didn't remember who I was. Even my mom. She kind of just circumvented our lives, stayed out of the firing line. But you. You've got this great relationship. How will you handle it if she forgets who you are?"

Getting up from the table, he walked to the far end of the kitchen, his gaze focused out the window.

"I don't think about it. That's how I handle it."

She rose and went to him. Standing right behind him, she murmured, "Ian, that doesn't mean it won't happen. It just means you won't be ready."

"You don't understand. If I think about it too much, it's like I'll make it happen. And I honestly don't know if I'll be able to handle it. This thing's not natural. It's not right. She's supposed to be there, always, to remember the important stuff that's happened. If she doesn't remember, then it's like it never existed. Poof. Just like my dad.''

"*You* will have those memories. You'll carry Daisy and your dad with you. It's something no person, no disease, can take away from you."

"It *has* taken it away from me. I'm not me anymore. I'm just some poor sap going through the motions. There's no future, and pretty soon the past will be yanked away, too."

Ian ran a hand through his hair and paced. "I had a really different life before. I wasn't always a nursemaid. I traveled, I partied. I had a job I loved and all the perks to go with it—a byline, lots of friends and…girlfriends. Then, one day it was gone."

Violet put herself in the path of his pacing. He stopped, toe-to-toe with her. She grabbed him by the shoulders, hard. "So somebody expected you to grow up. Big deal. Somebody needed you, poor Ian. You want me to believe that lifestyle meant so much to you? That's not what I see. I see a guy who's grown up enough to face what he's been dealt, without glory or recognition."

Vi paused for breath, wishing for an icy blast of airconditioning to cool her cheeks. Seeing him so defeated scared her. She couldn't let him turn his back on all the gifts he'd been given.

"Did you ever stop to think that maybe you were ready for a change? And that you should be grateful for everything you've had?"

"That's the reason I did it. I owe her."

Frustration pushed Violet forward, pushed her to get in his face. Shock him out of giving up. Because if he gave up, Daisy didn't stand a chance. And neither did she.

"Well, there's some serious navel-gazing. You figured you owed her. Bravo! Sure you owe her. For bringing you into the world. For loving you like crazy, no matter what you did. For rooting for you even though you couldn't find the ten if it came up and smacked you in the face."

His eyes got a hard gleam to them, his mouth set in a stubborn line. "I don't need this crap. You're supposed to be helping me. We're supposed to be on the same team."

"I *am* on your team when you're honest with me…and honest with yourself. This is just a load of bull."

"You want honest, okay, I'll give you honest. I put that woman through hell."

Violet wrapped her arms over her chest. "Go on."

"When Dad died, I flipped out. Dropped out of school. Just hung out, got loaded. Stole some stuff. Ended up in juvenile hall. All while Mom was trying to pick herself up and go on. Deal with her own grief."

"So what happened?"

"She moved us here. Was on my sorry case twenty-four hours a day. Until I finally gave in. Got my general equivalency degree, went to U. of A. The rest is history."

Understanding glimmered. "She saved your life, and now you want to save hers."

"Something like that."

God what a mess. "Ian, you can't save her. You know that, don't you?"

His face paled, his shoulders slumped. It was like watching the Incredible Hulk return to human form. Only she wasn't sure she wanted to see him as a mere mortal. He'd seemed so much larger than life all along.

"Maybe I thought I could."

"Until today."

"Yeah. Until today."

He moved back to the table and sat down. His expression was bleak as he picked up the sandwich, studied it for a moment, then tossed it back on his plate.

So how did she help him go on?

She'd already given her friendship, her support, her advice, along with a healthy dose of aggravation.

Vi stepped behind him and wrapped her arms around his neck, bending down to rest her head against his. "I'm sorry."

His hair was soft against her cheek. She rubbed her chin back and forth. Funny, it looked spiky, but felt so soft.

Ian sat rigid, until she whispered his name. Sighing, he leaned back and closed his eyes. He stroked her forearms, slowly working from wrist to elbow. His hands were so strong, supple even. Though he worked on her arms, it was her knees that wavered.

"Vi?"

"Yes?"

"I need you."

Her skin prickled as he placed a kiss on the tender flesh inside her forearm. He didn't need her to wash the dishes or take out the trash, or even watch Daisy. He needed her to help him forget for a little while.

She closed her eyes while his lips and tongue

worked toward her wrist. He nibbled on her palm, ran his tongue over the pulse point on her wrist.

She savored the contact. So simple, yet so persuasive. The guy who gave his all every day, finally, was asking.

Violet kissed his ear, and whispered, "Come with me."

She grasped his hand and pulled, gently. He was too damn honorable. He had to be sure it was her idea. "Please?" she whispered.

He stood abruptly, tipping the chair. It crashed to the floor, but he didn't seem to notice.

"Daisy?"

Violet pressed a finger to her lips. "Shhh. We'll check on her."

They tiptoed down the hall. Violet's heart hammered. What the hell was she doing?

This was dangerous. And not the titillating kind of danger, either. The kind she might regret later.

They stopped outside Daisy's door. Silently, with much practice, Ian opened the door a crack. Daisy was sound asleep, her arm flung wide, as if to welcome a lover. Her lips curved upward. It must be a wonderful dream.

He's a ten, Daisy. And I promise to take care of him.

Ian closed the door just as silently. He turned the lock on the handle, reversed to keep Daisy in, rather than him out. She'd be mad as hell if she woke up and was unable to go anywhere. The racket would be loud enough to wake the dead. Or intrude on an intimate moment.

Ian squeezed her hand as they went down the hallway. She returned the pressure.

When he hesitated at the door to her room, she shook her head. Too close to Daisy's, thick adobe walls or not.

He tipped his head to the side.

She smiled and tugged on his hand. His step lightened as they approached his room. She pulled him into the room and shut the door behind him. His lock had not been changed, so she twisted the little knob. There wasn't anyone who would roam the house, but it made her feel safer.

It was dusk, misty light seeping through the wooden shutters. The white walls almost seemed to glow in the half-light.

"Vi? Are you sure?"

That clinched it. If she wasn't sure before, she was now. The guy had her in his bedroom, ready to comfort him in the only way she knew how, and he was willing to send her away.

"Shh." She placed her hands palm-down against his chest, and pushed, gently, but insistently. He backed a step.

She followed. She pushed again, continuous pressure until he was against the bed. Then she shoved him down.

He raised an eyebrow, but didn't say a word. He leaned on one elbow and waited.

In the silence of his gray room, an odd thing happened. Ian's innate goodness gave her the courage to respond to him without reserve, to free a part of her she hadn't realized she'd saved—a shred of trust she'd set aside for someone special, someone heroic.

Violet shrugged off her T-shirt and tossed it in the corner.

Ian's gaze never left her. His eyes moved possessively over her shoulders, lit on the wisp of lace she called a bra. She would let him savor this moment, anticipate what little her bra hid. Her breasts were her glory, passed down from her grandmother.

Slowly, very slowly, she reached back and unhooked her bra. She let it dangle on her bent elbows, suspended over her breasts, tantalizing, teasing.

The metal clasp made a little click when it hit the tile floor. Ian's eyes widened. His surprise pleased her. Baggy T-shirts and business suits made wonderful camouflage. But there was a time and a place to showcase her attributes. The time was now. And Ian's bedroom was the right place.

Violet shimmied out of her jeans and threw them in the corner. Her hips swayed, her nipples hardened, as she drew ever closer to him.

Ian lost that indolent look. Relaxation was the last thing on his mind as he sat up and reached for her. She shook her head. Her hair whipped around her bare shoulders. Thrusting one hip forward, she savored the freedom of partial nudity. It was scary in a way, vulnerable. And yet, somehow like painting. He was the canvas and her body the paint. What they created would be a unique interaction between the two medias.

She grasped his shirt by the hem. Inhaling his scent she reveled in the absolute maleness of him. He was all hers. For the moment.

Vi pitched his shirt into the corner, where it skidded next to hers.

Then her nerve deserted her. The brush of cool air

against her breasts made her want to cover herself. She felt exposed instead of powerful.

She locked her gaze on the crisp sandy-brown hair sprinkled across Ian's impressive pecs. Wrapping her arms across her chest, she tucked her cold hands under her armpits.

This wasn't the way it was supposed to be. Not like a hooker performing a trick.

Then his hands were on hers, pulling gently to expose her breasts. She lifted her gaze and saw only his face. His gaze seemed to wordlessly ask her to trust.

Did she have any trust left? Probably not enough. But she did have admiration and gratitude. If they'd met under different circumstances, she sensed that would never have been enough for a man like Ian. He'd grown up at Daisy's knee, taught early on not to settle for less than a ten.

What was that silent promise she'd made to a sleeping Daisy? He's a ten and I'll take care of him. Physically, maybe even mentally, but it would take trust to touch his soul, to reach that ten.

She sighed, confused by the melancholy that stole over her, so close on the heels of euphoria. Too bad it couldn't have lasted a bit longer.

So she stood there and gazed into his deep, clear eyes and lied. Not with words, but with touch.

It must have been enough. Because he drew her back on the bed with him, allowing her the superior position. Power meant nothing to him. He would never make himself feel important by making her feel small.

He kissed her, tenderly, persistently. It was a start.

But she couldn't continue to lie to him, wouldn't promise something she couldn't deliver.

"Ian…"

"Shhh." He silenced her with a kiss. "I know, Vi. It doesn't matter," he whispered. "Just today. Now."

A low groan escaped her lips. She'd failed, miserably, to do what was right.

Violet accepted his kiss, shaping it with her lips and tongue into something that was theirs.

Today. Now.

He wasn't asking for forever, or even tomorrow.

Today.

She could give him that.

Violet wrapped her arms around his neck and claimed him. Then she braced herself on her palms and studied his face as she tickled his cheeks with strands of her hair. First one dimple appeared, then the other, right where her hair brushed.

An answering smile started at her toes and worked its way up her body, finally curving her lips, giving her such a wonderful fuzzy glow.

"Today…" she whispered.

"Today," he groaned.

VIOLET SLIPPED out of Ian's bed and tiptoed toward the heap of clothes, scooping up her underwear as she went.

One look at the tangled mound told her not to even bother dressing. Instead, she slipped on her panties and borrowed Ian's plaid robe. His scent drifted upward as she belted the soft flannel. She inhaled deeply, a smile curving her lips, memories weighing her eyelids.

Making love. It had been all that and more. They'd connected, as if on canvas, instinctively finding balance and grace. And passion—every work of art oozed it. He'd been the kind of lover she'd thought—graceful, powerful, with great stamina. Passion could be faked, but not selfless control. What was it she'd heard once? Manners were only a matter of showing more concern for another than for yourself. Ian had beautiful manners, both in bed and out.

Violet watched him sleep. The pads of her fingers tingled with remembered touch, ached to smooth the lines of his face, chase away the tension that still lingered there. It would be so easy to curl up beside him, pull up the covers and ignore the world at large. He would protect her. And everything would be fine.

She shook her head at the absurd thought. Teenage fantasies had no place in her life. She couldn't be there when he awakened. Wouldn't make any empty promises, if he even wanted them. Hell, for all she knew, he might thank her for a great, stress-relieving screw, then pointedly hint for her to leave.

No, not Ian. He was too damn decent for that. He'd simply wait her out.

Violet glanced at the clock on the nightstand. Her shift didn't start for another two hours, but she'd punch in a little early. Let Ian escape from his world of constant worry into the warm, fuzzy world of sleep.

Sadness washed over her as she shut the door behind her. Weariness dogged her steps as she headed toward the bathroom.

It wasn't for her, never had been. The girl from East L.A. didn't need any detours, even for a possible ten. Work was real. This was a fairy tale manufactured out of need.

A fairy tale of another kind faded as Vi tidied herself up. The fantasy that they'd been careful, so therefore, they were immune to complications. But apparently they had not been careful enough. The condom had broken and neither of them had noticed.

Taking a deep breath, Violet refused to panic. The timing was fine. No harm done. Crisis averted. It wouldn't happen again.

IAN OPENED Daisy's door a crack. She slept on, safe, sated, more peacefully than usual.

Then his gaze rested on the daybed, where Violet slept, safe in his robe, sated and restless. She flung a leg out, muttering something in her sleep.

God, how he'd needed her. Needed to sink himself into oblivion, surround himself with love and beauty. In Vi's arms he had forgotten, for a while, his responsibilities. Pretended he was free to make choices. But he wasn't. And Vi knew that. That's why she'd left him there, alone.

And she was right.

He couldn't commit to anyone. He had to be devoted to Daisy, one hundred percent. That meant his own life, his own wants and needs went on hold. He couldn't expect a woman to wait for him indefinitely, not knowing when it all would end.

Guilt stabbed at his gut. What kind of guy let the thought even cross his mind? A death wish, so he could live.

Ian let his gaze wander over Vi. Her deep brown hair swept back on the pillow, her lips parted slightly. Not seductively, not waiting for his kiss. But murmuring, muttering. She shifted onto her side as he watched, his gaze following the curve of her hip. She was flat-out gorgeous, and somehow he'd missed it.

Yeah, her features were symmetrical, her coloring striking. But the first time she'd opened her mouth, he'd missed her beauty. Seen only the bluster she wore to protect herself. It had been enough to put him off, so he didn't notice those breasts she hid so well, or the way her waist narrowed and hips curved. The woman was made to love. And she was determined to conceal that fact, from herself, as well as the rest of the world. Denial seemed to keep her going, seemed to keep her world safely spinning.

Just as she would deny what they'd shared. Not the physical act. She was too honest to lie about that. She wouldn't accept the emotional line they'd crossed. That's why she'd left while he slept.

He shook his head sadly as he closed the door. He knew what was coming, knew he couldn't stop it. It had nothing to do with him, but it still hit him like a physical blow.

He should be relieved. She was the perfect partner for a commitment-shy guy. Giving, loving, passionate, then gone. Poof! No strings. No promises.

But she meant much more to him than that. He cared for Vi. Maybe more than any woman he'd ever met. Her in-your-face attitude masked a sensitive soul and initiating lovemaking with him had been a gift. Not pity sex, but the gift of healing. And the only way she could bring herself to bed him. As a selfless act, designed to lift his spirits. Then it could be explained away. Only he'd be damned if he would just let her walk away.

But what could he offer her? A life sentence with the crazy lady? It could be six months, six years or anywhere in between. When would she start hating him, and hating Daisy?

Maybe it was for the best that she chose to be practical. But he'd never been raised to be practical. Toe-dancing, football-throwing Thessalonian had been raised to go for the brass ring. And that was Vi, no doubt about it.

CHAPTER NINE

"HEY, YOUR SHIFT'S OVER. No overtime remember?"
Ian leaned against a mesquite tree, enjoying the view.
He knew he couldn't have her, not permanently. But
it was nice to watch her anyway.

Vi used a bare forearm to brush the hair from her
eyes. Her cheeks were flushed, her eyes sparkled.
Jeans hugged her hips, and a baggy Cardinals T-shirt
hid her voluptuous figure. Yellow coated her hands,
like psychedelic Easter gloves.

"Daisy and I are going to paint. You go write your
book and leave us to our masterpiece." Violet looked
somewhere to the right of his face as she spoke. She
hadn't looked him in the eye yet.

Her tone was light, but the underlying edge told him
volumes. He made her nervous, so she wanted him to
get the hell out of there. But she couldn't say that,
because her kindness to Daisy was a direct result of
her kindness to him. A consolation prize of sorts—
*Don't expect any more recreational nookie, because
I'm too busy with your mom.* A way of giving, but not
giving. Interesting.

Ian crossed his arms over his chest. Why couldn't
he just leave it at that? It was best for both of them.
She needed him like she needed a hole in the head.
Although there were times when a hole in the head

was a good thing, necessary to survival in fact, by relieving pressure to the brain.

What they had shared certainly relieved *his* pressure. He hadn't felt so relaxed in years. And judging from the high color in Vi's cheeks, the experience hadn't been totally one-sided.

She eyed him warily, as if she expected a frontal attack. Her every word and movement screamed denial, and had for the past week. She didn't want to talk about it, didn't want to even admit it had happened.

He would let her think whatever made her comfortable. But he hadn't given up. He was simply taking the time to map out strategy.

"Thanks for spending the extra time with Mom. Book's really coming along. You don't know what it means to have that time without worrying about her. I've gotten more done in the past couple days than I have in months."

"No problem. Are you close to finishing it? The book?"

"I figure I can finish the first draft in a couple more weeks, thanks to you."

"I'm glad I was able to help. You deserve a break."

I sure do. And Vi was just the one to provide it.

He turned to walk away, then as if on an afterthought, turned back around.

"Oh, and by the way, Mrs. Rivers accepted Daisy and Joe back at the center. Judge Tanner located some more funding—enough to pay for another aide."

Violet stood stock-still. Joy, doubt and then out-and-out fear washed over her face as she apparently realized the implications. Six hours completely alone, with no Daisy to hide behind.

"That's great," she croaked.

"Isn't it?" He grinned with delight. Yes, today was one of the good days, no doubt about it.

DAMN.

Violet's hands shook as she placed a rock on the corner of their masterpiece.

The senior center. Tomorrow.

One part of her danced a victory dance for Ian and Daisy. The center was so important to them. Two glorious days a week to pretend life was normal—Daisy to "volunteer" and get out with other people, Ian to just have a breather. To write, jog, lift weights.

To make love.

It was one option of many. She knew it, and he knew it. His wry grin screamed evil intentions. No, not evil. Just destructive. And seductive.

The seductive part scared her. If she weren't tempted, it would be easy. All it would take would be a single sentence to flatten him, verbally castrate him so he never again had a remotely sexual thought about her. But her brain had somehow gone haywire, and the last thing she wanted to do was flatten him. Unless of course, it meant she were on top and involved unspeakable pleasure.

A small hand held out another smooth river stone within her line of vision.

"That canvas is good, but not nearly that good," the older woman said.

Violet shook her head. She'd been staring, sightless and motionless.

She smiled as she looked up at Daisy. She raised a hand to shield her eyes from the sun. "For a forgetful old woman, you sure don't miss much."

Daisy sniffed her disdain. "I remember what I want to remember. As for my age, well—" she gestured, her hand a graceful arc "—it's all relative."

It certainly was. Daisy was more vibrant than anyone she'd ever met. Certainly wiser. How could she have thought she was a crazy old woman?

Violet sat back on her haunches and grasped Daisy's hand. She gave it a squeeze and asked, "You think you can behave yourself while you're at the center this time?"

Daisy returned her squeeze. A knowing half smile tickled her lips. "Can you?"

Violet's jaw dropped, but she recovered quickly and snapped her mouth shut.

The question left her speechless. Transparency had never been one of her problems, unless it involved ambition and independence. Transparent need scared the heck out of her. She might as well hang out a Hurt Me sign.

"It's okay, dear. No need to answer." Daisy patted her shoulder. "But remember, the tens don't come along often. Grab it while you can."

With that the old woman turned and strolled toward the house.

VIOLET SHIFTED, her rear end protesting at long hours in the office chair. She twined her hands together, raised them over her head and leaned back. Her shoulders crackled, her back ached. She rotated her neck from side to side.

Glancing at her wristwatch, she was surprised to see it was almost one o'clock. Four hours since the senior center bus had chugged down the road, taking her chaperone with it. Four hours since she'd expected Ian to come find her, certain that he wanted nothing more than to seduce her.

Violet rubbed her eyes and yawned. Disappointment washed over her. She should be relieved, darn it.

Her hopes rose when, moments later, there was a tap on the door.

"Vi? You awake?" he asked softly. The concern in his voice was real. No lies, no games. Just a great guy.

"I'm here."

The door opened slowly. A plate and a sandwich came into view, much like a white flag. When no shots were fired, an arm appeared, and then the whole man.

"I brought you a sandwich. Thought you might be hungry."

His hazel eyes held an apology, one she couldn't understand. "I...thought maybe you were avoiding...the kitchen."

Clearing her throat, she said, "Kind of. The kitchen, I mean."

She accepted the plate and napkin. Grilled cheese.

He smiled, a half smile of regret, then turned to leave.

"Well, maybe not the kitchen."

Ian turned back, and cocked his head to the side, like Annabelle when she was really intent.

Violet looked down at her feet, where gray socks covered her icy toes. Her fingers felt like little clumsy Popsicles. But a drop of perspiration trickled down the side of her face.

He didn't say a word.

"It was you."

"Me?"

"I've been avoiding you."

"Why?"

It was a rhetorical question. His eyes gave it away. She suspected that he knew her fear as well as she did.

"The other night...I wasn't really ready—I mean not physically, everything was okay there—just... well, up here." She tapped her temple.

A frown tugged at his mouth. He ran his hands through his hair. "Vi, I knew you weren't ready. Just like I know you're not ready now. I needed you so badly, I ignored that. I'm sorry."

He had known. He'd tried to stop her. Halfheartedly maybe, but he had tried to stop. And he'd admitted he was wrong. Maybe she could be as honest.

"I'm working on it though...up here." She tapped her temple again.

Ian knelt by her chair. He pushed the hair behind her ear and cupped her neck. He rested his forehead against hers, his breath soft on her face.

"Vi, it's not something you should have to work at. It's either there or it isn't."

The emptiness in his voice scared her. He'd given up on her.

"No, you don't understand. It's there." The words rushed out, tumbling over her numb lips. "Really, it is."

He pulled back far enough to link his gaze with hers. She flinched and looked away. His hand dropped from her neck, leaving a void where her skin was exposed to the cool air.

He pulled away from her, but not before placing a kiss on the top of her head. His voice was thick when he said, "No, it isn't. You're trying too hard. I won't settle for that."

Tears scalded her cheeks as she watched him walk away. It was as simple as that. No persuading, no courtship. Just sad acceptance.

THERE WASN'T any sweet transition from sleep to wakefulness. Just intuition that jolted Vi upright, her heart pounding, her palms sweating.

Something was wrong. Really wrong. Violet couldn't quite figure out what it was, though. She frantically tried to focus in the dark. Night. Not the condo.

As her eyes adjusted, she could make out a twin bed, wrought iron headboard, whitewashed walls, thick-beamed ceiling. Adobe.

Her heart slowed its pace. Daisy's room.

She concentrated hard and focused on the twin bed. Empty.

Violet swallowed the lump in her throat and swung her legs over the side of the daybed.

The bathroom.

Surely Daisy was in the bathroom, maybe even asleep again. No need to worry.

She belted her bathrobe as she staggered down the hall. Reflective tape glowed, reminding her more of a crime scene than a hallway.

Violet peered around the doorway, ready to exhale her relief. But it caught in her throat, making her gag on her own air.

No Daisy.

A coughing fit doubled her over, while her mind raced. What to do? Wake Ian?

No. Not that. Probably find her wandering the house somewhere.

She kept her steps light and steady. No need to wake Ian in a panic. Everything would be fine.

Ten minutes later she had to admit everything would not be fine. She'd checked the house, thoroughly, except for Ian's room. Could Daisy have gotten confused, gone to Ian's room instead of her own? Anything was possible.

Violet tapped lightly on his door. No answer.

She twisted the knob and quietly opened the door. Ian was sound asleep, his arms thrown haphazardly above his head. He slept like he did everything else, with gusto and no excuses.

The sheets bundled around his waist, with his broad chest rising slowly, then falling. The dusting of hair on his chest reminded her of their evening together, exploring, caressing, memorizing his taste and textures.

She shook her head. Daisy.

One glance around the neat room confirmed her fears.

Daisy wasn't in the house.

The bed was soft and inviting where she knelt near Ian's pillow.

"Ian, wake up." Violet jostled his shoulder.

He mumbled something, then rolled over on his side. His unshaved chin scratched her bare knee as he snuggled against it, his arm instinctively wrapping around her hips.

"*Ian!*" she yelled.

He shot to a sitting position, bumping his nose on her knee. He felt for broken cartilage as his eyes focused on her.

"What the hell…"

"It's Daisy. She's gone."

"Gone?"

He shook his head and released his nose, his eyes alert now. "How long? Check the bathroom? The rest of the house? Outside?"

His terse questions ripped through her heart. "Not outside," she choked out. Tears threatened, but she brushed them away. This was no time to go soft. It wouldn't help anybody. "I came to get you when I couldn't find her in the house. I thought two of us could cover more ground."

"When's the last time you saw her?"

Violet's gaze leapt to the bedside alarm clock. How could that be?

She hung her head, like Annabelle the time her bum leg had hindered her from getting outside in time for a potty break.

"Ten," she whispered.

"Ten o'clock," he hollered. He lunged wildly for the alarm clock. "It's almost two now."

Violet cringed. Not because she was afraid of him. Because of the way she hated herself.

"I went to sleep around ten. As soon as my head hit the pillow. She must've gotten up to go to the bathroom and I didn't hear her."

Misery knotted her intestines.

Ian threw his legs over the side of the bed and reached for the phone. "I'll call 911."

The image of helicopters and bloodhounds made her

sweat. Then everyone would know how irresponsible she'd been.

"Maybe she's just outside. Maybe we can find her first."

"We'll lose time," he barked. "Better to have Search and Rescue on the way."

Violet clamped her lips shut to keep them from quivering. Her throat was raw with the effort of holding back tears.

Ian grabbed her hand and gave it a quick squeeze. "I've been through this before, remember?"

"Yeah," she croaked. She wasn't the only incompetent boob to ever lose a little old lady. But that didn't seem to make it any better.

VIOLET PULLED her knees up to her chest, the lawn chair shifting dangerously beneath her. She didn't care. All she wanted was to feel warm again, stop her teeth chattering. All she wanted was for the world to quit tilting and bring Daisy back to them.

She'd served coffee to Search and Rescue until she thought the tired men and women would explode. The kindness in their eyes made her feel even guiltier. So she fed them donuts and coffee and fussed over them, until the numbness took over. Then the chills set in.

Someone, she didn't know who, had wrapped a crocheted throw around her shoulders. It didn't come close to easing the icy dread that reached clear down to her soul.

Violet hated the helpless waiting. She'd offered to help search, but she didn't know the terrain. Then they'd be looking for two lost souls, instead of one, as Ian had pointed out.

More coffee. Grilled cheese sandwiches maybe.

Violet heaved herself out of the lawn chair and headed inside to the kitchen. She could feel the collective sigh of relief when she closed the door behind her. Insanity always made people uncomfortable. Now where was the darn cheese?

IAN'S FACE was lined with fatigue when he returned. Her watch told her it was almost five. Sunrise seemed a long, long time away.

"Any luck?" She asked as she tentatively touched his sleeve. She knew the answer before he slowly shook his head.

"It's too dark. We're gonna wait for dawn to search some more."

Ian collapsed on a lawn chair on the veranda, as rescue workers filed past, silently. A steadying hand on his shoulder, a nod toward Violet. They cared. Way too much to lie.

Violet went into the kitchen to get a sandwich and coffee for Ian.

She didn't know what to say when she put the plate and mug in front of him, so she, too, stayed silent.

When would it be okay to speak? At the funeral?

Be positive, be upbeat.

How?

"I'm sorry." It was the only thing she could say.

Ian didn't look up at her. He simply stared into his coffee cup for what seemed like hours.

"I know."

THEY FOUND HER at 11:18 a.m. At least that was what Violet's watch said when they radioed back. Shock, exposure, dehydration. The words from the C.B. radio were meaningless and impersonal as they washed over her. Daisy was alive, though barely conscious.

The helicopter pilot could be heard, explaining that he could only touch down in a field near where she'd been found. The terrain was too rough. Rescue workers needed an all-terrain vehicle to reach her. How in the hell had she gotten that far, in such rugged country?

Violet watched the sky for the helicopter to pass by. It was an excuse to pray, the first time she had prayed in a very long time.

Please make her okay.

She whispered the sentence over and over, to the wispy clouds, the insipid blue sky of autumn, to the stiff breeze that moved the leaves and branches.

The helicopter started as a tiny dot, growing bigger, until it lowered itself out of view. The thump-thump-thump of chopper blades was loud, as if it had landed in the yard instead of miles away. Amazing how noises carried out here.

An eternity later, it lifted off.

Please make her okay.

Violet stood up at the sound of an ATV moving at full throttle. Ian burst through the bushes, half standing to cushion the blow of tires bouncing on rock. The determination on his face told her nothing would stop him. He'd be at that hospital as fast as humanly possible.

As he leaped off the ATV, a sheriff's car swung into the circular drive, scattering gravel.

The squad car door was open and Vince was pounding across the dirt the second the car came to a complete stop.

"Hey man, I heard. Couldn't get away till now. Where're they taking her?"

"Central Neurological."

"Get in. I'll take you."

Violet sprinted to the squad car. "I'm coming, too."

Ian looked at her, really looked at her, for one terrible moment.

He couldn't shut her out. She wouldn't let him. It was *her* Daisy, too, dammit.

"Please."

Ian nodded.

It took a half a second for her to throw herself in the back seat and they were off. Violet wrenched her door closed as they swung out of the driveway, lights and sirens blaring.

IAN LISTENED to the doorknob rattle. He didn't have the energy or the inclination to get up and unlock the connecting door. He'd been running on pure adrenaline for the twenty-four hours since Vi had woken him up to tell him his mom was missing. Exhaustion weighted every muscle in his body.

Resting his shoulders against the headboard, he didn't think he could move if he tried.

But then the pounding started. The wood reverberated from the blows. "Ian. Open the damn door. I'll wake every last person in this hotel if I have to," Vi shouted, her voice muffled only slightly.

Ian sighed. He couldn't face her right now.

"I mean it. Let me in." More pounding. "You can't avoid me forever."

She was right. He couldn't avoid her forever, but he'd sure hoped to delay this conversation until he was somewhat rational and rested.

He groaned with the effort of standing. "I'm coming."

Flipping the lock, he opened the door.

Violet's eyes narrowed as she studied him from head to toe. "You look like hell."

"You don't look much better."

Vi shrugged. She reached out and plucked a twig dangling from his shoulder. "Are you gonna talk to me now?"

He folded his arms across his chest. How was he supposed to talk to her when his emotions were such a jumble, a nasty, seething mess of guilt, resentment and sympathy? So he said nothing.

"I'm sorry dammit. I've already told you a hundred times." She stalked over to him and stabbed at his chest with her index finger. "Mr. I'm-so-perfect-I-never-screw-up."

"I never said I was perfect."

"Yeah, but when *you* lose Daisy, it's a mistake, you learn from it and everything's okay. I lose her and it's a capital offense."

"Look, we're both tired. This isn't the time to have this conversation. We'll talk in the morning." Ian started to turn away.

"Don't—" She grasped his arm.

He refused to face her. He was afraid she might see the accusations running through his head. His voice was low and rough. "You could've gotten her killed."

"Don't you think I know that? Ian, look at me."

He knew he was a goner when he met her gaze.

Violet's eyes were brimming with tears. "I'm not asking for your forgiveness. I'm asking for your understanding."

"I understand what you're going through. The guilt, the rage, the helplessness." His voice was terse. "It was bad enough when that was all I had on my conscience. Now I've got you, too."

"What do you mean?"

"Who brought you into this whole thing? Who told you you could handle it? *Me.*"

Her cheeks flushed. "You really have an incredible ego, don't you? I thought you were blaming me, when all along you were accepting the guilt for the entire thing. You know, Ian, you'd make a terrific martyr."

Her tart observation made him feel about two inches tall. Was that what he'd become? Some whining, self-pitying martyr?

"That's a bunch of bull."

"Is it? I'm a grown-up. I can take responsibility for my own mistakes. Or is screwing up all your territory? Is that it? You're uncomfortable if the world doesn't hinge on what you do?"

Ian ran a hand through his hair. "I don't know. I'm so damn tired I don't know what to think."

"Then why don't you just admit it? You're human, not God. Not even St. Ian." Violet stepped closer, her eyes flashing.

"I can't talk about this now."

But Violet wouldn't let him back away from her or her accusation. She stepped forward for every backward step he took.

"Admit it, Ian. It makes you feel important. Better than everyone else."

"No. It makes me feel…like maybe if I try hard enough I'll be…I don't know…the kind of son she wants. Not the asshole who abandoned her."

Vi stopped in her tracks. Her voice was soft. "Don't you know you're *already* the kind of son she wants? Just the way you are?"

His throat got all scratchy, his eyes burned. "But I wasn't here for her when she needed me. This time, or before."

"But you're here for her now. You've done your damnedest, loved her with your whole heart. I'd say that makes up for your self-absorbed asshole days."

Somehow her argument made sense to his addled brain. He nodded slowly. "How about you? You've tried your damnedest. Can you get past your mistakes?"

Her shoulders sagged, the light of battle died in her eyes. "I was so afraid when Daisy was out there lost. I'd think about her hurt or scared and blame myself. She *believes* in me, Ian." Violet lowered her eyes. "That's something nobody's ever done before."

Ian drew her unyielding body close to his and smoothed her hair away from her face. "Nobody? Not even your folks?"

"No," she whispered.

A deep, dull ache started in his chest. He could imagine her as a little girl—big, dark eyes and enough spunk for six kids. But nobody to believe in her, nobody to bake her a birthday cake….

"Tell me about your parents?"

He felt her body tense.

"Hey, it's only fair. You know my secrets—I'm St. Ian, the martyr asshole." Grasping her chin, he raised her face. "I may be a lot of things, but you can count on me."

Her gaze roved over his face. He warmed under her scrutiny.

"It's not easy for me...to talk about." Her gaze dropped to his shirtfront.

"Try."

She took a deep breath. "My dad's a drunk and my mom pretty much threw us kids to the wolf."

Ian's gut tightened. "What was he like? When he was drunk?"

"He...he had a temper. And getting drunk meant he could whale on us kids and not feel guilty. Because if he was drunk, he couldn't be held accountable for his actions."

"He beat you." It was a statement, not a question. "I'd kind of suspected something like that. But hoped I was wrong."

She nodded.

"And your mother didn't step in?"

"She, uh, usually disappeared when he was in one of his...moods. Us kids were left to fend for ourselves."

"How many brothers and sisters?" he asked.

"My brother died when I was sixteen. Car accident. And I have a sister, Colleen, she must be something like twenty-three now."

"Something like?"

She hesitated for a moment. "Uh, yeah. We don't keep in touch much."

"And your dad and mom?"

"Mom left Dad shortly after Patrick died. Married some guy who owns restaurants and moved with him to San Diego. Colleen lives with Dad and keeps an eye on him. When he needs something extra that Medicare doesn't cover, she calls me.''

''The old guy beat you when you were kids, but Colleen takes care of him and you foot the bill?''

Violet shook her head. Her voice was taut with emotion. ''He never hurt Colleen. Just me and Patrick.''

''Why?''

''I don't know.''

She looked away, but not before he saw the sadness in her eyes. The betrayal.

''I kinda figured she was more loveable. I was stubborn. Defiant.''

Ian placed a kiss on her nose. ''That's what I like about you.''

''Patrick stood up for me. Got beaten worse because of that.''

''He believed in you.''

''What?''

''You said earlier nobody before Daisy ever believed in you. It sounds like Patrick did.''

She raised her chin, searching his face. Her eyes filled with moisture. A single tear slid down her cheek.

''I guess he did.''

CHAPTER TEN

VIOLET ABSORBED the truth of Ian's statement. Patrick had believed in her. Enough to risk considerable pain.

Ian lifted her chin. "You okay?"

"Y-yes." She avoided his gaze, afraid what she might see in his eyes now that he knew. Because no matter how many times she told herself it wasn't her fault, that she hadn't deserved the abuse, a part of her always felt ashamed.

He rubbed his thumb along the sensitive skin below her jaw. "*I* believe in you."

"After all that's happened today? And everything you know about me?"

"*Especially* because of today. Yeah, you made a mistake. But you faced up to it and you did everything in your power to make it right. It's obvious that you love my mom…. And I'm hoping you care about me a little."

Vi swallowed hard. Suddenly her idea of the perfect man had nothing to do with Armani suits and starched white dress shirts. Or maybe it wasn't so sudden. Maybe her views had been changing so gradually she hadn't been aware that her version of the ideal man was one who knew the worst about her, had *seen* the worst of her, and still believed in her.

Ian's statement hung in the air between them. It was

a challenge. So was the possessive way he looked at her.

She flushed under his scrutiny. Things were getting way out of control. Especially her emotions. "Uh, sure. You're a good friend."

"No, Violet. I'm not a good friend. And I don't intend to be. I want it all." He dipped his head, his breath warm on her face. His voice was merely a whisper when he said, "Whether you admit it or not, so do you."

She couldn't *not* return his kiss. He'd seen something she'd failed to recognize. That while she'd been busy adjusting to his world, she'd not only grown to love his mother, but she'd also allowed Ian into her heart, too.

He drew her close, and she melded to him like a second skin. His kiss was deep and welcoming, so natural, that her caresses mirrored his without any conscious effort. He countered, she balanced.

She didn't know if there was enough of her left to give to another person, but with Ian she desperately wanted to try. Pulling back, she ended the kiss. It took effort and will. And from Ian's rapid breathing, it took plenty of his will, too.

"Vi—"

"Shhh. You're right. I do...care for you." The words got stuck in her throat. "More than a little."

His smile removed any doubts she'd had about opening up to him. "I sure hope so, 'cause I think I'm falling for you."

Running her palm along his stubbly cheek, she marveled at the sheer perfection of the man.

He kissed her lips, her eyes, her cheeks, almost as

if he were worshiping her. He made her feel cherished and alive.

Vi broke the kiss a second time. "You know when you said I wasn't ready up here." She tapped her temple. "You were right. I wasn't ready to make love. But I'm pretty sure I'm ready now."

Grasping his hand, she led him toward the bed.

His steps slowed.

She turned.

His expression was such a mixture of delight and disappointment, she almost laughed. Almost. The disappointment part scared her.

"What's wrong?" she asked.

"Vi, please, please, *please* tell me you're on the pill."

"No, but I bet we could find condoms at the hotel gift shop."

Ian groaned. "That's what I was afraid of."

"Is that a problem? It wasn't the last time."

Clearing his throat, he moved closer, touched her hair, her face. "Did you notice that…um…the condom failed?"

"I noticed. I just kind of put it out of my mind. I've been so busy…."

"I figured you were on the pill—stupid assumption—so I didn't worry too much." His skin went white, then a strange greenish hue. "There's no chance that you're—"

"No. Wrong time of the month." Vi closed her eyes and willed it to be so. No use panicking the man when there was so little statistical probability.

"You don't know how relieved I am to hear that. My life is way too complicated right now for a baby.

That'll teach me not to steal condoms from Mom's stash. She's probably had them since the Carter administration.'' He chuckled dryly.

Violet's heard his voice as if he were speaking through cotton. Her heart pounded. "My life is complicated, too."

"Hey, snap out of it. No need to worry, right?" His voice was hopeful.

"Uh, no. No need to worry." What had she been thinking? To put herself in such a vulnerable position? "But you're right, we can't take a risk like that again. I'll see my doctor for a prescription ASAP. Good night, Ian."

"Good night?" he echoed as she closed the connecting door behind her.

"C'MON, DAISY, you've got to try," Violet cajoled. Her back cramped with fatigue.

She tried again.

Kneeling next to Daisy's chair, she'd dragged the canvas over to her. Getting the woman's shoes and socks off had been a battle, but she'd done it. Daisy's feet were dipped in orange paint, all she had to do was smear them across the fabric.

"Just wipe them off on the canvas, like mud."

The paint was starting to dry, leaving cracks across the tops of the old wrinkled feet. It would be a real bear to get her cleaned up. If removing Daisy's shoes and socks set her off, Lord only knew what water would do. Probably about the same reaction as her boss's when she'd asked for a short-term leave of absence for the full six weeks of Annabelle's recovery.

Her boss had relied on icy politeness to get his point across, whereas Daisy was much more vocal.

But he'd conceded in the end, maybe Daisy would, too.

Studying Daisy hopefully, she looked for any sign of softening. The older woman sat perfectly still, back straight, lips pursed, arms crossed.

Violet sighed in defeat, wiping the sweat out of her eyes with a forearm. She stood slowly and worked the kinks out of her back. She could lead a horse to canvas, but she couldn't make it paint.

"I know, you're just not back up to speed yet. But I'm certainly not going to let this gorgeous day go to waste." She glanced around her and inhaled deeply. A gentle breeze rustled in the mesquite, doves cooed, sparrows chirped. Being in love, or something like it, made her life seem to sparkle. "What a great day. A gift for November."

She eyed Daisy, but no change.

Violet poured blue paint in one tray, green in the another. Tapping her chin with her index finger, she decided. She'd need brown, for the tree limbs and trunk, too.

She lifted her cotton skirt and stepped into the blue. Cool, fluid, sensual around her toes. First she skated across the upper two thirds of the canvas, then went back across, feet together, hips swinging.

Raising her arms for balance, she threw in a clap and a spin for good measure.

An old rock and roll tune hummed through her as she worked, breathless, excited. The music in her head moved through her body, directing her feet.

At last, Violet stepped into the bucket at the edge

of the canvas and watched the water turn blue. She still hummed a tune, turning to survey her work. Her heart jumped in surprise.

"It's good," Daisy pronounced, clapping her wrinkled hands in time with Violet's humming, not missing a beat.

"But you need to work in a little white before it dries, for those clouds on the horizon."

Violet studied the expanse of blue. She was right.

"By all means." Violet gestured toward the canvas. "Would you do the honor?"

A grin split Daisy's face, her pique forgotten. "I thought you'd never ask."

With each swirl and turn of Daisy's feet, the clouds took shape. It was breathtaking.

Her arms dropped, her swaying stopped. She stepped onto one of the beach towels arranged around the edge of the canvas.

She gestured grandly toward the painting. "Your turn, my dear."

Violet curtsied deeply, honored to collaborate with such a gifted artist, such a great woman. "We'll finish together."

They both were out of breath when they stopped, side by side, on a beach towel. Violet draped an arm around the older woman's shoulders and exhaled deeply. It was wonderful.

But Daisy clucked her tongue impatiently.

"There's something missing." She tipped her head to the side and studied the painting. Then she walked to another towel and studied it from that angle.

"Bougainvillea," she pronounced.

"Where?" There wasn't a bougainvillea anywhere in the courtyard. Not enough sun.

"Not here." Daisy's words were clipped, impatient. "Here." She tapped her forehead. "Artistic license."

Then she pointed. "There and there. Maybe some there. Just a touch. A little magenta. Give some perspective on distance. Perk it up." She nodded emphatically. "See what I mean?"

"I think so...."

One big toe at a time, she dipped and squished, until there was a beautiful border of bougainvillea petals along the lower corners.

Daisy stepped back to check their handiwork.

Violet's heart pounded as she waited. It was like waiting to find out about a promotion, or a special school project. Only better.

"Maybe some shadowing there." Daisy pointed, Violet nodded.

"And a little light here...."

Genius. The woman was a genius.

When Daisy was satisfied, they stood back, arms linked.

Violet sucked in a deep breath. Gorgeous. Simply gorgeous. Like nothing she'd ever seen before. It glowed, it glistened. It flowed, an impressionistic version of the mesquite tree.

Violet couldn't speak, couldn't even push a croak past the lump in her throat. That she could be a part of something so extraordinary was too much for her to comprehend.

"That, my dear, is a ten."

Daisy hobbled off toward the house, leaving Violet to stare in wonder at their masterpiece.

"YOU SHOULD HAVE seen it, Ian. It was like nothing I've experienced before. Like everything just came together perfectly in that one moment. Like it was bigger than us, somehow destined." Violet sighed, leaning back against the couch, tucked in the crook of Ian's arm.

"I'm wounded," he declared, as he clutched his chest. "You mean to tell me making love with me wasn't like that? Like 'everything came together perfectly' and was 'bigger than us, destined.' Although it's been so long, your memory's probably a little foggy."

A frown formed on her lovely forehead. The woman was everything he wanted, but she needed to lighten up sometimes.

Her eyes widened. "It's the same thing," she breathed, wonder in her voice, awe shining in her eyes.

He brushed the hair from her forehead and kissed her softly. She was too good for him, but somehow that didn't matter to her. Somehow, she still wanted him.

Then it happened, kind of like one tequila shooter short of oblivion. All of life's mysteries crystallized for him as he caressed her lips, nibbled and tasted. Whatever else happened, somehow he'd landed in a pile of crap and come out smelling like a rose. All because of her.

Something rumbled up in his chest, his throat. It burned. It made his eyes water. And it wasn't the salsa from lunch. This woman made him want to bawl like a baby. Because she loved him.

He reluctantly ended their kiss, so sweet and pure. As penance, he leaned back on the couch, squeezing his eyes shut. His throat worked convulsively as he put a vise on his emotions. Guys didn't cry about stuff like this. *Especially* guys who danced.

Crying about death was okay, acceptable. Some movies even. Hadn't he gotten a bit teary-eyed at the last Vin Diesel movie? No problem, he could be as sensitive as the next guy. But not over women.

"Are you okay?" she asked.

He nodded, not sure he could find his voice in the cesspool of raw emotion. How did women do it, going around emotional like this? It felt like hell. Screw the endorphins. A good run could give him that.

Ian wiped his eyes and sniffed loudly, a great big, manly snort.

"Allergies," he choked out.

"I love a man with…allergies." Vi wiped a stray droplet at the corner of his eyes. "As a matter of fact, I think a man with…allergies…is extremely sexy. Almost as sexy as a man who cooks. And here it is, all in one package…." Her voice trailed off in a feline growl.

He opened one eye to peek at her. There was a devilish glint in her eye, her mouth curved in a wicked grin. He smacked his forehead with an open hand. What in the hell was he going to do with her?

He grabbed her and pulled her on top of him, giving her an answering growl.

"I made…you…lunch," he told her, between vicious nibbles.

"Mm-hum," she sighed.

"And I have a horrible case of…allergies." He punctuated the words with a trail of wet, open-mouthed kisses down her neck.

"Yeesss…" It was more of a purr, reverberating in her throat, directly under his caressing tongue.

"A release of endorphins might help."

"Huh?" She didn't really hear him, just wrapped a hand around the back of his neck and pulled him into better nibbling position.

"Making love…" he found that sensitive spot right near her jugular. "releases…all sorts of…ben…e…ficial…chemicals."

"Mmm," she agreed.

He reached for the hem of her T-shirt and tugged upward, over her rib cage.

Her hand stopped him before he even got a glimpse of her lacy, oh-so-full bra.

"Huh-uh."

"Huh-uh?" He pleaded, he begged, he gave her his best lost puppy look. But her eyes, so warm and erotic a moment before, now carried a hard glint.

"Hasn't it been a month *yet?*" It seemed like years.

"It's been three days." She raised three fingers, as if his hormone-fuddled mind needed visual aids. "That leaves twelve more days till my doctor's appointment."

"No way. It's been four *weeks* and three days, at least."

"Where'd you learn to count? The Pentagon Purchasing Department?"

He let out a groan of frustration. She wasn't going to let this slide.

Vi smacked him on the shoulder with an open hand. It stung. It wasn't fair.

"Besides, it's not my job to be gatekeeper. You

don't need a baby. We can't risk it. No matter how much fun we could have together.''

He had to smile. She had him there. Or he wished she had him there. It brought to mind all the wonderful things she could do with those strong, supple fingers.

He held up his hands in defeat. He knew she wouldn't budge, but it had been fun to try.

He deposited her next to him and threw an arm around her shoulders. She snuggled in to his armpit like a bunny finding a safe burrow.

''Don't get me wrong. I want kids someday,'' he pondered. ''Lots of them. It's an only child kind of thing I guess. Always saw myself raising them some-place like this—lots of room to roam, small school, small town.''

''And what about a mother for those kids?''

''Don't know. That part was always kinda fuzzy. I couldn't really put any of my girlfriends in that pic-ture. Just not the right kind of...I don't know... chemistry. Mom and Dad were madly in love till the day he died. I want that, too.''

She cleared her throat. Probably allergies.

Vi. If only he'd met her at a different time in his life. She was joyous, loving and a real pistol. Life would never get boring with her around. And their kids would grow up to be feisty, independent free-thinkers.

He smiled at the vision. Lots of little dark-haired, brown-eyed kids who could spit nails. Maybe even a blonde or two, just for good measure.

''Why the smile?''

He peeked sideways at her. ''Just thinking.''

''About what?''

"About what our kids might look like."

Her expression didn't change.

"Yours and mine."

Her eyebrows drew together in one straight, sable line. Was she mulling it over, or disgusted with the very thought?

He continued his pitch. "Not now, I mean. Like maybe years down the road. After things calm down...I mean, well...you know."

The sun broke across her face, so relieved was her smile.

"Of course. Well, someday, sure. When my career's at a stable point, if we're togeth— I mean...well, it's a possibility."

If they were together? Where'd that come from?

"Oh, come on, you have to have thought about it before, in the abstract at least. Probably not even me. Any old donor once you reached the corporate heights."

He'd meant it as a joke. But it hurt, to think he might not be good enough, or that she had so little faith that they were absolutely right for each other and always would be.

He replaced his frown with a grin. But Vi didn't even notice. She was too busy picking at a cuticle.

"I kind of figured kids weren't for me," she commented, her voice low.

She didn't look at him, just stared at her annoying cuticle.

"I mean, lets face it, my gene pool isn't a real prize. My DNA probably screams 'dysfunctional.'" She looked up then, just long enough to put a delaying hand on his arm.

He swallowed whatever reassuring comment had jumped to his tongue.

"No really. Alcoholism is inherited. So's anxiety and depression. You look at my family tree, we've got it all."

It was hard to fathom, that such a perfect woman could really see herself that way.

"Hey. Vi." He clasped her chin and made her look at him. Her gaze met his for a moment, then slid away.

"You wanna know what I see when I look at you? I mean besides a beautiful woman with an incredibly hot body?"

That brought a small smile. They were headed in the right direction, but had a long way to go.

"I see a fighter, a survivor. You could have rolled over and died. Could've used your family as an excuse to fail…or even worse, self-destruct." It hit him hard in the gut, the paths she could have taken and he would have never known her. Drugs, alcohol, suicide. "But you *used* it. You learned from it and used it to fuel your ambitions. You worked your butt off and got an education. You picked a career and got good at it. And you're smart as hell. So don't go telling me your genes are inferior. They're what make you *you,* and I wouldn't want you any other way."

Ian inhaled deeply, breathing hard, like he'd just finished a long run. He surveyed her face, searching for some sign that he'd gotten through.

She was quiet, absolutely still. His words hung in the air between them.

Then her upper lip twitched, then quivered. Her big brown eyes filled. A tear crept out, ran down the side of her nose, following the curve of her mouth to dangle on her chin.

He tasted salt as he rubbed his lips across her skin, erasing her sorrow.

"Nobody's ever loved me like that before," she murmured.

"Somebody should have." His voice was husky, his throat raw with regret. "But I'm honored to be the first."

Vi touched her lips to his, barely a flutter.

"Thank you." Her voice was as husky as his, tinged with wonder, coated with destiny. There was so much packed into those two words, he didn't know where to begin. All he knew was that he would never let this woman get away.

CHAPTER ELEVEN

VIOLET FAIRLY FLEW through the doorway. She couldn't wait to give Ian the good news. And Daisy, too.

"Ian," she called.

His muffled voice drifted to her ears, coming from the direction of his office.

It took only a few seconds to follow the sound. Tapping on the closed door, she entered Ian's inner sanctum. She was careful to step around the reference books scattered haphazardly on the floor. His desk wasn't much better. A well-aimed nudge from her hip sent a pile of computer paper sliding into a bad imitation of the leaning tower of Pisa. It swayed precariously as she perched on his desk.

He glanced up from the computer screen, a distracted frown his only acknowledgment.

"I've got the most fantastic news." She let her hands do most of the talking, gesturing in the air, while she punctuated the picture with key words. "The annual fall arts and crafts fair. We've got a booth. It's so huge, we can share with crafters from the center. It'll give Daisy a chance to show her work, bask in a little glory. I'll do the rest. Isn't it great?"

"Huh?" He stared blankly at her, before scowling.

"The crafts fair. Get with the program."

"Sorry," he grunted. But he didn't look sorry. He looked annoyed. What was his problem?

"Daisy's work is so spectacular, it ought to be shared. She deserves her day in the sun. The ladies at the center agree it would be just right for her. Get out and see lots of old friends, bask in their adoration, then go home for a long nap when she's ready."

"Daisy?"

This man was seriously deficient. She peeked over his shoulder and saw a screen full of words.

Violet balanced her hands on her hips. "You wanna talk later?" she demanded.

Ian grunted and turned back to his screen. It was a grunt of agreement, she assumed.

"Remember, Daisy'll be back from the center by three. I want your official okey-dokey before I give her the good news."

Another grunt.

Violet took the hint and tiptoed out, though she could have goose-stepped and saluted and he wouldn't have noticed. She closed the door gently behind her, smiling indulgently. So this was what he was like when the creative juices kicked in. She only hoped she was his muse.

Wandering into the kitchen, she was confronted by Annabelle and her soulful eyes.

"Walk, Annabelle?" She reached for the leash hanging on the wall near the dog bed. The vet had said she needed exercise, as long as they didn't take it too fast.

Annabelle pulled herself to her feet and barely limped when she approached Violet. Her tail swished from side to side with anticipation. She pulled back

her lips and gave a great big doggie grin. Her teeth
shone, her eyes sparkled. This was one happy dog.

Violet snapped on the leash and headed out the
door. She was careful to set a leisurely pace and soon
lost herself in the beauty of the day.

It was an afternoon made for calendars—deep blue
sky, golden sunshine, a gentle autumn breeze, with
just enough of a nip to remind her that there were four
seasons here, instead of the two in Phoenix.

Yes, Annabelle was almost healed. It filled her with
immense satisfaction to know she'd helped. And
maybe learned a little in the process. It seemed silly
now, to drive that way. Did the risk ever justify the
action? Judge Tanner had been right. She *had* needed
time to cool off, get things straight.

But what about when Annabelle was back on the
job? There hadn't been any invitation to stay. Her
leave of absence wouldn't last forever. If Ian did invite
her, what then? Prolonged shacking-up and an even
longer commute? Or maybe marriage and a long commute? He'd talked about kids, but never marriage.

Something inside her shrank at the thought of leaving him. Images of an empty condo reminded her just
how lonely her life had been before she'd met him.
And Daisy. She didn't want to leave her, either. She
wanted, no, maybe even *needed* to absorb as much of
her wisdom and spirit as she could. While Daisy still
remained Daisy.

Someday the painting would end. Communication
would become difficult, maybe even impossible. What
about then? Was she prepared to go the long haul?

Her heart said yes, her head said maybe. Then the
scared part, the part that clung to the safe old things,

wanted to say hell no! Baby-sitting a few adjusters and networking with upper management seemed almost easy in comparison, certainly less heartrending.

They needed to talk, she and Ian. Maybe then it would become clear.

Annabelle's nose came up. She stopped and lifted one paw.

A roadrunner crossed the trail several yards ahead, gangly legs a-moving, a lizard hanging from its long, thin beak. The lizard tail twitched, then was still.

It was beautiful, but sad. The circle of life.

Annabelle resumed her pace. They walked in a contented silence, the jingle of dog tags the only noise to break the stillness.

Something gray and furry blurred in front of them and was gone.

Annabelle quivered with excitement.

"Sit," Vi commanded.

The dog sat. But every microbe of her being strained toward the bushes where the jackrabbit had disappeared. She scarcely blinked, sending all of her considerable attention toward the brush.

"Easy, girl."

Annabelle swished her tail once, but never took her eyes off the brush. Thank God she was too well-trained to bolt. Thank goodness basic obedience training was part and parcel for an Alzheimer's assistance dog. She could just see it now. "Sorry, Ian, I lost your dog. Gotta go back to work. It's been real…"

Even with Annabelle there to help, it would be nearly impossible to leave, to go on like nothing had changed.

A paw scraped her pant leg.

She knelt down and took the great head between her hands. "No rabbits today, sweetheart. Sorry, girl. Ready to go back?"

Annabelle gave her a big, wet slurp on the chin.

"Okay, okay. I love you, too. Let's go see if Ian's done yet."

Violet stood, but things started to waver back and forth. She clamped her eyes shut, willing away the specks of light behind her lids.

Annabelle's nose nudged her thigh. The dog whined.

"I'm okay girl. Just stood up too fast. Maybe a little dehydrated."

Violet opened her eyes and the world righted itself. Too much sun, not enough water. It was easy to forget when the weather was so gorgeous.

"WE WERE SO LUCKY to get a booth this late." Violet gestured with a celery stick to punctuate her point. The Tater Tots looked heavenly. She inhaled deeply as Ian pulled the cookie sheet from the oven. Grease and salt, it didn't get any better than that.

"And one this large—it's just incredible."

Ian raised an eyebrow. "You think it's a good idea? All those people, the confusion…"

"We'll take Annabelle. Daisy can preside over the whole thing from her lawn chair. When she gets tired, or if she gets confused or frustrated, that'll be the cue for you to take her home. I'll do the rest." The celery stick waved like a baton. Her hands seemed to have a mind of their own these days. Words were so much more expressive with their help.

"Welll… It *is* just Echo Point. Everyone knows her."

"It'll be fine, Ian."

He slowly removed the oven mitts.

God, he had beautiful hands. They were large, with long, artistic fingers. She'd never seen him grip a football or a baseball bat, but it wasn't a great stretch to imagine him that way. Strong, sure, but always enjoying the game, with that goofy grin and a flash of dimples.

No, she'd never seen that intense jock side of him. But she'd seen him gently escort Daisy down the hall and seen him prepare her favorite finger foods with the attention of a five-star chef. And she remembered those hands on her body, intimate caresses as well as everyday touches that showed how much he loved her. Subconscious things like cupping her elbow to guide her to the dinner table, or featherlight touches at the small of her back as he followed her from a room.

Violet closed her eyes to block out the images. They were stranded here, stalled at a plateau when they desperately wanted to move to another level. It was torture, this enforced abstinence, but somehow exciting, too. Her fevered mind could transform an innocent gesture into foreplay. Ian's hands suddenly became erotic appendages promising great pleasures.

"Vi?"

She opened her eyes. He was right in front of her, a quizzical smile lifting his lips. The man hardly ever frowned. Only when she interrupted his writing.

It seemed like all she wanted was to hold him. Even the intoxicating aroma of food couldn't distract her from her purpose. She closed the short distance between them, yanked the oven mitts from his grasp and tossed them on the counter.

His lips twitched into a smile as she guided his hands to her hips. He took the hint and pulled her closer. Murmuring all sorts of promises, she wrapped her arms around his neck like she'd never let go.

His arms tightened around her as he led her into a slow dance. The man was divine on his feet. And off them, too.

Violet closed her eyes and absorbed the moment, the feel of him against her body, warm, strong, loving. How right it was to have her arms around him. His lips tickled as he nuzzled the curve of her neck.

She leaned her head against his shoulder and swayed with him. The top of her head fit perfectly under his chin. If she couldn't have him in her bed, this would have to do. She inhaled deeply.

His scent was so like him, straightforward, sexy, playful, with an underlying seriousness that made the games all the more precious. There was a time to play, and a time to grow, and he knew the difference, knew what was important. Family, loyalty, building a home and not settling for anything less than a ten.

Was she his ten? Daisy seemed to think so. Violet hoped so. Because this moment was perfect—slow dancing in the middle of the kitchen, their romantic dinner of Tater Tots and hot dogs growing colder by the minute. The meal didn't matter as long as she shared it with Ian.

The celery stick dropped from her limp fingers, before she curved them around the back of his neck.

He started to hum. It reverberated through her, filling up all the empty spaces. It was a promise. The same promise Edward had made to a young Daisy. The same promise that beckoned her to change the direction of her dreams, dream a little bigger, a little grander.

"I'll bring you a daisy a day, dear...." he whispered.

"I UNDERSTAND," Violet said into the phone.

But she didn't understand, not on any level that counted. Sure, it was standard operating procedure. Move up the ladder, change locations. The two went hand-in-hand. It was as if the great gods of insurance didn't want management to get too comfortable in one place. As if contentment equated laziness.

"Las Vegas. The first of the year," she confirmed through numb lips that refused to cooperate. She meant to say, "Forget it. Take your stinking promotion and put it where the sun doesn't shine."

But she didn't.

Instead, she searched for a pad of paper. Not a piece of scratch paper to be found. She leaned over the counter to grab her purse. Sticky notes would have to do. When at last she found them, she copied down the important stuff. Not that she could really forget.

Las Vegas. January 3rd, she wrote. *Call Realtor.*

"I'll list my condo," she mumbled, then placed the phone very carefully back on the receiver. She stared numbly at the kitchen tile, noticing that somebody needed to mop.

Las Vegas. This changed everything. Surviving a whole month in Cleveland for training seemed like a stretch right now. How in the world could she leave Ian and Daisy like that?

Vegas. Big, transient, all glitter, but no substance.
Why the hell couldn't she do the right thing?

Fear. A commute she could handle. A nice way to
dip her toes in the domestic waters with Ian, but still
have her job and condo as a safety net. It was total
commitment she couldn't do.

Violet threw the pen down and pushed away the
news, along with the cold, hard knot in her stomach.
It was a no-win situation and she had a canvas to prepare.

IAN SAUNTERED into the kitchen and stopped dead in
his tracks. No, anything but this.

Not the notes again.

Little bits of yellow were everywhere, littering the
counters, stuck to the fridge. He didn't have to look,
but he knew he'd find them in the strangest places.
Stuck to the TV, the bathroom mirror, on tables, lamp
bases, pretty much anything that was still. Even Annabelle, if she didn't move fast enough.

How the hell had it happened? He'd gotten rid of
all scratch paper, notes, cards, writing implements.
They were all locked away in a file cabinet in his
office.

Ian picked one up and read it. ''Get machine fixed
before X-mas. Pack.''

It was in his mother's shaky scrawl, but that didn't
surprise him. He groaned and hung his head. Pack.
Another frenzy. He didn't think he could go through
it again.

Violet shuffled into the kitchen and grunted. He au-
tomatically poured, then handed her his rugby mug.

The coffee was hot, strong and lethal, just the way she liked it.

Her eyes closed in bliss, but it was *his* heart that warmed and started beating faster. It made sense to see her this way in the morning. It was simply Vi. She got out of bed half-comatose and it was pure poetry to watch her return to human form.

She sighed and slurped noisily.

Her eyes started to lose that glazed look. Her gaze wandered around the kitchen, her forehead cramped into a frown.

"Looks like snow," she croaked, her bathrobe sleeves flapping as she gestured. "Yellow snow."

He shook his head, and it hurt. He could feel the knot starting behind his eyes. Soon the dull throb would take on a life all its own—like the notes.

"Daisy. She used to write notes to keep things straight. *Hundreds* of them. Said they helped her remember. But then she'd forget she wrote a note, so she'd write another, and another. I don't know what bug she's got up her a—what she's doing this time."

"What machine needs fixed?" Vi asked.

Ian scratched his head. "Hell if I know."

"Pack? You haven't been talking to her about a nursing home have you? It'd kill her. Strange place, strange people. She'd just curl up and die."

"Hellloooo. That's what I've been trying to avoid."

Vi set down her coffee. "Let's pick them up and see if we can get a clue, some insight. Maybe she's upset about something."

"This one's the same, and so's this one. I've seen her do this before. She'll write the same thing over and over and over. She'll obsess about it whatever it is. Let's sweep the whole place, get rid of these before she gets up. Maybe she'll have forgotten.''

They plucked notes from every surface. Just when they thought they'd gotten them all, another would sprout inside the microwave or on Annabelle's leash.

''Here's some notes I took yesterday. You don't think…''

''Let me see.'' Ian took the note from her limp fingers. ''What's this? Vegas, Realtor. Maybe that's where she got machines—slots maybe? Packing because of the Realtor? We may never know.''

Vi took the note and crumpled it into a little ball.

He grasped her by the shoulders and turned her to look at him.

''Hey, what's this all about? Vegas. Realtor?''

''I meant to tell you today. After I slept on it.''

''If you want to elope to Vegas, the answer's yes,'' he joked. He refused to look at it in any other light. It was the Realtor part that bothered him. Realtors weren't needed to plan a weekend trip, or even an elopement. Realtors meant permanent change, and not necessarily the good kind.

She wouldn't meet his eyes. ''Ian, you're making this even harder.''

Man, the kind of double entendres he could make with that one. But he'd keep it clean. ''So you eloping with Joe? Or maybe Judge Ralph?''

She chuckled, but her expression remained troubled. Her fingertips were soft as she reached up and smoothed his face.

He grasped her hand and held it to his cheek.

He'd never let her go, never.

But he would. Because she meant that much to him.

"What gives?" he asked softly. It was time to get the painful part out of the way. Rip off the bandage quickly.

"My promotion. I have to relocate to Las Vegas. It's fairly common. I mean they move the executives around quite a bit. Learn more that way. See how different regions work. Vegas is a huge responsibility. Lots of tourists, claimants come and go."

"You want this? *Really* want this?"

"I don't know."

"Would it help if I asked you to stay?"

She shook her head. Her eyes filled with tears. "I don't know."

"Violet, what we've got here is real. Just as real as insurance and promotions. You can't throw it all away because you're afraid."

She raised her chin to battle angle.

"Easy for you to say. The worst thing that happened to you was that you had to wear a tutu. Some of the rest of us weren't so lucky. I learned early how to protect myself. Think on my feet, anticipate. Read people, read moods. I didn't do that so I could break through the glass ceiling, make the cover of *Forbes*. I did it to survive. Here—" she tapped her temple "—and here—" she tapped her heart. "So you think I'm afraid? Damn right I'm afraid. But at least I admit it. You just joke."

He let his hands drop from her shoulder so there was no danger of his palms constricting into a bone-crushing grip.

Restlessness goaded him to pace. Distance was good. That was what she wanted, wasn't it?

He turned back to face her. "Yeah, I'm afraid.

There, I admitted it. I'm afraid because you can walk away and I can't. I'm stuck here. I can't just decide this isn't fun anymore and chuck it all. I've made promises, promises I won't go back on. And no matter how much I love you, I *won't* sacrifice Daisy to make it work. So, I can't beg you to stay. I can't pull out all the stops, get down on bended knee and promise you the world. What you see is what you get.'' He made a sweeping gesture around the room.

''Would you? Ask? If you could?'' she whispered.

''Hell, yes. You've got to know that, Vi. I love you so much it hurts. So much it makes me crazy, trying to figure out how we can make it work.''

He ran out of breath.

Then she did something so completely unexpected it rendered him speechless.

Vi got down on her knees in front of him and took his clenched hand in hers and kissed his white knuckles.

He felt her tears before he saw them, washing away her kisses.

''Then we'll figure it out. Together,'' she murmured.

VIOLET HAD even looked under her bed. But it wasn't there. Her mouse was gone. So were her notes from the last meeting. And other things, like her black flats and her brush.

Daisy had to be the culprit. But she'd checked her room last night, as discreetly as possible. Nowhere. Not in Daisy's closet, not under her bed. Not even in her dirty clothes hamper, where the vegetable peeler had been found.

It was a mystery. One that was driving Violet crazy. Not hard to do these days.

She still had to decline the promotion, but couldn't formulate the letter. How to turn down a fabulous opportunity, but leave the door open?

She couldn't. That was the crux of the matter. If she turned down this one, she'd never get another shot. She'd be relegated to the ranks of the unambitious. The mommy track, with no infant to show for it. The boyfriend track was even less desirable, downright foolish. It showed a real lack of judgment, willing to throw out her career for the first good-looking guy who came along.

No, the corporate guys upstairs wouldn't understand. Because they were from another time, another generation. Maybe it wasn't even that. Maybe it was just because they were guys. Most probably wouldn't understand that kind of sacrifice. Her dad certainly wouldn't. But Ian did. He'd made that sacrifice himself, for someone he loved. Wasn't that the first thing that had really struck her about him? Like Patrick, he'd put someone else first.

Guys like that were hard to find. And she wasn't about to let this one get away.

Violet reached for her briefcase and pulled out a legal pad. A pen, scrounged from the bottom of her purse, sufficed. She wrote her letter to management, simple, to the point, explaining why she could not accept the position.

She leaned back in her chair and threw her arms wide. Her shoulders were suddenly light. A smile started somewhere near her toes and culminated in an ear-to-ear grin.

IAN'S BACK was to her as he stared out the French doors. Vi wrapped her arms around him and rested her cheek against his back.

"Hey, handsome. Whatcha looking at?" she asked.

"Watching Daisy. Thinking."

"About what?"

"How glad I am you decided to stay. How glad I am I didn't have to choose her over you. It'd kill me to see you go." His voice was low, unusually solemn for Ian.

"I know."

She felt a pang of remorse that she'd caused him pain, even if just for a day. But at least the remorse dulled the ache of being chosen second when push came to shove. The ironic part was that she wouldn't respect Ian if he deserted Daisy to be with her.

Forcing a bright tone, she said, "I'm not going anywhere. Unless of course you give me the boot."

"No way."

"I'll commute during the week and spend weekends here. If that doesn't work, I'll make the drive every day if I have to."

"I don't want you to have to do that. Almost two hundred miles round trip. But we'll make it work somehow."

She didn't bother to tell him she'd drive to the ends of the earth for him. They stood, his back to her, wrapped up together in their own thoughts.

Finally, Violet asked, "What's she doing?"

"Sitting. Petting Annabelle. That's pretty much it. But she looks happy."

"She *is* happy, Ian. You've done a great job here." She squeezed him around the middle for emphasis.

He rested his forearms along the tops of hers and squeezed back.

"Ian?"

"Hmmm?"

"Have you seen my mouse?"

"No way. I promised, remember? No hanky-panky for another four weeks isn't it?"

"No, goofball. My computer mouse. But while we're on the subject, my appointment is Monday. After the craft fair closes this weekend."

"That's the soonest you could get in?"

"Cross my heart."

He turned and pulled her into his arms. "All this talk of hearts and mice is getting me all heated up. Wanna make out?" He waggled his eyebrows at her.

His banter lightened her mood. She batted at his shoulder. "Not now," she admonished. "When Daisy goes to the center tomorrow."

He dipped his head and kissed her. No pressure. Just promise.

"You got a date then, lady. Now, your mouse. Where could that pesky critter be?"

His hands started moving, seemingly everywhere. He trailed a finger down her hip and zigzagged to her inner thigh. "I think I saw it around here last time...."

She grasped his hand and pushed it away. Heat suffused her cheeks, she swallowed hard. "How about my brush?" She tried another tack, but it backfired. It was really getting hot.

Ian grinned from ear to ear, as if he could see every lurid thought in her head.

"I'm not even going to go there. Let's check

Daisy's room.'' He grabbed her by the hand and pulled her down the hall.

''I already checked,'' she protested.

''Not in the right places.''

It didn't take Ian long to find her things. He pulled two suitcases from Daisy's closet and laid them on the bed. He slowly unzipped them and threw the lid back with a flourish. *''Voilà.''*

There they were. Amid a jumble of other junk was her mouse and her brush. In another suitcase, her files fought for space with an iron and something that had once been edible. All that was left was a big blob of squishy brown stuff. A plum maybe?

She gingerly lifted out her files, grasping them between her thumb and forefinger.

''How'd you know?'' she asked.

''Simple, Watson. The notes. Packing. She'll do this till the house is emptied out or I hide her suitcases. She must have found them in my room. Come to think of it, I'm missing a few things, too.''

''I'll leave you to it.''

Violet beat a hasty retreat, half afraid to see what else he might find in the depths of Daisy's suitcases.

CHAPTER TWELVE

IAN DIDN'T KNOW how she'd done it, but somehow it had worked. All that colorful cotton and hemp was now "framed." Not in the traditional sense, but lashed to long poles constructed of tree branches. Some were little bitty sapling branches, others were good-sized. Strapped to the frames were Daisy's masterpieces. And they looked magnificent.

He watched as Violet explained about the mesquite picture to a small group clustered around. Her face flushed with excitement, her eyes sparkled. And her hands never stopped moving, as she gestured here, underscored there. Something in their grace and expressiveness nagged at him, something familiar he should recognize.

Daisy.

He walked over to the lawn chair where Daisy and Annabelle held court.

He grasped her hand and squeezed.

"Hello, Mom."

"Isn't it wonderful, dear? We've had three offers already today for 'Dancing Tree.' A woman from Scottsdale wants us to do a showing there. And then there was some idiot with ideas to mass produce shower curtains and sell them in those chichi shops in Sedona." She snorted with disgust.

Good thing Dad had left her fairly comfortable, or they might have to consider the shower curtain idea to finance her future care.

"Having fun?" he asked.

"Certainly. Haven't seen some of these people in years. Oh, there's George Phillips over there." She gestured in the direction of the Indian fry bread stand. "Yoo-hoo, George, you handsome thing you," she trilled, loudly enough that at least ten other people turned, in addition to lucky George.

The man in question saluted her with a honey-laden circle of fry bread and winked, before he stuffed half of it in his mouth.

"Ralph Tanner stopped by a few minutes ago. And Edith Templeton, why I would've hardly recognized her—dyed her hair red, of all things. But it was good to get caught up."

"I'm sure," he commented dryly. Vi had been right. Daisy was in her element. "I'll go say hello to Violet." He patted Daisy on the shoulder and sauntered off to where Vi was surrounded by customers, most of them men.

Who wouldn't want to get close to her, smell her sweet perfume? Watch the way her gorgeous eyes lit with excitement. Try to steal a kiss from those mobile lips.

He elbowed a couple of 'em out of the way and rested his arm on her shoulder.

"Hello, Vi," he growled, letting it drop off to a suggestive purr.

"Hi." She smiled up at him and accepted his kiss. He pulled her close and deepened the kiss, just to make sure everyone knew exactly where they stood.

"Whew," was all she could say when he finally released her. But her cheeks flushed a rosy red, and her gaze wandered over his face. She gave him a dreamy smile, before turning to her entourage.

"Ian, I'm sure you know Luke and Mike. And that's Ralph, Jr. of course. And Mrs. Marshall, the high school art teacher."

He shook hands and nodded until he felt like one of those stupid dogs he used to see in car windows. The damn things grinned like idiots and bobbed their heads up and down until it looked like they might fall off.

"I'm gonna steal Vi away for a second. You guys just keep on appreciating the art." When three sets of eyes followed the sway of Vi's hips, he amended, "The pictures." He pointed to redirect their attention, then found Vi already sitting on a hay bale. She patted the empty space next to her.

"How's it going?"

"Wonderful. I couldn't have asked for a better response. Everyone's been so enthusiastic. And this dealer from Scottsdale is interested in having a showing. Just stuff from people with Alzheimer's. All sorts of arts and crafts and photography. Kinda show the hopeful times, since most people already know the dark side."

"Sounds interesting. And ambitious."

He watched Violet watch Daisy hold court. Her lips twitched into a smile, her eyes glowed with affection.

"Good thing I'm a secure kinda guy, or I might wonder if you loved me just because of my mother."

"Hmm?" She pulled her gaze away from Daisy and

linked her arm through his. "You're such a wonderful guy because Daisy did a good job raising you."

"Damn near perfect," he agreed.

"Damn near."

He saw that mischievous smile, just before she raised a paper cup and took a long drink of soda.

"So what's your excuse?"

"Pardon?"

"What's your excuse for being damn near perfect. It's not that quaint upbringing of yours."

The sparkle in her eyes faded.

He wrapped an arm around her and drew her close. "I'm sorry, Vi. Don't answer that. It was a stupid…"

"No. It's okay. I turned out okay because somebody loved me enough to go to bat for me. My brother—"

"Patrick."

"Uh-huh. I couldn't invalidate everything he did for me by giving up. Then all his sacrifices would have been for nothing. So I pushed and worked and fought to be something better."

She reached up and ran her palm over his Saturday stubble.

"And you know what?"

"What?"

"I think he knows. And he's proud."

"I think you're right." He squeezed her tightly against him, and thanked God for Patrick.

He was startled out of his reverie by Annabelle nudging him in the chest with her nose.

Jumping to his feet, he commanded, "Where's Daisy?"

Annabelle turned and trotted off toward the fry

bread stand. Ahead, he could just make out Daisy's form weaving through the crowd.

"Mom," he hollered, and sprinted after her.

It seemed like everything moved in slow motion, including his legs. His brain commanded *run*, but dread, like quicksand, sucked at his feet. Dodging around a kid here, an adult there, he was finally able to gain on her.

By the time he reached her, Annabelle was sitting patiently at her feet.

"Good girl," he wheezed as he stroked her silky head. He doubled over, struggling to catch his breath. Finally, he was able to suck in air without a burning pain in his chest. He was a long distance runner, not a sprinter.

"Come on, Mom, no wandering off." He placed a hand on her elbow and tried to draw her back to the booth.

Daisy wrenched her arm away. "I'm *not* wandering off. I'm not a child. If I want a…a…one of those things…" She stabbed a finger in the direction of George Phillip's Indian fry bread. "I'll have one."

"Sure, Mom," he soothed. "I'll get you one."

"I'll get it myself. Now where's my purse?"

"You didn't bring a purse."

"I *always* carry a purse." Her voice rose, people started to stare. She stabbed a bony forefinger in his chest and screeched, "You stole it. You stole my purse!"

More people turned and stared. He could feel his neck getting hot. Crap. What should he do now? Throw her over his shoulder, kicking and screaming?

A burly man he didn't recognize stepped toward them.

Just then Violet strolled up, a bright smile pasted on her face. Her own purse dangled from her fingers.

"Here's your purse, Daisy. You left it over there." She pointed vaguely in the direction of the booth.

"Oh, thank you, Evelyn dear." She frowned and turned the purse over in her hands. "But this doesn't look like my purse. My purse is black and this one is brown."

"It's new," Vi improvised. Bless the woman. No lynchings today, thanks to her. "See, you just had time to put some money in from your old purse." She opened it up for Daisy to see.

Daisy clucked her tongue. "I know I had more money than that."

Ian rolled his eyes in exasperation.

"Maybe it's in your old purse," he got out through clenched teeth. "We'll check when we get home."

"Yes, dear, whatever you say."

"Why don't you go get your fry bread. I'll go with you."

"Fry bread? You know I don't eat fry bread. All that grease, calories would go straight to my hips."

His blood pressure ratcheted up, no matter how hard he tried to keep his cool. "You *said* you wanted fry bread."

"Don't be silly." She reached up and patted his cheek, like *he* was somehow deficient.

He could feel a flush spreading up his face, but bit his tongue.

"Maybe Ian could take you home and make your favorite lunch. Grilled cheese and tomato soup." Vi wrapped a sisterly arm around Daisy's shoulder and turned her in the direction of the car.

"Yes, Evelyn, that's a wonderful idea. You've always been such a good friend." She patted Vi on the arm and chattered about their dance school days.

At the booth, Vi hugged Daisy goodbye like a long-lost friend and turned to Ian.

"Remember, Ian, grilled cheese just the way she likes it, lightly browned on the outside, but the cheese good and gooey on the inside."

"Sure, *Evelyn,* anything you say, *Evelyn.*" He lowered his voice to an evil growl. "Lightly browned, gooey cheese. And if she accuses me of theft one more time, I might be tempted to slip a sedative in her juice."

"MORNING, GORGEOUS," he whispered, as he leaned over to nip Vi's earlobe.

She absently batted at him without really even looking at him. Instead, she leaned against the counter, coffee cup poised in midair.

"You're sure she was up to going to the center today?" Her eyes clouded with doubt, her brow puckered.

"After Saturday, I would have packed her off kicking and screaming."

That remark only deepened Vi's frown.

"I'm only kidding. She had a long nap yesterday, should be good as new today. The routine's good for her."

"I'm not sure today was such a good idea. She seemed...tired."

"We all are, Vi. You could torture yourself to

death, but what it comes down to is that we need a break, and so does she. Believe me, they'll call if she's not up to it.''

He drew her into his arms, her coffee cup wedged between them. It was like a hard, unforgiving chaperone, keeping them from getting closer.

Ian settled for caressing the thick terry cloth that encased her shoulders. Her hair was pulled into an oddly angled ponytail on the top of her head.

''I thought maybe we'd have a date.''

''A date?''

''Yeah, you know one of those things where two people find a mutual interest and indulge in some carefree play time.''

''We have a mutual interest. Daisy.''

''We have another mutual interest,'' he whispered into her ear. ''Remember?''

He pried the coffee cup out of her fingers and drew her close. He wrapped her into a hug, close enough so she could remember exactly what she did to him.

She shifted her hips, maneuvering even closer, until they fit together like the pieces of a jigsaw puzzle. She let out a whimper as he closed in for the kill. He slid his mouth over hers and let his lips and tongue show her just how much he'd missed their closeness, just how wonderful his memories were, and how much it tortured him to know they couldn't continue. Yet.

Violet responded, drawing him in, making little puppy noises of need. She remembered all right.

Ian sucked in a breath as she ground her hips against him, almost sending him over the edge. He tried to pull away, but she wouldn't let him go. She grasped the collar of his golf shirt and pulled him even closer.

He wrenched his head away to exhale, grab another quick breath before he went down for the count. "Vi, this isn't—" Oh, man, he shouldn't have let her loose with those lips. She'd devised new ways to torture him, though it was getting harder and harder to remember just why he resisted.

So he didn't resist, just sank to the floor. Maybe she'd just leave him there, like some old jelly fish, no spine, no free will. Completely defeated.

But she didn't leave him. Instead, she followed him down and pushed and prodded at his lifeless limbs until she had them positioned to her liking. Climbing aboard, she pushed him back onto the cold tile.

She threw her head back, exposing the long, golden column of her throat. Then hooked her index finger into her ponytail. The twisty thing that held it bounced off the fridge with a clang. Her hair whipped around her face, settling back to caress her cheek, her throat. But it was her eyes that held him transfixed. Tiger eyes, watching her prey. A feral smile curved her lips, her pointy little tongue darted out to lick them.

Where in the hell was the gatekeeper?

It wasn't supposed to be like this. He teased, she withdrew. It was a lovely, innocent game.

This, this was downright warped. Did she expect him to refuse? Or was it a test?

He hated tests and this was no different.

Her pink robe gaped as she leaned forward, revealing one perfect breast, taut, supple, tempting.

She shifted into a more comfortable position. Or at least it was comfortable for her. For him it was torture, sheer torture. Through his thin nylon jogging shorts he could feel her heat, pressed against him in invitation.

His head swam, the room seemed to whirl around him.

"No," he strangled on the word.

"No what?" Her eyes danced with glee. Wicked woman.

"No, thank you," he gasped weakly.

Her hair brushed his chest as she leaned forward. Her breath was sweet on his lips, her mouth millimeters above his, as she whispered, "I love…"

He closed his eyes, ready to surrender. His lips parted, giving in to the inevitable.

"…a man who says please and thank you."

He licked his lips, opened his mouth to receive her hot kiss. He lifted his head in anticipation, but found nothing but a mouthful of her long, dark hair as he mumbled, "Thank you."

Violet had left his mouth for more promising territory. She inched her way up his body, one slow tortuous hip wiggle at a time, until that one exposed breast was suspended above his waiting lips. Time seemed to stand still as he anticipated the sweetness, the tight texture of the nipple surrounded by satiny smoothness. He raised his head, but she adjusted her position, keeping just out of reach. And of course, each adjustment of position required her to wiggle those hips, caress the length of him with that hot, wet area he vaguely knew should be off-limits.

But for the life of him he couldn't remember why. It was somewhere in the back of his mind, but the sight of her silky hair brushing her golden areola, exactly where his lips should be, drove all rational thought from his brain.

He made a lunge for her, but she was too fast. She wrenched backward, tucked and rolled, and was gone before he reached his objective.

By the time he managed a sitting position, she towered over him, adjusting her robe. He made a grab for her ankle, but she danced away.

Damn caffeine. Made her too agile.

He admitted defeat and dropped back to a prone position, letting the tile cool his fevered blood. Slowly, his breathing reached a normal pace.

"Vi?"

"Hmm?"

"Next time just shoot me."

"Gladly. Now I want my date. Brunch would be a good start, maybe that little greasy spoon along the highway. Then a movie, a good chick flick. No, I take that back, we can rent a movie on our way back. I'd like to see those Indian ruins near the falls. After brunch, of course. We can stop for an ice cream on our way back, that cute little old-fashioned ice-cream parlor…"

"Are we going to eat our way through this day or what?"

"The 'or what' part is out of the question, so yes, I guess we will eat our way through this day. We can even bring something back for Daisy." She turned on her heel, humming a satisfied tune.

VI'S HAND was toasty warm, tucked safely in Ian's as they strolled down the street. The ice cream melted in her mouth and trickled down the back of her throat.

Double mocha swirl, the next best thing to heaven. Rich, smooth, sinful.

She glanced sideways to watch Ian eat his cone. He mouthed it with his lips, then swirled with his tongue. Nice technique.

He swung her hand in an aimless contented arc as he eyed the electronics store window.

The bookstore came next and his steps slowed, then stopped. He gazed in the big plate-glass window, his eyes fixed on the bestseller display. There was a tenseness in his shoulders, an energy crackling as he seemed to stretch toward the rack of books. Famous books. Acclaimed books.

Ambition. It was a weird thing to associate with Ian. But he wanted to be on that bestseller list, wanted it badly.

She watched him for a moment, letting the idea sink in.

"You want to be famous?" she asked.

"Me?" He seemed to come out of his trance and realize they had been standing there for a while. He shook his head and grinned sheepishly.

"Naw."

"Everybody's got dreams, Ian. It's okay."

"No, it's not."

"Why is it okay for everyone else, but not you? St. Ian again?"

They strolled on, he swung her arm again, only this time it seemed to help him think.

"Because it means I'm taking that part of me away from Daisy. Like maybe I'm not giving enough of myself to her if I want the other too much."

"Is that how you feel about me? Like there's not enough love to go around."

"Love, yes. I've got plenty of that for both of you. Time? Not so sure."

Something cold and sticky ran down her hand. Her ice cream was melting, forgotten and neglected. She swirled her tongue around the bottom, rotating the cone as she went.

"Where's that leave us? Tuesdays and Thursdays, nine to three?"

He stopped dead still and turned her toward him. His grip on her hand tightened. "It's not what I want. I have dreams about us, too. Things I want to do together, places to see. Do you realize how badly I want to read the Sunday paper in bed with you? Sleep late, make love, read the paper? Neither of us setting foot out of bed till noon."

"Sounds heavenly." She closed her eyes. The weak afternoon sun was warm on her eyelids as she imagined the day he described. "Then maybe a walk with Annabelle," she continued for him. "Catch a movie. Make dinner together, something wildly exotic that requires all sorts of sharp utensils."

"Those dreams don't include Daisy, do they?"

She opened her eyes and smiled wistfully. Ian's face was scruffy and dear beneath her palm as she loved him, with her eyes, her hand, her heart.

"No, they don't. We'll make new dreams. Ones that include Daisy."

"Okay. How about Daisy stumbles on a plot to overthrow the government." He gestured grandly, including the horizon in their little dream. "We flee, pursued, one step ahead of the villain. But we outsmart him, save the government, and everyone lives happily ever after.''

He bowed, ice cream cone and all.

''Bravo, sir,'' she pronounced, talking past the lump of ice cream stuck in her throat. Why the hell did she ever think this stuff was creamy?

She tossed her cone in the trash and reached for Ian's hand. It was sticky and familiar. They'd tackle their villains together.

IAN WENT OUT to meet the bus when it rumbled to a stop. Violet watched him from the front window.

He held his hand out to Daisy, steadied her as she descended the steps. She said something, and Ian leaned forward to hear her.

The afternoon sun played with his hair, highlighting a few strands, leaving others in shadow. His dimples peeked out as he laughed at something Daisy said.

He was afraid there wasn't enough of him to go around. But somehow it would have to be enough. She'd just have to quit wishing for more.

Violet opened the door for them as they approached. The smile died on her lips.

Daisy stopped in her tracks, her eyes narrowed, her lips compressed to a thin, angry line. Her face flushed as she stared at Violet. Her mouth worked, but no words came out.

Then they came, but they didn't make any sense. Disjointed, out of context. It was like starting a foreign movie midway through, waiting for the subtitles to make sense.

Then they did, and that was even worse.

''What's *she* doing in *my* house?''

"This is Violet. Remember?"

The old woman snorted and stabbed a bony finger in Violet's direction. "Can't you see? It's Olivia Randolph. Tramp," she spat out the word.

"It's me, Daisy. Violet, the other flower woman." Violet reached toward her, silently begging her to remember.

"Don't touch me." Her eyes grew hard, glittered with hate. "I told you if you ever came around here again, I'd pull every last hair out of your head."

The gnarled old fingers reached for her. Violet backed away, trapped. Panic bubbled up inside her. Where to go? She couldn't get out unless she went past the mad woman on Ian's arm.

She simply froze.

"Vi...I mean, Olivia was just leaving," Ian soothed, then turned to her. He winked, then his features went rigid with anger. He advanced a step toward her, and she involuntarily backed away.

"Now, Olivia, I told you to get out of here and never come back."

He moved Daisy to the side to let her pass and jerked his head toward her car.

Violet dashed around him, not daring to look back until she reached the car. She got in and slammed the door, locking it behind her.

Ian and Daisy slowly made their way into the house. Without her.

She lay her head on the steering wheel and let the tears seep from beneath her eyelids. She was too tired and wrung out to even make a sound.

A KNOCK on the glass made her jump. She sniffed and looked blearily around, trying to remember exactly why she was in the car. It was dusk, everything out-lined in the soft gray light, palo verde trees, rocks, cacti.

Then it came back in a rush. Olivia, they wanted her to be Olivia.

The door handle rattled. She didn't move to unlock it.

Then Ian pressed his face against the glass, worry etched in the lines radiating from his frown. His nose left a funny little smudge.

He knocked again. "Come on, let me in."

It hurt too much to comply. He'd denied her, like Violet had never even existed. First it was Vi, now they rejected Violet. Not shrinking Violet, but the new-and-improved version, the real deal. How could he pretend that she never existed?

The tears trickled anew as she probed her wound, the horrible abandonment. It was just make-believe, but it hurt.

Hurt so much, she needed someone to hold her.

She flipped up the lock and waited, arms crossed, tears running.

He opened the door and wrapped his arms around her. She fell into them and cried as if her heart were broken. Because it was.

"I'm…not…Olivia," she pushed out between sobs.

"Of course not," he soothed, awkwardly patting her back.

"I'm…V-Violet," she hiccupped.

"I didn't mean to upset you. It was the only thing I could come up with."

"*She* doesn't know who I am. The other flower

woman.'' The sobs started all over again as pain slashed at her heart. The betrayal of being thrown out of their special club was almost more than she could take.

''I don't know what's going on, Vi. But I'll find out. She was pissed off about something that happened at the center, some woman took her chocolate cake.'' He smoothed her hair out of her eyes. ''I don't know why. But I'll call Dr. Greene.''

''Was it Olivia? Who stole her cake?''

''No. Olivia was a neighbor back in New York. Mom was convinced she was after Dad. Who knows what it all means now. Probably nothing.''

He wiped the moisture from her face.

She was able to give him a weak smile through the blur of tears.

''It's stupid to be upset. I've just been…well…so emotional lately.''

Maybe love did this to a person. Made *all* emotions became just that much more intense. How did people do it then, subject themselves to this kind of torture for forty, fifty years?

Ian's face was dear, so close to hers. Worried. He had so much on his plate, and then she had to go and add to it.

She flung her arms around his neck and squeezed him to her.

''I'm so sorry.''

He pressed his forefinger to her lips. ''Shh. Just come in the house. Daisy's asleep. She probably won't even remember all this when she wakes up. And Vi?''

''What?''

"She loves you, every bit as much as I do. Don't ever doubt that."

It was like a shot to the heart. Like one of those darn commercials where the daughter dances with her father at her wedding and they flash back to her childhood.

A fresh wave hit her, wrenching sobs from deep inside. Her stomach ached, her throat burned. But it felt so good to cry.

"Oh, Ian. That's the sweetest thing anybody's ever told me."

He just gave her a puzzled smile and patted her shoulder.

How could a man truly understand the supreme mysteries of life and love, the whole incredible cycle of it all?

CHAPTER THIRTEEN

PLUSES AND MINUSES danced before Violet's eyes.

Until she squeezed her eyelids shut to block out the images. Only then was she able to open them and focus on the business at hand—the letter from her boss, regretful, but somehow offended. Sure the company was "disappointed" in her decision not to accept the District Management position. The stiff tone, from people she'd known for years, made her feel as if *her* personal decision reflected badly on them. As though her change in circumstances somehow invalidated their faith in her for the past eight years.

Had it really been only six weeks ago that her job had been her whole world? Now she could barely muster an ounce of interest.

Much more fascinating was the kitchen timer she'd rescued from the trash yesterday, another victim of Daisy's organizational attempts. Two more minutes and it all would become clear. The pluses and minuses would crystalize. Too bad her thoughts wouldn't crystalize. Everything was fuzzy, the pros and cons.

It was something she'd never thought much about, except in the purest abstract form. Six weeks ago there was no reason. Her life was well charted, her career goals right on track. Then Annabelle's fuzzy green tennis ball had rolled out in front of her car, and everything had been crazy ever since.

No, not Annabelle. It had started with Ian, the "mad man," hauling butt out of the brush. So scary she'd feared for her life. Now that fear seemed ridiculous. Even more ridiculous that he could remind her of her father, in any way, shape or form.

Her heart skipped a beat as the timer dinged.

Her legs wouldn't obey her command to stand.

So she sat there at her desk like a limp noodle. Unable to stand and walk if her life depended on it.

Maybe it did. The pluses and minuses could have a profound effect. Not only on *her* life, but also Ian's.

IAN WATCHED Vi for a moment, soaking in her beauty. Even in sweatpants and one of his old T-shirts, she was flat-out gorgeous, up to her elbows in soapy water.

"We need to talk," he told her.

Violet jumped, as if he'd snuck up on her and shouted, "Boo!"

"Daisy's taking a nap. Doctors' appointments always tucker her out. Probably from trying so hard to put one over on them. To pretend nothing's changed," he explained.

Violet said nothing. Her eyes were wide, shadowed by something he couldn't quite put a finger on. Maybe she knew. Sensed what had come as such a shock to him. Funny, he thought he'd prepared and prepared, but when it really happened, it had taken him by surprise.

He handed her a dish towel to dry her hands. She usually used the dishwasher, but now every glass in the house was lined up on the counter, dried and spar-

kling. He peered into the sink, where bowls and silverware lurked beneath the suds.

She dried her hands slowly, as if to put off the inevitable. Man, she was one telepathic woman.

He took her hand in his and led her to the front
room. Her hand was cold, as if she'd been rummaging
in the fridge instead of up to her wrists in warm, soapy
water.

"Let's sit. Get comfortable."

Her face paled, then she obeyed. Her rear hit the
couch like a ton of bricks, as if her legs wouldn't hold
her a minute longer. He'd had no idea it was going to
be this hard.

He sat next to her and rested his arm around her
shoulders. Drawing her close, he began, "Something's
happened we need to talk about."

He reached for her hand. Still cold. He warmed it
in his, while absently smoothing his thumb over her
palm.

"You're right," she agreed. Her voice croaked, like
it did before she'd had her morning caffeine fix.

"I don't know how this will affect us, you and
me...." He didn't want to give her an out, but he had
to. "I'd understand if you chucked it all. I wouldn't
wish this on my worst enemy."

Silence.

Ian tilted his head, trying to see her shadowed eyes.

It hit him like a sucker punch. Her eyes were moist,
shining with hurt.

How had he hurt her? He was only trying to make
it easier.

"Hey, don't cry. I didn't mean to make you cry."

He wiped away a trickle from her cheek. "At least say *something*."

Her lips wobbled. She opened her mouth to speak, but nothing came out. Then her voice was high, strained. "I don't want to chuck it. I never really knew how I'd react if it happened. But now, it's real and I want it more than I've ever wanted anything in my life. I'd...I'd hoped you might feel the same. But it's okay, I'll handle it on my own. You don't need to do anything."

Her babbled words made absolutely no sense.

"You're *happy* Daisy's condition has deteriorated?"

"Wha—What?"

"Daisy. She can't remember you because the Alzheimer's has progressed. She's losing more and more of her memory. It's progressive, working backward in time. Soon she may not even remember...me."

"Oh, Ian," Violet cried. She squeezed his hand tightly. Her gaze flew over his face, calculating the damage to his soul. "I'm so sorry. I had no idea it would be this soon."

It helped, having her there. Having someone who cared, who could relate.

"Me neither. You warned me to be ready. But somehow I blocked it all out."

"No wonder she doesn't know who I am. But she knows that I'm familiar so she gives me a name from her past."

She let go of his hand and placed her palms on either side of his face. They were still cool, somehow comforting. Sane. "How long? That she can remember the rest, I mean?"

"Don't know. Months, maybe even years. I just have to deal with it as it comes."

The words were simple, easy. But how would he do it? From here it was all downhill. Big time. Up until now, he'd had flashes of the mother he'd always known. And in between, the new Daisy had grown on him. Like a new friend.

"I can only imagine how hurt you must be. It explains so much. In a way, it makes it easier for me. It doesn't seem so much like she's rejecting me. Or abandoning me. She has no control over it."

"You're saying that to make me feel better. So I won't lose it when she doesn't know me anymore."

"Oh, Ian, *you* will always have those memories inside. Where's the guy who told me what I am now is a result of where I came from?"

"And you, lady, are perfect, just the way you are. Now, what gives? You acted like you already knew, like you were upset."

She withdrew her hands and held them in her lap, her knuckles white.

"I, uh, had something else on my mind."

He tucked the curtain of hair behind her ear so he could see her expression. She gnawed on her lower lip, her eyes were filled with doubt.

"What?"

"Not now, Ian. It's not a good time. Not with all the other stuff you've got going on."

"Vi…" He lifted her chin, and turned her face toward him. "You can tell me anything, anytime. Okay?"

She nodded, but her eyes were still clouded.

"Vi, I've got enough to worry about now, without

worrying what you're keeping from me. My imagination will go wild, and before you know it I'll think you're terminally ill, or a fugitive from justice or—''

His gut lurched.

''You're not…sick, are you? Cancer? Heart problems?''

She actually broke a smile, a small, trembling smile.

''No, silly. I'm not sick…yet.''

''Yet? I don't like the sound of that. Tell me.''

She sighed, and would have turned away from him, but he grasped her shoulders and blocked her escape.

''You can tell me anything.''

The tension went out of her shoulders, the fear from her eyes. Relief washed over her face, relaxed her frown.

''I'm pregnant,'' she whispered.

''What?''

''Pregnant.''

''Oh.''

The room started to spin and so did his head. He leaned back weakly against the couch.

Her voice seemed to come from far, far away. ''I know it's a big shock, but once I got used to the idea…well, I kind of liked it. I hoped maybe you'd feel the same way.''

Like the idea? How could he like something he couldn't comprehend?

''You said it was the wrong time.''

''Just call me the Queen of Denial.'' She laughed hoarsely. ''I guess the rhythm method was about as reliable as Daisy's condoms.''

Ouch.

A baby.

Their baby.

Somewhere around his toes, a weird, unexplainable feeling started to spread through his body, one cell at a time. It worked its way up his legs, his torso, his neck and erupted in the biggest shit-eating grin. He let out a whoop of sheer, unadulterated pride.

"We made a baby."

He grabbed Vi and pulled her off the couch. Life had never seemed sweeter as he danced her around the room, swinging and dipping for joy.

Her cheeks flushed, her eyes sparkled. The doubt was gone, replaced by joy.

Then shock stopped him dead in his tracks. Momentum kept her body going, but he hauled her back. He held her to him, tightly, willing her to agree. "This is a *good* thing, right?"

Her face was like the desert sunrise, one minute dark, the next the most luminous sign of hope. Her smile was almost as wide as his.

"It's a *very* good thing."

They resumed their dance, this time a slow waltz. Vi rested her head against his chest. He kissed the top of her head. He would remember this moment always.

Gradually, his feet slowed. He hugged her tight, wedged her hand, clasped in his, under his chin. Eyes closed, he savored her. The smell of her hair, its softness against his chin, the way she felt in his arms. Suddenly this was the A-Number-One best day of his life.

"You'll marry me?" he blurted out.

Big, dumb jerk. No flowers, no music, no bent knee.

Vi raised her head and looked into his eyes. Whatever it was, he must have done something right. Because the happiness shining in her warm, brown eyes just about bowled him over.

"Of course I will."

He sealed it with a kiss. She clung to him, and he to her, as they slow danced around the living room floor. It seemed forever, and a split second. It expanded in his chest until he thought he would explode with his own good fortune. This fabulous woman loved him and carried his child. She'd agreed to become his wife. What a fantastic hand fate had dealt him, at a time when he'd least expected it.

"Vi?"

"Hmmm?"

"You think there's a reason? For Annabelle running out in front of your car?"

"Maybe," she murmured. "Kismet and all that."

"Or maybe even something bigger. Supreme being…God."

"He's got one heckuva sense of humor."

"He sure does."

"Who's got a sense of humor?" A voice behind them demanded.

Ian turned to see Daisy shuffle into the room, her hair poking out in all directions. Her nap had been a restless one.

"Uh, Judge Tanner," he improvised. A deep discussion of God wasn't one he wanted to get into. With Daisy's confusion, it could go on for days, each circle more mentally exhausting than the previous.

She cackled with glee. "The old coot does kind of crack me up. Did I ever tell you what he wears under that black robe? Women's panties."

"Yes, Mom," he sighed, relaxing his grip on Vi. "You sure did."

As he turned, Violet turned with him. Daisy's eyes narrowed.

"You didn't tell me we had a visitor." Her face went blank.

Vi stiffened in his arms.

Please God, not again. He couldn't handle another Olivia scene right now.

Daisy patted her hair into some semblance of order and straightened the skewed neckline of her dress. "Why, Evelyn, you should have told me you were coming."

He could feel Vi's shoulders relax. She looked up at him and winked.

"Yes, Daisy. I've come to stay for a while, remember?"

Daisy frowned for a moment, then her face brightened. She smiled and rushed over, extending her hands. She grasped Vi's hands in hers. "Of course, dear, it will be so lovely to have you. How long did you say you were staying?"

Vi looked up at him, one eyebrow raised.

"She'll be here for a long, long time," he supplied. "Isn't that great?"

"Yes, wonderful. We'll catch up later." She patted Vi's hand and drifted out of the room.

"How are you going to explain? About us?" Vi asked.

"I don't know," he muttered. "I'm not sure how much she understands. Maybe time doesn't mean much anymore. She may not see anything odd about her school friend romancing her son.'' He shrugged his shoulders.

Vi's shoulders started to shake, and he drew her close.

Please, not another crying jag.

How in the world was he going to live in a household with one perpetually confused woman and another hormonally challenged one?

Her giggles caught him off guard. He leaned back to look at her. Her eyes shone with merriment as she threw back her head to laugh. All he could do was shake his head and hang on for the ride.

''Just wait…'' Another wave of laughter took her by storm. She hiccuped, then continued, ''Until I start to show.''

The woman had a warped sense of humor. Maybe that's why he loved her so much.

''Oh, no,'' he groaned. ''I can see it now, 'Mom, your friend from school, the one who's at least seventy. Well, she's knocked up. And I'm the father.'''

Violet leaned against him, weak with a fresh burst of laughter. Tears rolled down her face.

At least somebody found it amusing.

He gently untangled her arms and moved out of her embrace. Easy for her to laugh. But then a great idea hit him. ''Maybe I'll let Evelyn break the news to her.''

The laughter died on her lips.

''THERE, THERE, DEAR,'' Daisy soothed as she held Violet's hair back for her.

Violet's hands shook as she wiped the moisture

from her eyes. All she wanted to do was rinse out her mouth and die.

"It's to be expected, dear. I was sick as a dog with Ian. It'll pass though." Her hand was gentle as she rubbed between Violet's shoulder blades. So this was what it was like to have a mother, a *real* mother.

"I'm okay now." She braced her hands on the cold, smooth edge of the toilet and levered herself up. Cool water splashed on her face and a slurp straight from the faucet made her feel almost human again.

She turned to Daisy and wrapped her in a big hug.

"Thanks," she whispered. "I don't know what I'd do without you."

The older woman placed her palms on Violet's cheeks and held her gaze. Her eyes were wise, loving. "And I you, dear."

They walked from the bathroom, hand in hand.

Ian looked up inquiringly when they reached the living room. His brows puckered in a worried frown.

"You okay?"

"I am now."

"Evelyn's going to have a baby, dear," Daisy informed him.

"Uh, yeah," he cleared his throat. "That's what I hear."

"Isn't it wonderful?" Daisy fairly beamed.

Ian's face softened into a smile. "Yes, it is."

"Evelyn dear, why don't you go freshen up."

"I guess I will."

Ian watched Vi leave the room, the sway of her hips, the tilt of her head. He winked as she passed. She winked back and smiled a small, secretive smile.

"Ian," Daisy whispered.

"Yes, Mom?"

Daisy grasped his hand and squeezed. "We need to be supportive. Now is a difficult time for Evelyn. No need to mention the rascal that left her in this condition. Poor innocent girl…no need to upset her. Now promise me, no questions, no talking about the father."

Ian couldn't have been prouder of his mom than at that moment. Dazed and confused though she might be most of the time, she had a heart of gold.

"Okay. Mom…?"

"Yes?"

"I love you."

She ran her fingers down his face, as if lovingly memorizing the details. "So much like your father," she whispered. Her smile faltered for a moment, the corners twitched downward. Then she shook her head and smiled gently. She leaned over and kissed him on the cheek. Her scent, constant and unchanging, enveloped him in the security of her hug. It brought a dull ache to his chest, to know she wouldn't always be able to offer comfort.

"I love you, too," she said. "Now, we need to get Evelyn a snack."

"But she just threw up."

"Yes, but frequent snacks will help. Get her some soda crackers and maybe some cheese. Lots of calcium for that baby."

"Yes, ma'am." He saluted. Thank goodness one of them had been through this before. "Lots of snacks, lots of calcium."

Daisy wandered out of the room before he even finished his sentence.

"Mom?"

No answer.

After a moment he followed her down the hallway and glanced in her room. She lay on her bed, face-up, fully clothed. His heart jumped into his throat, until he noticed her chest rise, almost imperceptibly.

He went in and picked up the crocheted afghan off the daybed. Shaking out the folds, he covered her. She muttered something, then rolled on her side.

Someday it would be different. He'd look for that telltale rising of her chest and it wouldn't be there. What would he do? Handle it, whether he was ready or not.

Ian tiptoed out of her room and closed the door.

He headed for the kitchen, where he found Vi.

"Coffee?" He raised an eyebrow in disapproval.

Vi's gaze slid away from his. Guilt hunched her shoulders.

"I tried. But I can't do it cold turkey. Puking up my guts every morning is bad enough. The withdrawal headaches are excruciating. It helps. A little caffeine and a lot of milk. Milk's good for the baby." She raised her chin to a mutinous angle. "Daisy said so."

She tipped the cup toward him so he could see. It was the truth, though he'd never doubted her—a little coffee and lots of milk.

He snaked his hand behind her neck and drew her close. She rested her forehead against his chest.

"It's okay, Vi. You're doing your best. That's all anyone can ask."

Sniffling sounds came from beneath her bowed head. Her voice was muffled when she spoke. "I tried.

I really tried. I want this baby so bad. Healthy, ten fingers, ten toes.''

''We both do. Just do the best you can. Moderation's the key, okay?''

He tipped her chin up so he could see her face. Her lovely skin had an ashy tone, her eyes were red from crying. Her hair was pulled up into one of those ghastly ponytails. ''You are the most beautiful woman I've ever seen.''

She clasped his hand and slid it down her side, then took a detour to her stomach. Flat. It was hard to believe there was a baby inside, but it was true. His baby. *Their* baby.

His hands had a mind of their own, fighting to wander even lower. It had been so long the memory was faded around the edges. He wanted to experience her again, love her again. This time knowing her so much better and loving every inch of her.

''The vet's okayed Annabelle for duty,'' he murmured, placing featherlight kisses at the corner of her mouth. She tasted of milk and sugar, with a zip of coffee thrown in. Delicious.

''Really?''

''You know what that means? We can spend the night together.'' He trailed kisses down the side of her neck, luxuriating in the softness of her skin. ''Like a normal couple, in the same bed. All night.''

She moaned, low in her throat. She wanted him. Now.

''Daisy's asleep.'' He pulled her robe low on her shoulder, nibbling, kissing.

Her moan was hoarse with need, raw.

He continued the downward exploration with his

mouth. He wanted her, like he'd wanted no other woman. She trembled under the caress of his lips and tongue.

This time her moan had a strangled quality, as if she couldn't wait a minute longer.

She wound her fingers into the hair on his scalp. He was really getting to her now. Adrenaline surged, testosterone surged, hell everything in his body surged.

"Ouch," he mumbled against her breast.

The nerve endings in his scalp screamed for mercy as she wrenched his head back. A simple no would have been fine.

The tension on his scalp eased as he looked into her face. Green—definitely green.

"Let go...." she panted.

He let his arms drop to his sides.

She slapped her hand over her mouth and dashed out of the kitchen, robe and ponytail flying.

He followed her down the hall.

He was several yards from the open bathroom door when the familiar sounds reached him.

This was a first. Rejection he could handle. But not to the point of vomiting.

"NO. ABSOLUTELY NOT. I refuse." Vi placed her hands on her hips and glared.

"After the wedding planner, we can stop by. Check it out," he wheedled.

The senior center bus had just rounded the corner out of sight. That meant six glorious hours by themselves.

"No."

He sighed. The fire in her eyes told him it would

be a long argument. That only made it harder. It was an argument that had waged in his mind since they'd gotten the diagnosis.

He grasped her gently by the shoulders, rubbed her arms. "It's something we've got to face. Whether you or I like it, it will eventually happen. Believe me, my whole life the past two years has been wrapped up in keeping her home. It's the best thing for her…right now. But what about later? She *will* need round-the-clock professional care. Maybe not next week, next month, maybe even not next year. But we have to be prepared. You said so yourself. That way we know we've taken our time and picked out the very best place."

Tears filled her brown eyes. It brought an ache to his chest, not just her pain, but the fact that she loved Daisy so deeply.

"But there's hardly been any change since I've been here. Well, besides the name thing." She fingered the collar of his golf shirt. "What if they're wrong? It happens you know. Wrong diagnosis."

"Not this time. I've gotten a second opinion, third opinion."

"There's two of us now, plus Annabelle. We can handle anything," she pleaded.

"Vi, I hope so. But we have to be prepared for the worst."

"But this is her home, Ian. She will always need her home, her things. Us."

The pleading in her eyes just about killed him. It would be so easy to give in. Stick his head in the sand and pretend it would never happen. He'd tried that once, but the disease wouldn't wait for him to come around. It would progress at its own whimsical pace, whether they were prepared or not.

"The last thing I want is to be caught unprepared. She might end up in some really horrible place. This place—" he gestured around the familiar white walls and rough-hewn wood beams "—won't always be her home. Someday, things'll get more confused, and she might not even remember it. But we'll still be there for her. Just not in a twenty-four hour a day way."

She clasped his hands in hers and bent her head. Her tears burned their way down his knuckles.

"I feel like we're giving up," she sobbed.

"We're not giving up. Not by a long shot." He grasped her chin and raised her face to him. "We'll keep her here as long as we're able. I promise."

Her gaze wandered over his face, searching for the truth.

She nodded.

"Okay."

IAN'S SILENCE unnerved her. His expression was carefully controlled, as if he didn't want her to know what kind of poker hand he held.

His hands on the steering wheel were steady, relaxed, as he guided the Wrangler through traffic.

"What'd you think?" Violet prodded.

"I'm okay with it, if you are."

"She didn't impress you as kind of…well…pushy?"

He glanced sideways at her as if to assess her mood.

"She was okay."

His voice was mild, too mild.

"You hated her didn't you?"

"No, not at all. I'll do whatever you want."

"Aha! Just what I thought. You hated her and you're patronizing me because I'm pregnant."

He lifted an eyebrow. His lips twitched into a smile.

"Okay. I admit it. I hated her. She was a bossy, condescending twit. But I'd put up with her if it'd make you happy. Because I love you."

Her throat got all scratchy and her nose prickled. She reached for his hand and pressed it to her cheek. "You are just about the best guy ever," she sniffled.

"Oh, no," he groaned. "Here we go again."

"It's okay. It's a good cry," she murmured between sniffles.

"A *good* cry? Boy, have I got a lot to learn," he moaned.

Her heart skipped with the sheer exhilaration of it all. She could feel a grin spread across her face, even as the tears flowed. "It's okay. I'll teach you."

He shook his head and patted her hand.

"Ian?"

"Hum?" he answered.

"Let's ditch the wedding consultant."

"You got it."

"Ian?"

"What?"

"Do you think Judge Tanner would do the honors? Tomorrow?"

Silence.

"I mean, if that's too soon, we can wait. Or if you wanted a big wedding, I guess we could. I just thought it'd be nice, romantic kind of, since Judge Tanner brought us together. Something simple, a few flowers, a pretty dress. Daisy, Joe and Vince as witnesses...."

She was babbling and she knew it. He could jump in any time now and ease her worries. Maybe he didn't really want to get married. Maybe he was just doing the old-fashioned right thing.

She glanced at him and was stunned by what she saw. He met her glance for a split second before returning his attention to the road. But what she saw was such overwhelming love, mixed with humbleness and gratitude.

"It's perfect. Just perfect. I'll call him when we get home."

"What about that place, the Oasis Care Center?"

"It'll wait a little longer. We've got a lot of things to do."

Relief seeped through her. He said it was putting off the inevitable, but she was just superstitious enough to think it would have been tempting fate. Daisy was fine. No need to worry.

"Vi?"

"What?"

"I love you."

"I love you, too."

CHAPTER FOURTEEN

IT WAS THE JITTERS all right. The flowers shook, her knees shook, just about every hair on her head shook.

Violet waited outside the courtroom, counting squares of yellowing linoleum. She got to twenty-six before she let her mind wander to her purpose for being there.

It hardly seemed possible that two months and two people had made such a tremendous difference in her life. Come to think of it, there were so many more people involved. Fate maybe?

Marriage. Motherhood. Neither had been in her plans. Well, marriage maybe. To some successful, intelligent, completely *safe* attorney. She'd have had her work, he'd have had his, then they'd meet up in the middle for an elegant dinner out.

What she'd gotten was so much more. A built-in family, with built-in problems.

A smile twitched her lips as she thought about what she was getting into. She wouldn't trade it for anything in the world.

The door opened and Mrs. Rivers from the center poked her head around the corner. Somehow the news of the ''secret wedding'' had traveled like wildfire and people appeared out of nowhere. Half the senior center patrons were there, along with the whole Moreno extended family.

"They're ready for you," Mrs. Rivers said.

Violet smoothed the skirt of her dress—shimmery cream lace over a soft wool shell. Sleeveless, it hit her midthigh and showed off her shoulders and legs. The classic A-line sheath didn't hide her waist, but didn't accentuate it, either. It was the one and only dress she'd tried on and it was perfect.

She cleared her throat and stepped through the doorway. Warmth crept up her cheeks as everyone turned to stare at her. The little old ladies from the center were dressed in their Sunday best. The men, too.

Violet tried not to think of the phone calls she'd tried to make last night but simply couldn't—calls to her mother, her sister, her father. But her instincts screamed that her family would suck all the happiness out of her special day and somehow taint her marriage.

Shaking away the negative thoughts, she focused on Mrs. Rivers. The woman beamed with pride, as if she were the mother of the bride. These people were her family now.

A sweet sense of belonging washed over her, making her want to open her arms wide and give each and every one of them a hug. Or cry.

No, no crying. It would ruin her makeup.

She let her gaze move on, to the front row where Daisy sat, hand in hand with old Joe. She looked lovely in her favorite green party dress, hair curled, a soft blush and lipstick blending away the years.

Her eyes glowed with fondness as she watched "Evelyn" walk down the aisle.

And next to her, sitting proudly in the aisle, was

Annabelle, with a big green bow draped around her shoulders. Even she turned to look at the bride, her wise brown eyes aglow with happiness, just like Daisy's.

Ian held his breath as he watched Vi float down the aisle. At least that's what it looked like to him, an angel of a woman floating on thin air. He still couldn't believe she had agreed to be his wife.

His throat closed up as she smiled at him, her eyes alight with love. Her dark hair, shining with vitality under the harsh overhead light, brushed her cheek. His gaze skipped over her shoulders, kissed a golden brown from the sun. Then downward, to endless legs, all delicate curves within shimmery off-white panty hose. And somewhere in the middle, was his child. Their child.

It was something he'd dreamed of a long time ago. A dream pushed aside for unimportant stuff—traveling, sports, the excitement that went along with it. He'd never brought the dream out to examine it, not even after Daisy became ill. Just put it on hold like everything else.

Then Vi came into his life, all prickly and hell-bent on leaving, *pronto*. Until somewhere along the line, she'd relaxed, let down her defenses. And then the impossible became possible. She loved him nearly as much as he loved her.

Vi stepped up to take her place next to him, putting her hand in his. This was it. The moment of a lifetime.

Judge Tanner polished his glasses with the sleeve of his robe as he beamed down at them.

"I'm honored to be officiating at this important occasion. Doubly honored because I brought these two young people together.''

Vi squeezed his hand, he smiled down at her. Thank God she had a lead foot.

"I've watched them grow and learn. A fine couple they are, if I do say so myself."

The audience chuckled appreciatively. Ian sneaked a glance over his shoulder, and every last one of them smiled, like collective matchmakers.

Daisy dabbed at her eyes, as if she really deep down understood. She'd taken their announcement in stride, congratulating him on doing the right thing for dear "Evelyn."

"You kids want to exchange vows? That seems to be the way it's done these days." Judge Tanner frowned in disapproval.

Ian's stomach dropped to his toes, his ears burned. Vows? He glanced around for inspiration. It didn't come.

His collar tightened like a noose.

He cleared his throat.

Vi looked at him expectantly. Her lips parted in anticipation.

"Vi, I, um, didn't prepare anything." His ears were on fire, so was his neck. A fleeting shadow crossed her lovely brown eyes, gazing into his. Hell, he'd hurt her already, and they weren't even halfway through the ceremony.

Ian pulled in a deep lungful of air. He willed the rest of the room away. It was just the two of them, and she deserved to hear what was in his heart.

He grabbed both of her hands and squeezed.

She winced at his tight grip. But her encouraging smile was back in a flash.

"Vi, you're everything I ever wanted in a woman, but I was too stupid to know it."

Her smile widened at that.

"I wake up every day and this light kind of washes over me, because I know I've got you. And maybe I don't say things just right, and I don't always do the right thing, but somehow I must do *something* right because of the love I see in your eyes, and I see myself through your eyes and I'm so much more than I really am. Vi, I'll spend every minute, every day, living up to being the man you think I am, the man I know I can be. With you by my side."

Vi withdrew her hand from his and laid it against his cheek. Tears glittered in her eyes.

Please, *please,* have them be the good kind of tears.

"Oh, Ian," she breathed.

He reached up to her hand and cradled it with his own.

"My mom and dad had a great love. A ten. And I'd just about given up on finding that…till I met you." His vision got all blurry, a lump lodged in his throat. "There's a song Dad used to sing to Mom, all about loving someone till the rivers run dry, and pretty much beyond eternity. That's the way I feel about you."

He drew Vi close, her hand still on his cheek. Placing his free hand at the small of her back, he held her as if she were the most precious thing in the world. Because she was.

"I'll bring you a daisy a day, dear…" he sang, softly, just loud enough for her to hear. The tears dribbled down her cheeks. "I'll bring you a daisy a day," he choked out.

But he managed to get it together, and the next verse was louder. With a full back-up.

Ian turned to their guests. Daisy stood slowly, blending her beautiful voice with his. One by one, their guests, their family, stood and joined in.

There wasn't a dry eye in the house.

VIOLET STRETCHED her arms over her head and smiled. It was a lovely, lovely day. That light Ian had talked about during the ceremony crept from the tip of her toes to the top of her head.

She turned on her side to look at him. It was good to see his face so relaxed, so boyish, even with the stubble of whiskers.

A sigh escaped before she could block it. Guilt niggled, regret prodded. Regret that it couldn't always be like this. That they couldn't play and love and bask like other newlyweds. Guilt that she even had those thoughts.

Today was special, so she pushed away the negative thoughts.

They had an entire day without responsibility and it made her almost giddy just to think about it.

Ian shifted next to her. His eyes opened slowly. A smile spread across his face as he realized where he was, that she was with him. *That* was real, and forever.

She could almost see that wonderful light pass through him.

"Morning," he whispered.

"Morning." She leaned over to kiss him.

He smelled good, totally Ian. All musky, and male and all hers.

He slid his hand down her bare hip, his touch light, his fingers dancing.

Goose bumps prickled where he'd caressed.

Oh, what this man could do to her. Over, and over and over. And never stop.

Vi rolled on top of him, intent on showing him just how much she loved him.

That's when it hit her right between the eyes.

That dull, throbbing, all-encompassing ache.

"Coffee," she mumbled, as she untangled her legs from the sheets and managed a clumsy dismount.

Ian grunted as her heel ground into his thigh. At least she hoped it was his thigh.

Coffee, coffee, coffee, tattooed inside her skull, like those little bitty mallets xylophone players used. Only this tune was far from soothing.

"I love you," filtered through the din as she headed out the bedroom door.

A fresh pot was brewed and the mallets were muted by the time Ian sauntered into the kitchen, hair damp, feet bare. Instead of his customary sweats, he wore an exceptionally nice-fitting pair of jeans. For such a big guy, he had lean hips, not an ounce of fat. Just vast expanses of muscle.

"No jogging today?" she inquired over the rim of her rugby cup.

He reached over her head and flicked open the cabinet. "Nah. I figured I'd make the most of our time...*alone.*"

He shot her a lopsided grin as he pulled out a cup with Echo Point Senior Center emblazoned on it.

"Mmm," she commented, savoring the scent of freshly showered Ian that filtered past the aroma of coffee. He smelled almost as good clean as he did after a long night of lovemaking.

"The world is at your feet, Lady Vi." He gestured with his cup, sloshing some over the side. What a waste. "We'll do what you want to do. Eight more hours, just you and me."

He waggled his eyebrows at her. "Make love all day? Let me memorize every millimeter of your body? Your wish is my command."

It brought some tantalizing visions to mind.

She sipped her coffee, wondering how to broach the subject.

"Ian, I love you with my whole heart. The time we spend together is so precious. Making love is the very best of that. But we've got some stuff we need to hash out, now, while Daisy's gone."

Ian didn't like Vi's phrasing. It didn't come anywhere close to what he wanted to do with her. It sounded, well, adversarial.

"It's our honeymoon. Surely 'hashing out' can wait for later," he wheedled.

"No, it can't. We need to work things out while Daisy isn't here—she might misunderstand." She leveled one of her serious manager looks at him. "What's the money situation? Are we prepared financially if Daisy has some catastrophic injury? I've heard something as simple as a broken bone or bad cold can really throw an Alzheimer's patient for a loop. And you keep talking about looking at rest homes, but is that really necessary?"

Ian grabbed a bar stool and swung it around so he

could straddle it. He rested his arms on the counter and contemplated his wife.

"Honeymoons are supposed to be fun."

"Sure. Under different circumstances. But we have to have our game plan straight, get organized. To care for Daisy, the baby. It's not going to be easy, but we can make it work."

She sure had a way of killing his romantic thoughts. But she had a point. And if plans and lists made her feel safe, he was all for it. "Dad's pension and a few investments pretty much keep this place going. My book's almost finished. When the money comes rolling in, it'll be a piece of cake."

Vi raised an eyebrow. "And if Daisy takes a turn for the worse before your ship comes in?"

She really had no clue. The book was going to be big, really big.

"Then I'll sell this place. It's paid for. The profits would pay for several years in a nursing home."

Vi contemplated the inside of her coffee cup, as if it held tea leaves instead of a few drops of very diluted coffee.

"What about insurance?"

"Daisy's got Medicare."

"I mean for you."

"Don't need it. Never get sick."

Violet slowly shook her head. "I'll keep my job. Take a pay cut and go back to adjusting. Telecommute, like I have been. That way we've got insurance for the baby. We can sell my condo, bank my few thousand in equity. But we'll be back at juggling schedules with an infant thrown in to boot. Midnight feedings and all that stuff."

"We'll be fine. Annabelle will help with Daisy. Heck, maybe we can even teach her to change diapers. Teach Annabelle, I mean. Daisy already knows." He chuckled lamely.

Violet didn't even crack a smile.

"Guess we didn't think about much of this," he commented, his honeymoon high crashing.

She stepped behind him and wrapped her arms around his shoulders. She leaned her head against his.

"We'll do it somehow. Together."

"Okay, planning time done. That leaves us seven hours and fifty minutes to have fun. First on the agenda," he said in his most serious manager-guy kind of voice, "is the artwork for my *New York Times* best-selling novel, yet to be titled. You go get one of those big old sheets or whatever it is you use for painting, and I'll bring the rest. Probably the studio would be best. I don't want you to catch cold. Lots of red and black paint to foreshadow the murder and mayhem. And did I tell you, clothing is strictly forbidden. You think you can create stunning art with your feet, wait till you see what I have in mind." He leered, just to make sure she caught his drift.

Vi's eyes widened. Then she grinned from ear to ear and hotfooted it out of the room.

VIOLET BLINKED at the wavering flames amid darkness.

Candles. There were candles everywhere. Short ones, tall ones, fat ones.

She held her breath as she stepped through the fairy-land of lights.

More candles. Every conceivable shape, every color, all twinkling with light.

Her eyes adjusted to dark, day turned into night by bamboo shades drawn over the huge studio windows.

Ian reclined in the center of an array of throw pillows. He lay on his side, his head propped on his bent elbow. A wicked grin underscored his nakedness, but love warmed his green eyes. She let her gaze travel over his chest, down his muscled stomach to where a blue-and-green checkered comforter frustrated her view. Flannel, it had to be flannel, so cozy—she could crawl in and lose herself.

And next to the makeshift pallet was a picnic basket. Flames reflected off the delicate crystal of fluted wineglasses. She opened her mouth to protest, when she read the label on the bottle. Sparkling cider.

Her throat got that familiar scratchy feel and her eyes burned.

"Ian," she breathed. "It's wonderful."

"You didn't think this was going to be all work and no play did you?"

"I thought the work *was* the play."

"You insurance people, you're all alike. No imagination. Come here."

His hand was outstretched, asking her to play his little game.

She wanted to reach out to him. To join him in that lovely, cozy cocoon. But her feet wouldn't move. All she could do was stand there and marvel.

"You did this...for me?"

"Just you. Although I might reap a few benefits, too. You need to relax. Now come here."

He held another bottle aloft. She strained to see it in the gloom.

"Massage oil," he supplied.

Her feet started to move. Before she knew it, she was naked and wrapped in warmth and security. She sipped the sparkling cider, then let Ian's persuasive hands roll her over.

Her eyes fluttered as he massaged her hands, one finger at a time.

"Mmm."

Who could have known fingers could be so tense?

Then it was her wrists. The pressure was just right. Shoulders, great. No more computer neck. Shoulder blades, the small of her back. Oil warmed in the palms of his hands. If this wasn't heaven, it was pretty darn close.

"Better?" he whispered in her ear.

"Little," she mumbled into the pillow.

His hands, strong and supple with oil moved down over her hips.

She groaned in ecstasy. A month's worth of muscle tension floated away on his fingertips.

Then the real massage began. One that made her skin tingle, her scalp tingle, pretty much every inch of her tingle. When she couldn't handle it a moment longer, she twisted around and opened her arms to him.

She eyed him through lowered lashes while he waited, sitting back on the balls of his feet, his thighs bunched, his forearms braced on his knees. His chest flexed almost imperceptibly as her gaze roamed upward toward his smile.

"Come here," she invited.

He raised an eyebrow. "More massage?"

"No. Some other relaxation techniques. You *do* want me to relax don't you?"

His gaze was intent, his voice husky. "I want the world for you, Vi. I want you to have everything good in life. And I want to protect you and cherish you forever and ever."

"For a man who doesn't rehearse vows, you do pretty darn well." Violet smiled through the mist blurring her vision. She'd always wondered how it felt to be cherished. Now she knew.

Opening her arms wide, she invited him to fulfill the promises he'd made here and at the wedding. And she made a few of her own, silently, in her heart, as she made love with him.

"THIS ISN'T FUNNY, Vi," Ian shouted as he rattled the studio doorknob.

Her giggle from the other side of the door told him she found it immensely entertaining. Almost as entertaining as making love on the polished hardwood floors of the studio, with throw pillows strategically placed for comfort.

Afterward they had painted, slathering each other with nontoxic, washable paint. At least he *hoped* it was washable. Nontoxic would be a plus, too, come to think of it.

"Come on, Vi, this stuff is starting to dry. *Everywhere.*" He glanced down at his most sacred area and winced. Seemed like a good idea at the time. "It's starting to scare me. The red and black is bad enough, but the paint's cracking as it dries. Who knows what they *really* put in that stuff."

He tried the knob again. No good.

"Our baby could be an only child. And it's no fun, let me tell you."

The door flew open and Vi rushed in, her eyes as big as saucers as she surveyed the damage.

"It was just a joke. You always said I need to lighten up. You don't think—" she stifled a chuckle, or maybe it was a scream "—there's any permanent damage?"

"Just my pride. And it was worth it to see you laugh. Now hand me a towel and let me shower off."

She reached up on tiptoe to kiss him as she wrapped the towel around his hips.

He reached to pull her close.

She danced out of his reach. "No way, buddy. I've had my shower. You need to wash your paint, uh, equipment if you ever want to get close to me again."

CHAPTER FIFTEEN

IAN TURNED OFF the ignition and got out of the Jeep. Strolling around to the other side, he opened the door for Violet. "Allow me."

She looked at his outstretched hand, then his face. "You're not humoring me because I'm pregnant, are you? Because I really am healthy as a horse. Except for the morning sickness stuff."

"No patronizing, I promise. Just a sincere desire to touch you every chance I get."

"How do you always know the right thing to say?" Her mouth wobbled as she smiled.

"Because I'm honest. And I leave out the parts you might not appreciate. Like how I have visions of you tripping and hurting yourself or the baby. Or how I know you're one hundred percent capable, but I feel this compulsion to protect you anyway...."

"Ahhh, the St. Ian bit again. But that's one of the things I love about you." She placed her hand in his.

He held on tightly until she was standing next to him. "You're sure you're up to hiking? It's not too much? We can just take in the view." He gestured to encompass the scenic panorama of mountain and high desert.

Vi strolled toward the lookout point, edged with a waist-high stone wall designed to keep people away from the steep drop. "No way, buddy. I want to see it all."

"We can see quite nicely from here." It was the truth. The Superstition Mountains rose against the sky, the purple, jagged expanse threatening to slice the wispy clouds above.

"It's beautiful," Violet breathed. "Absolutely beautiful."

Ian studied her profile, the clean line of her jaw, her delicate nose, the downright sinful tilt to her lips. "*You're* absolutely beautiful."

Her cheeks flushed, she turned her face away to look at the view. "It makes me uncomfortable when you talk about me like that. I'm not used to compliments."

"Surely I'm not the first guy to tell you that you're beautiful?"

Her eyes were wide and solemn as she looked up at him, reminding him of the children in the DeGrazia artwork. The kids' huge, dark eyes had always seemed to reflect a sad knowledge of the world way beyond their years.

"You're the *only* person who's ever told me that."

Ian whistled under his breath. "No prom nights where your date or your folks told you how gorgeous you looked?"

Violet shook her head. "Nope. I didn't go to the prom. And if I did, I wouldn't have had my date pick me up at home. Because my dad could be counted on for one thing—that he'd be drunk and sure to embarrass me. He never failed me there." Her chuckle was dry and scratchy.

"Then I'm glad you did't invite him to the wedding. I might have wrung his neck for what he put you through."

"I was a coward, Ian. I didn't invite him because I didn't want him to spoil our day. Not just the getting drunk part. But the way he makes me feel. Like I'm small, somehow."

Ian absorbed her admission. He'd never loved her more than at that moment when she placed her trust in him. Then the primal part of him took over in a rush of white-hot anger, demanding retribution from the man who had made this intelligent, loving, gorgeous woman feel small.

When he could control his emotions enough to speak, he pulled her close and said, "Aw, sweetheart, you have to be one of the bravest, *un*small people I know."

She smiled weakly, as if she didn't really believe him.

"How about your mom? Does she make you feel small?"

"No. She makes me feel invisible. In some ways that's worse."

Stunned, Ian didn't know what to say. Didn't understand how two human beings could do such a number on this woman's ego, apparently without remorse.

Holding her, he whispered reassuring nonsense into her hair. She sniffled once, then sighed.

He was batting zero for two. Did he dare ask about her sister? Ian's confidence faltered. He'd leave it alone. For now.

Rubbing her arms, he watched a tour bus pull up and disgorge a group of Japanese tourists. Within seconds they were nearly swallowed up by the group of chattering sightseers too busy taking pictures and pointing at the horizon to notice they were interrupting what had been a private moment.

"Come on. Let's hit the trail." Ian said.

Violet gazed up at him and wiped her eyes. "I'm so silly these days." Straightening her shoulders, she gave him that great big, screw-the-world grin. "Lead on, Scoutmaster Ian."

"Hey, I resent that. I've been demoted from saint to scoutmaster in less than an hour."

Violet prodded him in the side. "Go. I haven't told you what happens when the scoutmaster finds the lost Sierra Club wench, have I?"

Ian threw back his head and laughed. Life would never be boring with Vi. He grabbed her by the hand and started parting the sea of tourists. "Come on, lusty Sierra Club wench, I have plans for you."

"I said *lost* Sierra Club wench, not lusty."

"Lost, lusty, it's all the same to me. There's the trail over there."

VIOLET TOOK IN the beauty of the canyon. It seemed as if she and Ian were alone in the world. A slight breeze rustled the brown desert grasses, quail called to their young. Sipping from her water bottle, she craned her neck to see the outcropping near the top. "I wonder who named it? Echo Point, I mean?"

She felt the warmth of Ian's breath on the back of her neck. His arms slid around her waist, and he rested his chin on the top of her head.

"The story is that some old prospector went crazy looking for gold. Went to the top of Echo Point and hollered. His own voice echoed back to him, but he was convinced he was hearing the ghosts of all the miners who'd died on the mountain—thought they were telling him the secret to finding the mother lode. He died of exposure up there. But not before he went hoarse shouting to the ghosts.''

"What a sad story. They named the town after it?''

"Yep. Probably figured the story would bring in tourists. I'm surprised you haven't heard it before.''

"I'm a California girl, Ian. When I came to Phoenix, I was more concerned with building my career than learning local lore.''

"You missed out then.''

Violet smiled at the thought of how full her life had become. "Yes, I did. But our child will be different. He or she will embrace new experiences, savor everything that life has to offer. Never consider accepting anything less than a ten, because he knows deep down he deserves every last shred of happiness and love life has to offer.''

"And when will you learn that?'' Ian whispered.

Facing him, she wrapped her arms around his waist. His eyes were shadowed, his features solemn.

"I'm learning it every day. With you.''

She traced the laugh lines of his face, though he wasn't even smiling. Her fingertips instinctively knew where his dimples should be. Standing on tiptoe, Violet kissed him, willing him to realize how much she loved him. To realize that, in a way, her life had started the day she met him.

IAN PRETENDED to stagger under the weight of his precious load as he crossed the threshold.

Vi swatted his shoulder. "I told you we didn't have to do this."

"It's tradition. Besides, we forgot when we came home from the courthouse yesterday. Now we can do it properly. And reenact the wedding night, too." He waggled his eyebrows. "By my calculations, we have exactly forty-five minutes before Vince brings Mom home."

"Only forty-five minutes? We'll have to utilize some serious time management then." Violet wound her arms around his neck and kissed him like he'd never been kissed before, straight to his heart and clear down to his toes. Other regions in between reacted enthusiastically, too.

Ian pulled away a fraction and murmured against her mouth, "You check the messages, and I'll start a bubble bath for two."

"Excellent time management. But you have to put me down first."

"That's why you're management. You think of everything." Ian nibbled her neck then slowly set her on her feet, loathe to let her go, if only for five minutes. He glanced at his watch. "Hurry up and meet me in the master bath. We have only forty-*one* minutes left."

IAN SANK INTO the tub with a sigh of bliss. Life didn't get much better than this. He leaned back and closed his eyes. Next thing he knew, Violet was standing in front of him holding out a towel.

He noticed her eyes were wet, her lips trembled. And she wore too solemn an expression for a woman anticipating a bathtub tryst.

"What gives?" he asked, praying it was another of

the hormonal surges that made her more emotional than usual. But the tightening in his gut told him it was more than that. He got out of the tub and accepted the towel.

"We had a message from Vince."

"Please tell me they're running a bit late bringing Mom home. Or better yet, they're all having such a good time, they want to keep her one more day."

"Ian, Daisy's at the hospital."

"Something happened to Joe, right?" he prodded. "They took Daisy along because they didn't want to disturb our honeymoon."

Vi shook her head.

"She fell, Ian. Broke her arm, went into shock."

He sighed with relief, standing there, frozen to the fuzzy green bath rug.

"Broken arm. That's…that's okay. Not real serious. Sure, she'll be sore for a while, have to take it easy. But she'll be fine. Good as new."

"I hope so," Vi murmured.

He bit back a retort as he brushed past her. Frustration fueled his steps as he stalked across the bare tile. Why couldn't she look on the bright side for once, take the positive? Reassure him.

Violet padded behind him to his room. He turned his back as he pulled on a pair of jeans and a T-shirt. *Socks. Need socks.* Where in the hell were his socks?

His arms dropped to his sides, paralyzed, helpless.

Vi grasped his elbow and squeezed. "Ian?"

He didn't answer, *couldn't* answer. The only movement he could manage was to throw his head back and squeeze his eyes shut. Shut out the images. The only thing he managed to squeeze out were a few hot, hopeless tears.

Gentle hands pulled him over to the bed, forced him to sit. The bed sank when she sat next to him. Then the same gentle hands pulled his shoulders down, to cradle his head in her lap.

"It's okay," she soothed.

Now that she pretended everything would be all right, it really didn't make him feel any better. She knew as well as he did that Daisy might not recover. Broken bones, even simpler injuries, could be the beginning of the end.

"What do we do, Vi?"

"We drop back and punt. And get our butts to the hospital now. She needs us."

VIOLET SAT in the waiting room, staring sightlessly at the generic mauve and blue desert print hanging on the wall, wondering who in the heck had chosen the color scheme. Though the colors might seem soothing, the insipid tints weren't anywhere near the tans and sages of the desert. Or the fiery sunsets.

"She's doing better now. The private room seems to help." Ian's voice was a welcome interruption to her internal artistic critique. His news even more welcome.

Rising from the pseudo-comfortable upholstered chair, Violet went to Ian and put her arms around his waist. "I'm so glad. So she's out of danger?"

"For now. But she's *never* really out of danger. You know that as well as I do."

"It gives us a little more time with her though. I'm grateful for that."

He glanced at her sharply. "I don't know how long you'll feel that way. She's being…difficult."

"Her routine's all thrown off. She's in a strange place with strange people. Not to mention the physical trauma."

"I hope you're right."

"Will they let me see her now?" Vi couldn't keep the eagerness from her voice.

"Uh, no. They're trying to keep the distractions to a minimum. To be honest, they don't want to set her off again."

"And I set her off."

"Aw, Vi. It's not like that. It's whoever she imagines you are at any given time. None of us could handle another Olivia Randolph scene…especially you."

"I suppose you're right," she murmured.

"And I *know* I can't handle seeing her in restraints again." His voice was husky.

Violet couldn't believe her ears. Her pulse raced at the mental images of Daisy tied down. "You didn't tell me that. When did they have her in restraints? If I'd known that, I would have told the doctor a thing or two."

"That's why I didn't tell you. As much as I hated them restraining her, it was necessary. She was totally out of control. She could have easily hurt herself or someone else."

Violet tried not to feel hurt that he'd kept something that important from her. It was hard to believe that only hours before they'd been blissful newlyweds, closer than she'd ever imagined two people could be. Now they were keeping secrets, telling half truths, pulling away from each other. Her heart ached at this growing pain in their marriage.

"Ian, we'll get through this. Together."

His expression was bleak. "I sure hope so...."

"Vince wanted me to tell you he'd be back tonight after his shift. And his sisters send their love."

Ian smiled, but it was a mechanical motion. "Good. They've been great. Maybe Vince can help me get Mom home. Dr. Greene says she might be ready to go home in a couple days."

"That's wonderful," she breathed. "I'll do anything I can to help."

Drawing her close, he planted a kiss on the top of her head. "I know you will. I don't know how I got so lucky to have you."

"We're lucky to have each other."

"Yeah. I just hope she settles down once we get her in her own home with familiar stuff."

VI FUSSED with the cushion behind Daisy's back. It wouldn't lay flat, wouldn't do what it was supposed to. And everything had to be perfect for her first day home from the hospital.

Ian had stayed behind to talk to the social services lady at the hospital. See what kind of options they had for physical therapy, how much of it Medicare would cover, any other help that might be available. It was an exhausting maze of paperwork and phone calls, and she was more than happy to get Daisy settled, with Vince's help, and avoid the red tape.

Vi gnawed on her lower lip as she grasped Daisy's hand. Once she'd stabilized, there hadn't been any further outbursts. Instead, it seemed as if Daisy had withdrawn into herself. Vi touched her wrinkled cheek, looked for some spark of recognition in her eyes, but there wasn't any.

The doctor had said it might be this way. The medication might have side effects, amplified by the Alzheimer's.

She knelt by Daisy's chair, reaching out to brush the tangle of matted gray hair from her eyes. "Hey, where's my favorite flower woman?"

She locked her gaze with Daisy's, waiting for her to remember their connection.

Nothing.

"How about some painting? You love to paint."

No response. The lights were on, but nobody was home. It was like a shell, like the very essence of what made her Daisy had been sucked out.

"Tell me about Joe. The first time you met him."

Blank. Nothing. No stories about the horny old goat.

Okay, they'd try for the long-term memory.

"Edward. What was Edward like when you first met?"

Something seemed to spark in her tired blue eye. Her fingers twitched, her mouth worked. The memories were there. It just seemed like Daisy couldn't get to them. Or couldn't verbalize them.

"He was tall, like Ian, wasn't he?"

Daisy's mouth worked, but nothing came out. Her eyes were bright with frustration. Her mouth pulled downward, her hand beat the air.

She slapped away Violet's ministrations, refusing to be soothed. Spittle flew, her open hand connected with Vi's cheek.

The sting, the shock, the horror vibrated clear down to her toes. The humiliation.

Violet raised a hand to her burning cheek, but couldn't bring herself to touch it. If she confirmed it, then it really happened. It meant that the woman who'd invited her in, encouraged and loved her—had lashed out at her. In anger, in frustration.

Violet squeezed her eyes shut, trying desperately to stop the tears from seeping out. Trying desperately not to see the tears pouring down Daisy's face. She clamped her hands over her ears to block out the hoarse, animal-like keening noises.

It was Daisy making that horrible noise. At least that's what she thought, until strong, gentle hands pulled her balled fists away from her ears. Only then did she realize that low guttural grunts were the best Daisy could do. The shrieking came from her own mouth, erupting from a place so deep and scary, she refused to believe it was hers.

"Shhh," Ian soothed.

Her knees shook, her fists shook. It felt like every inch of her body shook. Her teeth chattered. Cold. It was so damned cold.

Ian wrapped her in his arms, but couldn't block out the sight of Daisy. Rage mottled her sunken cheeks a ghastly purple. Fear rolled her eyes to the back of her head. With every panicked breath came a grunting sound, like an animal in pain.

"Vi, go lie down in your room."

How could he expect her to leave the safety of his arms and travel all the way down the hallway by herself? The shaking, the chattering, the way her stomach heaved?

"C-c-can't."

"Sure you can," he soothed. His hands were already shoving her in that direction, but he kept his eyes glued on Daisy. "Lock your door when you get there." His tone was conversational. No urgency. Just a run-of-the-mill event.

She almost bought it, until she looked into his eyes and saw fear.

Violet forced one shaky foot in front of the other. She even managed a wobbly smile, just for him.

"Good girl," he murmured.

She turned her back on him and made her way down the hallway, the glow of reflective tape the only thing keeping her going. She could hear his comforting words and murmured reassurances. The grunting slowed, then finally stopped.

Slowly, deliberately, she locked the door and wedged a chair beneath the knob.

Then she allowed herself to slide down the wall and settle to the floor in a heap.

CHAPTER SIXTEEN

A KNOCK ON THE DOOR jarred Violet awake. The room tilted as she shifted to look at the clock. She couldn't see it—everything was gray. How long had she slept?

"Vi?"

The knob rattled.

"Vi, let me in."

Ian's voice wasn't nearly as calm as the last time she'd heard it. He sounded rough around the edges, as if he couldn't take much more.

She ignored the stab of pain in her lower back as she stood, every muscle in her body cramped and complaining.

Ian needed her.

The chair legs screeched in protest as she dragged it away from the door. Then she opened the door and flung herself at him.

He held her tight, and it seemed like hours that they stood there, silent, his scent washing over her in reassuring waves.

Finally, Vi backed out of his embrace to look at him, feel him, make sure he was okay. His cheeks bristled with stubble, his eyes were bloodshot and tired. He looked like that first day in court, when she'd thought he was hung over.

But it wasn't a hangover. It was fatigue and worry that pulled at him. Hopelessness dulled his eyes and slowed his speech.

"You okay?" he asked, brushing the hair from her eyes. His fingers trembled, beating a feather-soft tattoo against her temple.

Violet swallowed hard and nodded. Ian was here and everything would be all right.

"I'm so sorry, Vi." The anguish in his voice tore at her heart.

"Don't," she croaked, placing a finger against his lips. "It's not your fault."

"It *is* my fault. I brought you here, I allowed myself to fall in love with you, without thinking about the consequences. I screwed up. Royally."

She grasped him by the shoulders. "Hey. Don't apologize for loving me, or for loving her. It's what makes you you. It's why I love you."

Violet leaned against him, rubbing her cheek against the rough weave of his shirt. "I made my own choices."

"Maybe circumstances had a hand in it. The baby…"

"Are you saying the baby is the reason I married you?"

Ian ran a hand through his hair. "Yeah, I guess maybe I am."

"I married you because I love you."

His face softened, but only for a moment. He started pacing. "You didn't know what you were getting yourself into. You survived your father, you moved forward. Got away from it, built a new life. Then I put you back in that same situation, where someone you love lashed out, hurt you.''

He stopped in front of her. "I saw the look in your eyes, Vi. You can't hide it from me or pretend it wasn't there.''

"But—''

"It just about broke my heart seeing you hurt—the humiliation, like you'd done something wrong. Like it was your fault.'' He looked away, cleared his throat.

Violet's nose prickled. The empty place inside opened up again and threatened to swallow her whole.

"I want you to go.'' His voice was firm, his back straight as a board.

"You don't mean that,'' she whispered. He *couldn't* mean that.

Ian lifted her chin to look in her face. His lips were unbelievably tender as he kissed away the tear suspended on her jawline. "It's the only way I can protect you.''

Violet stiffened. She tried to wrench away, but he wouldn't let go.

"I don't need you to protect me. I can handle myself.''

"Can you? Handle the rejection, the lashing out?''

"I—I know it's the disease, not Daisy. She didn't mean to. You could tell how much it upset her.''

"And your dad's disease? Did the alcoholism make it easier to take? Did his remorse make it any better, or just confuse the hell out of you?''

"It's not the same.''

"It *is.* The way it affects you is exactly the same.''

"I didn't have anything to fight for then. Now I

have you. And our baby.'' She placed her palm on her stomach. *Their baby.* They could do it, make it work somehow. "I'm not giving up."

"You have to. If not for my sake, or for your sake, then at least for the baby's."

He placed his hand protectively over hers. She could almost feel the tiny heartbeat she knew was somewhere beneath their palms. All the fight went out of her. And something inside died—hope.

"What will you do?" Her voice was husky, her throat raw with regret.

"I'll get by. Like I always have."

"You won't have time to work on your book. The nurse said Daisy isn't sleeping. When will you sleep? How will—"

"I'll handle it. What I can't handle is worrying about you. And the baby."

His hand twitched, then clenched hers.

Liar, she wanted to scream at him. It was the divided loyalties he couldn't handle. It had been written all over his face as he tried to decide between helping Daisy or helping her. It was in the panic in his eyes when he realized he couldn't sacrifice one to save the other. He'd vowed to keep Daisy safe and happy at home, and he'd follow through on that vow until the very end. But he'd made a vow to her, too. Was it meaningless now?

Not meaningless. Just not at the top of the list. He wouldn't choose her over his mother. The knowledge formed a hard knot of regret in her chest. Shame blurred her vision as she looked down at their clasped hands cradling her tummy. She didn't want him to choose her. His loyalty, his devotion, made him stand head-and-shoulders above any other guy she'd ever met.

No, Vi didn't want him to walk away from Daisy, ditch his responsibilities. All she wanted was to share them.

"This might just be a reaction to the pain medication. Call Dr. Greene. Maybe there's something else they can give her."

Ian pushed a hand through his hair, now shaggy. "Yeah. You might be right. But stay clear of Daisy till I find out. Promise?"

She exhaled with relief. "I promise."

VIOLET DASHED into her room and slammed the door behind her. Safe.

For nearly a week, she'd lived in her room. Her frequent trips to the bathroom were a tactical nightmare. If Daisy so much as caught a glimpse of her, the thrashing and grunting started all over again.

The old woman couldn't go to the senior center in her condition, so Tuesdays and Thursdays weren't safe, either. The sheer unpredictability of Daisy's schedule made Vi's life a logistical mess. Day and night seemed to have ceased to exist for Daisy.

Several times a night, Violet heard Annabelle's toenails click on the tile outside her door. Every once in a while, the knob would turn. Whispered gibberish interspersed with English reached her ears. She'd lay in her bed, her heart pounding at the thought that she might have forgotten to lock the door.

And she only saw Ian a couple of times a day when

he shoved a plate of food through her hastily opened door. It was as if she were in solitary confinement.

Her few stolen glimpses of him broke her heart. Fatigue rimmed his eyes, his hands shook from too little sleep and not enough food. Simply feeding the three of them had to be a monumental task.

Violet gazed at her reflection in the mirror as she brushed her hair. Her skin was pale, her cheeks hollow. Her hair was limp and dull.

What had happened to the woman who'd determined her own future? Relied on no one? She was a virtual prisoner.

Violet swallowed her pride, her dreams. She had to take her future, and the future of her child, back into her own hands. And to do that, she had to admit defeat. A foreign word, until now.

Crossing to the door, she pressed her ear against the rough wood. Silence.

Violet took a deep breath and unlocked the door. Twisting the knob, she leaned outside. A quick check in both directions, like a child crossing the street alone, showed the hallway was clear.

She padded past Daisy's closed door. It was locked on the outside. Ian was probably making dinner while she napped.

The sight that greeted her as she rounded the corner into the kitchen told her things were worse than she'd imagined. Much worse.

Dirty dishes overflowed the sink and covered the counter. Two bulging garbage bags stood sentinel by the back door. The trash can brimmed with empty soup cans and paper plates.

Violet sniffed the air. Stale, slightly rancid and smoky. She checked the great room, but no Ian. Returning to the kitchen, the smoky odor was even stronger. Like something burning. It came from the stove.

She dashed over and grasped the frying pan handle. Pain seared her palm, shot up her arm. Her fingers froze around the handle like some obscene death grip.

Then her brain cells kicked in and she threw the pan in the sink. Flipping on the cold water tap, she held her palm under the running water.

All sorts of curses stuck in her throat. Every time she moved her hand from beneath the stream of water pain shot along her palm to her brain.

Where the hell was Ian?

As if summoned by her thoughts, he ran into the kitchen.

"Violet! What happened?"

"Where were you? The pan— Th-the sandwiches— They were burning—"

Ian's eyes widened as he focused on her hand and the running water. "Are you okay?"

"A burn. Nothing bad," she lied.

He turned on his heel and left her. Alone. Scared. And in pain.

She bit her lip to keep the tears at bay. She'd cried enough the past few weeks to last a lifetime. Hormones or no hormones, it was time to buck up.

Ian returned with the first aid kit.

"Here. I'll dry it with this sterile gauze. Once it's covered, it won't sting."

Drawing her hand away from the soothing water, he

gently applied the gauze. He'd lied. It stung like crazy. But not as bad as when the air hit it.

Then he sprayed it with some aerosol stuff and it quieted to a dull throb.

"Thanks. Where were you?"

"Uh...in the bathroom. I don't get any union breaks to take care of business. Gotta grab a minute when I can."

His face flushed with embarrassment.

Her heart contracted when she realized all the sacrifices he'd made in the past week alone. Trying to keep peace in the household had taken its toll. Not only did he have to care for Daisy, he'd had to wait on her, too. Instead of helping him, she'd simply added to his load.

He glanced over his shoulder. Clearing his throat, he shifted nervously from one foot to another. "You better get back. Daisy'll be waking any time now."

"Did you talk to the doctor again? About her new meds?"

"Uh-huh. They might affect her ability to speak. Or it might be the next progression in her disease. The moodiness, the frustration, there's no way of knowing if it's permanent. In all likelihood it is. I meant to talk to you about it this morning, but I couldn't keep my eyes open any longer. I can't stand putting you at risk. You, or the baby. Can't you see, there's no other way?"

She did see. But she'd hoped and prayed for a miracle. That the new medication would return Daisy to them. That they could resume being a family. That she and Ian could raise their child together.

Sadness washed over her, darker and deeper than she'd ever known. She couldn't put him through it. And she couldn't endanger their child.

Violet went to him and wrapped her arms around his waist. He drew her close and pressed a kiss to the top of her head.

She nodded slowly.

"I'll leave tomorrow morning."

VIOLET STARTED when the phone rang. Very few people called her at the condo. The silence had been an adjustment at first. She still woke up in the middle of the night, sure she heard Daisy calling. Or reached for Ian, even though they hadn't had the luxury of spending much time in the same bed.

Picking up the cordless, she breathed a sigh of relief at the sound of Ian's voice. She paced around the wicker coffee table as she talked, more to keep her mind working, and her mouth from babbling.

He asked how she was doing. What was she supposed to say?

"Great, great. I'm big as a house, and I've still got three months to go. How are you holding up?" Her voice lowered an octave, even though she tried to sound unconcerned.

"Uh, great. Sorry I haven't called for a couple days."

"I was a little concerned. I tried calling, but got some recording about the phone being out of service. If I didn't hear from you today, I was going to call Vince."

"Sorry, I didn't mean to worry you. But...I couldn't find the phone."

Anyone else she would have accused of trying a really lame excuse. But with Ian it was entirely plausible.

"Daisy threw the cordless in the garbage again?"

"Not exactly. I need to give you my cell number. I've disconnected the house phone."

"Ian, I know it's inconvenient to look in Daisy's hiding spots, but I'd feel more comfortable if you had a land line. That way if you call 911 they can trace the call."

Ian cleared his throat. "Uh, that was the problem. Daisy kept dialing 911. After three or four false alarms, the sheriff's department was kinda fed up. Vince suggested I get a cell phone. I carry it on me all the time."

"Why the 911 calls all of the sudden?"

"Daisy thought there was a burglar in the house."

Violet quit pacing. "Burglar?"

"She kinda...forgot who I was. Saw a strange man in the house and called 911."

"Oh, Ian," she murmured, needing like crazy to be with him, to hold him. "I can come this weekend."

"No, that's not a good idea." There was a trace of panic in his voice.

"Ian, if you don't want to see me, all you have to do is say so."

Vi sank to the couch. Where in the heck had that come from? "I'm sorry. I know it was a disaster last time I visited. For everyone."

That was an understatement. It had taken days for

her back to quit spasming. Babies and tension were hell on her body.

"It's just that I know how hard it must be for you. How much it hurts, even though you know it shouldn't be personal."

"Hey, I'm doing fine. It's you I'm concerned about. How are you feeling? How's the baby doing?"

Vi's heart contracted at the longing in his voice. It helped to remind her that he really *did* want to be there with her. That he wished things could be different.

"The baby's doing just great. Kicking and poking and prodding. I don't think my internal organs will ever be the same."

She smiled as she patted her eyes dry with a washcloth. Much as she looked forward to their phone calls, they were hard on her hormone-fuddled emotions. Next she'd need one of those huge bath sheets to mop up all those tears. Silent tears. Ian never knew. She kept her voice light and reassuring. Only positive thoughts during such an impossible time.

"By the way, I have my ultrasound next week. It'll be our one shot to see if we have a boy or a girl. It's next Tuesday, Daisy's day at the center—didn't you say she was back? Think you can make it?"

She could kill herself for even asking. Then she could kill Daisy for making this joyous time so impossible. Then she could kill Ian for being such a loyal guy, running himself ragged trying to make all of them happy. It was a no-win situation.

Not the baby though. She'd pretty much decided it was a boy. He was the only thing that kept her going. The only person she had to talk to about all these things. She couldn't dump on Ian, and certainly couldn't confide in anyone at work.

She was now the office pariah. Any mention of Ian, her mystery husband, elicited raised eyebrows. *Sure* she had a husband. So she was deemed unmarried, unmotivated and completely unacceptable. Her pregnancy was never mentioned, though she'd started wearing maternity clothes several months ago.

Instead, she was given a desk in the last row of the last bay of adjusters. Out of sight and out of mind.

Returning to the front lines had been tough. She'd almost forgotten the nonstop phone calls, irate customers and ever-increasing productivity demands from upper management. Funny, they hadn't seemed nearly so demanding when she merely passed along the bad news, soothed the ruffled feathers. Now it was *her* blankety-blank feathers, and dammit she'd had enough.

"Maybe you could catch a nap in the morning, then meet me for the appointment?" she wheedled.

Vi smacked the washcloth to her forehead. Only a self-centered bitch would suggest that he drive all that way in his exhausted state.

Ian sighed heavily. "I'll try."

Biting back a short response, she tried to find that last shred of understanding in her heart, but came up empty. She needed him, too. But his worst fear had come true. There wasn't enough of him to go around. Maybe not even enough for Daisy alone, and that worried her. Burnout dulled his voice to a monotone, nothing seemed to inspire any of their old shared jokes.

"You go get some sleep, Ian. And take care. Bye."

I love you.

She couldn't tell him that. Not now. It seemed too much like a guilt trip.

Violet sighed in frustration. She tossed her phone on the couch. It sunk deliciously in the down-filled cushion covered in Egyptian cotton. An optimistic splurge to make the condo seem cozy, homelike. But it took more than a designer floral print and goose down to make a home. Even if the print held special significance—daisies and violets interspersed with huge cabbage roses.

IAN SPRINTED across the parking lot, taking the steps two at a time. He'd meant to be there early. Steal some time just to be with Vi, to drink in all her beauty and reassurance. God knew he needed both.

He shook his head to blow away the fog. It was there all the time now. The fog, the dull ache that made it almost impossible to think. Impossible to plan ahead.

He hadn't meant to fall asleep. He'd just sat down long enough to read the paper, see what was going on in the outside world. It was the only thing that made him feel connected anymore. That and the phone conversations with Vi.

A reflection in the medical clinic's glass door made him hesitate, let the older guy go first. Then he turned and looked over his shoulder. He was the only one in the parking lot. Slowly, he turned to the man reflected in the door. Rumpled, haggard.

The old guy was him.

He ran a hand through his messy hair. Needed a haircut. Needed sleep. Needed so many things.

Shrugging his shoulders, he threw open the door, dislodging the image.

"I'm looking for Violet Davis, no, Smith."

The young receptionist's gaze slithered to the right of him, then the left. Finally, she managed to look him straight in the face. Her eyes were wide with uncertainty, her hands shook as she picked up the phone. She murmured into the receiver. Too quietly.

Ian braced his knuckles on the polished reception desk and leaned forward.

The receptionist pulled back as far as her chair would allow.

"I'm here to see my wife. Where is she?"

The scared little thing looked like she might bolt any minute. Another time he might have soothed her ridiculous fears. But now, he had to see Vi. Show her he hadn't let her down.

"The of-f-fice manager will be here in a minute s-sir."

Ian stood, his spine taut with the effort not to wrap his hands around her pretty little neck and *make* her tell him where Vi was.

"I don't have time for this shi—"

That's when the battle-ax entered the fray. No wonder they saved her for protection. The woman, Zee, according to her shiny brass name tag, had to be at least six feet tall and was built like a linebacker. Except for the mountainous peaks that entered the room a full second before she did, like a cattle guard on a train, only higher. Ebony skin, cropped white hair. She looked like she could mop up the floor with a lesser man. But he was a man with a mission.

"Ma'am, I'm here to see my wife—Violet Smith. I'm late already. I've got to see her. Now."

The battle-ax looked him up and down. Her gaze locked on his. Desperation kept him from looking away. Finally, she nodded.

"You'll have to forgive Kristi for jumping to conclusions. One of the other patients has a…domestic situation that gets sticky. You understand our caution?"

"Uh, yeah. I'm harmless, really."

A smile twitched at her lips. "This way, son. She'll be glad you're here."

Ian exhaled.

He followed her ground-eating stride, nearly colliding when she stopped abruptly at room number two.

She paused, her hand on the knob.

"Relax, son. It'll be okay."

Then she winked at him, flung open the door and was gone.

Vi lay on a pink vinyl examining table. She looked up at him, her eyes ringed with fear. Helpless, flat on her back and alone. Completely alone.

"Ian," she breathed.

He rushed to her side.

Her lips quivered as he kissed her. He grasped her hands in his, rubbing them to return some warmth.

"Am I too late?"

"They haven't done the ultrasound yet. I've been waiting for *hours*."

He glanced at his watch. "It's only ten-thirty. Your appointment was for ten o'clock."

She grabbed his hand and clenched it in a death grip.

"It's been hours I tell you. They gave me these ridiculous instructions to drink like a gallon of water. It was a typo, it had to be a typo. Nobody can drink that much water."

Ian tried to think of something soothing to say, but for the life of him he couldn't.

"Okay, so you drank like a gallon of water...."

"I did *not* drink a gallon. I drank a *reasonable* amount of water and they kept me in the waiting room for days and then they told me I didn't drink enough water and then they made me drink more and then left me here..."

Come to think of it, that last cup of coffee was screaming for release.

"So they haven't done the ultrasound yet. Good." He pointed to a second door. "It was a long drive. I'll just run to the restroom real quick and—"

"You will *not!*" Vi shrieked. Panic squinched up her face, her eyes were all whites.

"Huh?"

She grabbed him by the shirtfront, twisted a great big handful in her white-knuckled fist, and pulled him until they were nose to nose. "If you pee, I'll hear you. If I hear you, it's all over. If so much as a faucet drips in the next county, I'm going to lose it—all fifty gallons. Right here. Right now. Then we'll have to start over again."

"Okay." He gently disengaged her fingers from his

shirtfront just as a smiling blond woman in a white coat bustled into the room.

"Sounds like you're about ready now. Let's give it another try."

Paper rustled as the woman pushed up Vi's dressing gown.

He barely noticed the junk the technician squirted all over Vi's belly. It was the belly that held him transfixed. There was an honest-to-goodness baby in there. The last time he'd seen her naked, her belly'd been just a little puffed out, like she'd had too much Mexican food. But now, now there was a real baby in there.

Ian reached blindly behind him, locating the chair for visitors. The chair for dads.

He pulled it behind him without taking his eyes off his wife and this awesome thing that was happening.

The technician tinkered with the computer, punching buttons. Then she took an overgrown computer mouse and ran it all over Vi's tummy.

In certain spots, she'd stop, nod and punch in more stuff on the computer. He craned his neck to see.

The lady glanced at him, smiled, then turned the screen so he could see better.

"Here's the head, and here you can see a little hand." She pointed to different areas on the screen. He tilted his head one way, then the other.

"Yeah…I think I see it."

He dragged his gaze from the screen for a split second to look at Vi. Her huge, wondrous smile was a twin to the one he knew split his face. The moisture was the same, too, right around the eyes.

Allergies.

He sniffed and turned back to the screen.

There was a face. A face with two eyes and a mouth. And it *moved*. The wiggly thing she'd said was a hand moved up to the face.

Disappointment surged through him as he willed the baby to move its arm, quit blocking his view.

Then it did the most extraordinary thing. It maneuvered the hand to its mouth, clasped the fingers closed and located the thumb. And sucked.

He glanced at Vi to make sure she'd seen that most amazing event, too.

Her smile, the awe on her face, told him she had.

"Do you want to know the sex?" the technician asked.

He looked at Vi and raised an eyebrow.

"One miracle in a day is enough, don't you think?" he suggested. He clasped her hand in his, kissing her knuckles.

"Yes," she breathed. "I think it is. Let's be surprised."

VIOLET DRANK IN the sight of Ian sitting across the table from her, actually eating with her. Using utensils even.

"I've missed you," he mumbled through a mouthful of lasagna.

His appetite made hers look tiny in comparison.

"I've missed you, too."

She wanted to reach across the red checkered tablecloth and touch him, run her palm along his gaunt cheek. But with the way he wolfed his food, he needed sustenance. The hollows in his cheeks worried her.

"Have you been eating?" she asked.

"Mm-hm." He finished chewing and took a pull from his long-neck beer. "Have you?"

Vi had to laugh at that. She spread her hands wide. "It should be obvious. I never stop."

Ian grabbed her hands, and his gaze roved over her face. "You look beautiful. Absolutely beautiful."

And she felt awful. Not physically. Just that deep pit of aloneness that threatened to swallow her whole.

"You know what I miss most?" she asked.

"My hulking presence?"

"Of course I miss that. But what I miss most are your jokes. And talking, just sitting and talking. Not about anything earth shattering. You always know how to make me laugh."

She reached across the table and cupped the side of his face, rubbing her thumb across the lines at the corners of his eyes.

"You're my best friend, Ian. My only friend." The words caught in her throat. She'd been determined, if he showed, to make this appointment guilt-free. He had enough to deal with without her angst on top of it. "I mean, what's a good joke, without you to share it with?"

"I miss *making* you laugh. The way your nose crinkles, the way you throw back your head. The way you look at me that tells me we're the only two in on the joke."

"Our child will definitely have a warped sense of

humor.'' Good, change the subject. Getting too maud-lin. Plenty of time to cry after he was gone.

Ian toyed with his food, pushing it from one side of the plate to another. He needed to eat, get rid of that gaunt, on-the-edge look.

''Bread stick?'' She waved the basket under his nose.

''Sure.'' He grabbed one, tore it in two and placed the pieces next to the neglected lasagna.

''Some of the retired ladies at the condo pitched in and got us a stroller. Isn't that nice?''

''Stroller. Yeah. You'll need one.''

God, this was hard.

''Yes, *we'll* need one.''

Ian stared at his plate. He picked up a bread stick, gnawed on it for a minute, then dropped it on his plate.

''We can't go on like this.'' His voice was low, thoughtful.

His words echoed hers, the ones she whispered in the dark, when she was all alone at night. But the alternatives were even scarier.

''How's Daisy?'' she asked brightly.

''Bout the same. Except she's packing again.''

''Oh, no, not again.''

''Yeah. And this time it's to go back to New York. Back home. She seems to think she's visiting someone in Echo Point, a guest in her own house. Just doesn't remember anymore.''

''What about Annabelle? How does Daisy react to the dog?''

''Annabelle's like another part of Daisy now. She shadows her constantly. I worry that she's going to stress out...or whatever dogs do. I have to force her out in her run. She goes out, does her business, then comes right back in. Oh, and she's not Annabelle anymore. She's 'Dog.' And I'm 'My Friend.' Only a small part of her vocabulary returned after the pain pills were taken away.''

There was something in the flat acceptance in his voice that scared her. As if all hope was gone, and there would be no tomorrow.

Vi reached across and grasped his hand. *Hold on, Ian.*

How could she tell him that when she was doing such a lousy job herself?

She couldn't. So she resorted to platitudes instead.

''Ian, it doesn't matter what name she calls you. She still knows deep in her heart that you love her and you're someone important to her.''

''Yeah, sure. When she's not dialing 911 to report me as a burglar.''

The somber sarcasm scared her, too. Where was the guy with a goofy joke for everything? The guy who told her to lighten up?

''The technician says she'll call me when the videotape is ready. You want me to send you a copy?''

A smile broke across his face. Not the old carefree, cocky grin she was used to. No, this smile was just a little too wide, a little too desperate. ''Yeah, would you?''

''Of course.''

''I think about you all the time,'' Ian said, his gaze fixed somewhere just left of her face. ''Both of you.''

''Me, too.''

"This isn't fair to you, Vi. I can't ask you to wait in limbo forever."

"It won't be forever." The minute the words were out of her mouth she realized exactly what she'd said. It meant a death sentence for Daisy. "I mean, we'll figure something out. I'm working on that telecommute thing. If it's approved, I'll move to Echo Point, maybe rent a place nearby...."

"Thought you said your chances of that were slim-to-none."

Violet twisted the blood-red cloth napkin around her index finger. "When they get over my...change in career plans they'll come around."

"Sure. Whatever you say."

He pushed his plate away and nursed his beer.

Until he caught her watching him, caught the worry she knew was written all over her face.

He grinned, a smile that didn't quite reach his eyes. Raising his beer bottle, he toasted, "To the baby. And the future."

"The baby, the future," she echoed as she raised her water glass high.

CHAPTER SEVENTEEN

IT WAS THE SICK, sliding out-of-control feeling that told Ian he was in trouble. Big trouble.

He pumped the brake, turned into the slide. Dust filled the air, clouds of it.

The Wrangler went on two wheels. He was going over. The damn Jeep would never make this turn, not this fast.

He waited, while his hands and feet made the futile attempt to slow down and take the curve. He waited for his life to flash before him, show him the error of his ways, show him the things he'd done right.

But there was nothing. Just that same empty, dead space in the pit of his stomach. Like maybe he was already dead, but nobody'd bothered to tell him.

Things seemed to move in slow motion. The Jeep, teetering on two wheels. His clenched hands going limp on the steering wheel. The whole ironic inevitability. He'd die here, where his life had begun. The spot where Vi'd almost missed the curve, but landed where he needed her most—right in the middle of his life.

He didn't bother to brace himself for the roll. What was the point?

But the roll never came. The truck teetered for an

eternity, then dropped softly back to four wheels, as if pillows cushioned the drop.

Ian jammed on the brake, the vehicle listed to a stop.

His hands gripped the wheel lightly, surely. His breathing was slow and steady. It could have been a Sunday drive, for all the reaction he could muster.

Man, things were getting weird.

Why'd he take that corner like that?

Worse yet, why couldn't he feel anything? No fear, no shock. Just that hollow feeling, like the life had trickled out of him over the past two months. It had started the second he'd seen Daisy's hand suspended above Violet's head, then heard the sickening slap. The woman he loved was gone and had taken his heart and soul with her.

He shook his head to clear the fog.

Daisy. Had to get back for Daisy.

The center wouldn't take her anymore. She needed more care than they could provide. So Tuesdays and Thursdays, his very lifeline, was gone. He couldn't tell Vi. She worried enough as it was. Worry was bad for the baby. Had to be—look what it was doing to him.

Ian shifted into first and eased toward the house.

The circular drive greeted him, like a great yawning abyss, waiting to swallow him whole. His heart plummeted, his stomach complained.

Anywhere but here.

Like an old man, he stumbled out of the Jeep. His steps were slow, almost a shuffle as he approached the scarred wooden door.

It wasn't a home anymore. Certainly not Daisy's. Home was somewhere in her distant, fuzzy memory.

And it certainly wasn't a home for him, not since Vi had left. Home was where Vi was, pure and simple.

His key scraped in the lock, protesting. Nobody wanted to be here, least of all him.

He took a deep breath, plastered a grin on his face and stepped through the doorway.

His shins bumped in to something, almost sending him sprawling. Suitcases. Two old, ugly, bursting-at-the-seams suitcases.

Not again.

Vince ambled in from the kitchen, a beer in each hand. He handed one to Ian.

"Figured a nice cold one might be good after that drive."

"Thanks. For everything."

"No problem."

Vince chose the old leather recliner. He sat on the edge and waited for Ian to sit.

Only Ian didn't want to sit. That meant admitting he was here, caged for however long until somebody spelled him again. And the only somebody who could handle Daisy was Vince. His good buddy Vince, who had a life of his own and old Joe to care for.

The fog rolled in, over his brain, his heart, his soul, as he let his knees buckle. There. He sat. He was back on duty.

"How'd it go?" he asked, even though he didn't want to hear the answer.

"Okay. She got the door unlocked, but the suitcases slowed her down. I caught up to her before she hit the driveway."

Vince's forehead furrowed. Guilt chiseled grooves in his normally smiling cheeks.

"I'm sorry, Ian. She was asleep, I went to the bathroom. Looked in on her again and she was gone."

What now? Vince was his only hope, his only backup while he tried to keep things going with Vi.

"I know." Ian sighed heavily. "Every time I get some new childproof gadget, she figures it out."

"It's my fault, Ian. Her arm, all this."

Vince gestured to the suitcases, the sparse room, without a knickknack or magazine anywhere.

God, what had he done to his best friend? First Vi and now Vince.

"Nobody blames you. How were you supposed to know they'd try to jitterbug? Try a lift for God's sake? You were the only one who could help, who *did* help. You, your whole family. It meant a lot that your sisters pitched in, too. You gave us a honeymoon, a few hours away from all this. A few hours to be like normal people. Today, you filled in for me so I could see my baby for the first time. Do you know what that means to me?"

Vince didn't meet his gaze, just nursed his beer.

"What's it like?" he asked. "The baby thing?"

Ian leaned back against the couch and sipped his beer. "It's like the most fantastic thing I've ever seen. You can tell it's a baby, fingers, toes, a face."

"Boy or girl?"

Ian grinned as he remembered seeing the image on the screen. He didn't care. It really didn't matter, one way or the other.

"We're going to be surprised."

"Have you—" Vince cleared his throat, peeled the label from the beer bottle. "Thought about what you'll do?"

Ian tilted his head back and closed his eyes.

"That's all I think about. When I'm awake enough to think. I go round and round with it in my mind, figuring out some way to make it work."

"When it's Violet's time, you let me know. I'll bring in the whole family to watch her. Sit on her if we have to."

Ian opened his eyes, a smile twitched at his mouth. The mental vision of twenty or thirty Morenos camped out to watch one confused old woman made him laugh. But then he realized it was true. It was more than one human and one dog could do. Daisy needed a clan, and dammit he couldn't provide one.

"THIEF," his mom shouted, pointing a bony finger at him. "You stole my suitcases. You're keeping me prisoner. I want to go home."

"This *is* your home," Ian stated patiently for what seemed like the zillionth time.

"I remember my home quite clearly and this isn't it. There are two stories, a beautiful hand-carved banister, elm trees out front. And when it snows—" Her voice broke. She had tears in her eyes. "Edward and I take Ian sledding."

"I know you do."

His memories of those idyllic days had worn rough around the edges. He could barely recall the times when he was loved and cared for and everyone knew who he was. Now *he* wasn't even quite sure who he was.

His mother stepped closer, focusing on his face as if seeing him for the first time. Her lips trembled into a smile. "Edward?" she whispered, as she reached up to touch his face.

"No, Mom, it's me. Ian." He could barely get the words past the lump in his throat.

Daisy's eyes widened. "No, you can't be Ian. He's just a little boy." She glanced around wildly. Her voice rose to a shriek. "Where's my son? What have you done with him?"

She flew at him, clawing wildly.

He dodged, but not quickly enough. Her fingernails raked his cheek.

Grasping her wrists, he held on tightly. She squirmed, she screamed, she kicked. But he kept holding on—a restraint system in human form. Only he didn't feel human anymore.

Daisy suddenly quit fighting. He hoped she'd finally worn herself out.

Ian tentatively released her left hand. When she didn't attack, he stroked her hair. She clung to him, sobbing. Her body shook with the depth of her despair.

"I want my son. My husband. My *home*."

"Mom, this *is* your home."

Raising her head, she glanced around. Her eyes had an unfocused, glazed look. "No, this isn't my home. My home has two stories, a beautiful hand-carved banister and elm trees out front. And when it snows, Edward and I take Ian sledding...."

VIOLET TRIED to pretend she didn't notice that she was the only woman in childbirth class without a coach. She placed her own pillow at a comfortable angle, leaned against the wall instead of a partner.

She also tried to pretend she didn't see the pitying

looks from the married women. She was doing a lot of playacting these days. Pretending she didn't know Ian was killing himself trying to care for Daisy, pretending she didn't know that Daisy was slipping away day by day. Never acknowledging that she called Vince every once in a while to wrangle the truth from him. It was a pretty pathetic existence.

But slowly, she was coming to terms with being in limbo. What was the alternative? The thought of letting Ian go was something she couldn't face.

The petite, blond instructor entered the room and asked if anyone wanted to share news or ask any questions. One woman raised her hand. "My husband says he wants the baby to be born on the 18th so he doesn't miss the golf tournament. Would you tell him I don't have any control over when the baby comes?"

The instructor smiled. "She's right, Jonathan. The baby will choose its own time to come. Unless, of course, you're having a C-section."

The husband's face brightened. His wife elbowed him in the ribs. "We're not having a C-section," she hissed.

The woman's question reminded Violet of her biggest concern. Raising her hand, she asked, "I've read that labor with first babies is generally twelve hours or more. Is that pretty much true? My…um, husband lives out of town and I'm concerned he won't be able to get here in time."

"Where is your husband coming from?"

"Echo Point."

"Beautiful place. He'll have plenty of time. Not to worry."

Violet sighed with relief. She desperately wanted Ian there.

"However," the instructor continued, "there are rare occasions when first-time mothers give birth in an hour or less. The odds are in your favor, though, Violet."

Vi was beginning to wonder. Nothing had gone right since the second day of her marriage. And Ian had to find someone to care for Daisy before he could leave for the hospital.

Smiling wanly, she said, "I guess I'll hope for a long labor then."

The teacher nodded sympathetically. "You're the first woman I've *ever* heard say that. And it's the first time I'll tell a woman I hope she has a long labor. I can understand how much it means to you to have your husband there."

"Thank you," Violet murmured. *You have no idea.*

THE BABY KICKED, then rolled, like a ship on the sea.

Violet absently caressed a knee, or maybe it was an elbow. She chewed on the end of the paintbrush she held in her other hand.

More green maybe?

No. The tree was perfect. It was the lighting that was off. There was no magic here. She found it hard to work from a photo, without the ambience of the real adobe to reflect light.

Violet closed her eyes and reveled in the aroma of paint. *Now* she could feel the magic of the courtyard, see the fairy dust at sunset.

Peace crept over her.

She winced as the baby landed a good one to the ribs.

More ocher maybe? She just couldn't decide.

The baby settled down as she wandered around the condo, cleaning brushes, moving the canvas to the corner. He liked movement, liked sound. Then he would sleep.

Six weeks to go.

At times she couldn't wait to see the baby, hold her son or daughter. Then other times it scared her so bad she almost hyperventilated. Giving birth was scary enough. Even scarier when she thought of going through it completely alone.

"You and me against the world," she whispered, stroking her taut skin. It couldn't possibly stretch another millimeter, could it? The teacher had simply smiled and nodded, handing her a tube of cocoa butter.

Ian was a coach of sorts, she supposed, if only from a distance. His last call had been over a week ago. He'd tried to be enthusiastic, but it was the plastic kind, meant for her, but not him.

At night, alone in the dark, she'd wonder what she would do if he dropped out of the picture completely.

Keep doing what she was doing. These days her plans, her goals, centered on the baby. She made a good living. Her child would be safe and secure. More and more she visualized them as a family of two, the way it would appear to the outside world—a single mom caring for her child.

The little old ladies in her complex did their best— clipped diaper coupons, gave her nutritional advice, even crocheted a beautiful soft yellow and white cap and booties. For those drafty waiting rooms at the doctor's office, they said. A crib blanket was next, she suspected, quickly hidden away when she joined them at one of the patio tables out in the park area.

She suspected things would fall into place. But her heart ached for Ian.

For what he was missing, what she missed without him.

The doorbell interrupted her brooding. Probably one of the ladies with more diaper coupons.

She pasted a smile on her face as she opened the door.

Her smile froze.

"Hello, Vi." Ian's voice was a caress, low, loving. His eyes shone, his cheeks were fleshed out, no longer gaunt. He looked like he'd had a week at Club Med.

She reached up to fluff her hair, until she realized it was piled on top of her head, held in place by an old terry cloth scrunchy.

"What're you doing here?"

She leaned around him, looked left, looked right. The walkway was empty, except one of her ladies peeking around the corner, eyes big as saucers. So now they knew. This was not an immaculate conception.

"I want to take you somewhere."

"Ah, I'm not really dressed to..." She gestured helplessly at her paint spattered denim overalls.

"You look beautiful."

"Well, come in. I'll get my purse."

She was acutely aware that he was checking her out from head to toe. His gaze paused briefly at the basketball wedged between her suspenders, or at least that's what it probably looked like.

"You look great."

He wouldn't take his eyes off her. Wherever she moved, turning off lights, finding her purse, his gaze followed her. Hungry.

"It's Saturday, Ian. Where's Daisy?"

"Daisy's fine." His cheeks dimpled as he grinned from ear to ear.

He stood and held his arms wide, eyes sparkling, dimples calling.

"Come here, Vi. Let me hold you."

She couldn't move. Not if her life depended on it.

"Ian…I don't understand."

Here he was, out of the blue, offering himself to her. No explanation, no time to adjust, nothing. If he only knew how hard it had been, training herself to accept what little he could give. Not to pine for more.

His smile faded when she didn't move. He came to her, wrapped his arms around her, whispered reassurances into her hair.

"I know this is sudden, a surprise. I should've called first. But I just didn't want to waste a second."

She sank into his embrace, allowing herself to believe that he was here, really, physically here.

It was just as she remembered, his scent, the way they fit together. How his arms could make it seem like everything would be fine. He pulled away and looked at her. Just looked.

"Why the goofy grin?"

"It's so great to see you. I mean really *see* you."

Wonderful. She looked like hell and he finally decided to take stock of her.

He leaned forward, his eyelids lowered, ready for a welcoming kiss.

She gave it to him all right. One punch to his very solid bicep. Not hard, but enough to get his attention.

"Hey," he yelped, rubbing his arm. "What was that for?"

"That," she enunciated clearly, "was for dropping out of my life for nearly five months. Worrying me, putting me through hell, all this stuff alone, with a zombie for a husband. Then you show up at my door all bright-eyed and bushy-tailed and expecting to take up where we left off...well, take up where we never were...I mean...I don't know what I mean."

All she knew was that the tight knot of aloneness hadn't gone away the minute he'd walked through the door. There were too many unanswered questions. Too much time being strong, carrying on alone.

Ian let his arms drop, walked over to the chrome bar stools. He pulled one out as if to sit down, then left it there, while he wandered around her apartment.

"I'm sorry. I was so excited, it never occurred to me you might not be glad to see me."

"I *am* glad to see you. It's just a shock. These past few months have been...hard. I developed a routine, a life that doesn't depend on you being here. I had to. Your calls got fewer and further between. You were so...distant when you did call. I forced myself to accept what it meant. That you wouldn't, *couldn't* include us in your life."

He pulled her into his arms, resting his cheek on top of her head. His voice was raw. "I know. And I couldn't see any other way. I'm sorry I put you through that. Sorry for all the time I missed with this little one." He placed his palm on her rounded belly.

The baby did one of its great sea rolls, then elbowed Ian's hand for good measure.

"That…that was the baby?" he whispered.

Violet nodded, blinking back tears.

"Wow."

"Yes. Wow."

"Come with me?"

She nodded again, not trusting her voice. She'd go just about anywhere with him.

THEY PULLED UP alongside the curb in one of the older residential areas: wide sweeping lawns, fifties era ranch homes, tidy sidewalks.

The house was gorgeous, set back from the road. Green, green grass and all sorts of trees—not so common in Phoenix. The spacious home was painted a muted lemon-yellow offset by crisp white trim.

"Why are we here?" Violet asked.

"You'll see." Ian's grin only heightened her curiosity.

He hopped out of the Jeep and came around to help her out, more a necessity than a common courtesy these days.

There was a spring to his step she hadn't seen for a long, long time. A whistled tune floated on the warm breeze. The scent of orange blossoms tickled her nose.

"Hey, wait up. I'm not as fast as I used to be."

Ian waited, swinging his arms back and forth, like he *had* to keep moving.

He grasped her hand, and together they walked up the tidy walkway. She stopped for a moment, entranced by the colors in the flower bed. It bordered the front walkway and flowers spilled everywhere, lush, vibrant. Pinks, purples, every shade imaginable. It contrasted so nicely with the yellow paint.

Ian tugged at her hand, pulling her out of her reverie.

"I'd like to paint this house."

"I'm sure you'll get plenty of opportunity."

That stopped Violet in her tracks.

"Did you buy this house?"

"Nope. Any home we buy, we'll pick out together. This is a friend's place."

Friend? Obviously a close one. The only close friend that she knew about was Vince, and he would never leave Echo Point.

Violet's steps dragged as they got closer to the door, white, with diamond-shaped glass.

Ian knocked.

The door swung inward and out came the biggest woman Violet had ever seen. She towered above, nearly as tall as Ian. Snow-white hair cropped close to her head in an afro and dark, dusky skin. No lines, except for crinkles around her eyes and grooves in her cheeks, when she gave them a big, easy smile.

The woman grabbed Ian in a bear hug and kissed him on both cheeks.

"Ho," Ian grunted. It probably started out as "hello," but got compacted in her hug.

Violet backed up a step as the barge advanced on her. She'd squeeze the baby right out.

"And you must be Violet." She gently grasped Violet's hands in hers. "I've heard a lot about you."

Ian gestured toward the woman. "Vi, this is my very special friend, Marge. She owns this house. You might recognize her—her sister's Zee, the office manager at your doctor's.''

"Ah, yes, I think so."

"And she's a very special friend of Daisy's."

"Come in, honey. We don't want you standing around in this heat."

Marge shepherded her into a lovely entryway. Light and bright, there was an air of peace. Marge exuded it, the walls reflected it.

Violet glanced around the living room. Neat and tidy, very few knickknacks. A beautiful filigreed silver cross on the wall.

"Now, dear, I'll just get you a cool glass of lemonade and some ginger cookies."

"Some for me, too," Ian threw at her retreating back. "Marge makes the best cookies on the whole face of the earth." He patted his abs and sighed, "I must've put on five pounds this week."

"You needed it. I was worried."

Marge bustled into the room, a little crystal plate of cookies balanced on the rims of two long, tall glasses of lemonade.

Hot on her heels came...

"Daisy!" And, "Annabelle?"

CHAPTER EIGHTEEN

VIOLET TENSED out of habit, waiting for the onslaught. Waiting for Daisy to flip out at the very sight of her. But her presence didn't even seem to register with the old woman.

Daisy waved gaily, but her eyes never left the plate of cookies. Neither did Annabelle's.

"Now, Daisy, you rest your skinny little behind over here, and I'll bring you a plate of your own," Marge directed. She winked at Violet. "Saves fighting if they each get their own plate of cookies."

Daisy picked a seat next to Ian on a floral print couch not so different from Violet's.

Marge bustled from the room, only to return almost instantly with Daisy's snack. The big woman moved quickly and quietly.

Daisy gulped her lemonade from a big plastic spill-proof coffee mug. Her arthritic hands had no problem with the large handle. She slurped greedily and shoveled a cookie in her mouth. Then she slipped a piece to Annabelle, sitting at her feet.

"I'll leave you folks to chat. If you need anything, just holler."

"Thank you," Violet murmured.

She couldn't think of a thing to say, just stared at Ian, then Daisy, then back to Ian again. It was like watching a tennis match, only she had no idea of the score.

"How are you Daisy?" Ian asked.

"Good," she mumbled through a mouthful of ginger cookie.

Good? She looked great. Almost like her old self.

"When we finish our snack you can show me and my friend around."

Daisy nodded, birdlike, her eyes bright, clear.

"You?" she asked Ian.

"I'm your friend. I come to visit every day."

She nodded again, satisfied with his explanation.

"Her?"

"Another friend."

Violet finally found her voice. "Daisy, it's good to see you and Annabelle so…happy."

A puzzled frown pulled at the old woman's forehead.

The Lab's tail thumped against the carpet.

"Annabelle. Your beautiful dog."

"Dog. Mine." Her hair, more gray than gold, bounced as she nodded and smiled. It was clean and had been recently brushed.

Annabelle's tail thumped again.

"I can see that. She loves you very much."

"Edward?" Daisy's hand stilled, the last bite of cookie suspended near her mouth.

"He's not here right now," Ian explained.

Violet held her breath.

Daisy nodded, satisfied with his simple explanation.

"Marge and the other house mothers have helped a lot. They know way more than what the books tell you. We deal with whatever reality Mom is in on any particular day.''

"Like make-believe."

"Kind of. Only it's not make-believe for Mom. It's what her brain is telling her is real."

Violet tried to wrap her mind around what Ian was telling her. "So she visits here. Kind of like the center. A day camp kind of thing."

"No, Vi, she lives here."

The world dropped out from under her feet. She glanced at Daisy to gauge her reaction. She didn't appear to have heard them, too intent on getting the last cookie crumbs to stick to her wet index finger.

"B-but we hadn't discussed…this," Violet gestured around her, "lately."

"Bye-bye." Daisy waved at them as she worked her way up off the couch. She and Dog went their merry way, probably in search of more cookies.

"Just give it a chance. Look around, see what it's like. Then we'll talk. Okay?"

"Okay."

He led her through the house, his stride easy, relaxed.

The great room was just that—great. Big screen TV. Lots of firm chairs, a few recliners and another floral print couch. The windows were open, with fresh spring air billowing the white eyelet curtains. Clean. It smelled clean. Not the disinfectant kind, but sheets-on-the-clothesline kind.

To the left, there were card tables set back from the intimate TV grouping. Four gray-haired ladies played cards, while several more watched a popular game show. Daisy was one of them.

"No men?"

"Nope. They have two facilities, one a few blocks over, for the men. This one's for the women. They get together for parties and stuff, but separate dorms puts the brakes on the hanky-panky."

"No hanky-panky," Daisy parroted as she did a graceful modern dance toward them. Nobody even blinked. The TV watchers watched TV, the card players played cards.

"Daisy's a born flirt. She must hate the restrictions," Vi observed.

"Not really." He grasped Daisy's hand as she waltzed by. "There's a dance Saturday night, isn't there?"

Daisy's eyes lit up. "Boys. No hanky-panky."

She wandered off, Annabelle close behind.

Violet folded her arms over her aching chest. "Okay, she *seems* happy enough. But what about when we're not here. I've heard all sorts of horrible stories...."

Ian hugged her close and squeezed.

"No hanky-panky," Daisy chirped as she floated by.

Ian's chest rumbled. Then he threw back his head and laughed.

"A little late for that, isn't it?" he whispered in her ear.

"This isn't funny. I'm worried."

"That's become a habit, hasn't it? Worried about me, about Daisy. Maybe a little worried about the whole motherhood thing. This time I intend to dispense with all those worries. Put a smile back on your face."

How could she process this sudden change and give him what he so obviously wanted—her stamp of approval?

Her ambivalence about the place had to be written all over her face. But Ian didn't seem to notice. None of the little old ladies in the room noticed. But Marge strolled in, wiping her hands on a dish towel.

"Ian, why don't you show Violet the garden?"

"Excellent idea."

They were in collusion against her. She felt like Alice in Wonderland. Like she wasn't sure what was real and what was fantasy.

Ian grasped her by the elbow and propelled her out the door.

And they stepped into paradise.

Vi sucked in a breath.

It had to be the most beautiful garden she'd ever seen. Flowers, all kinds, everywhere. Herbs and vegetables woven in here and there. Hummingbirds zipped back and forth, hovering long enough to sample a bright-red desert poppy here, a yellow bloom over there.

Monarch butterflies fluttered about, all orange and black, drifting on the balmy spring breeze. Smaller, yellow butterflies followed in their wake.

And the scent—it was intoxicating. Wildflowers and orange blossom.

Violet glanced around, searching for the orange trees. They had to be nearby. Sure enough, beyond the garden area were citrus trees scattered here along the emerald lawn. Glossy dark leaves, brilliant white trunks.

Her feet seemed to have minds of their own, leading

her down the red brick path that separated the rectangular planting beds.

Ian strolled beside her. "They grow most of their own fruits and vegetables. The women help in the garden if they want to. I couldn't sleep one night—must've been Tuesday—so I came to see Mom. Just after dawn. Figured I could watch her sleep, or keep her company if she was restless."

"You just dropped in? At dawn?"

"Sure. Marge told me to come any time. There's always someone on duty, even at night. Then there's a guy I met, his mother's in the room next to Daisy's—he works second shift. Sometimes he visits right after work. About three in the morning. Anyway, I came to visit about dawn, and you know where I found Daisy? Sitting out here, watching the sun rise, talking to the flowers. At least I think it was the flowers."

He grasped her hand and led her to a bench—a wooden slat wedged between two square planters.

Violet sighed as her rear hit the wood. Not very comfy, but a welcome relief. She massaged the small of her back, knotted from standing and worrying.

"Okay, so you can drop in any time. That's good. If there's something going on, if they're abusing her, you can catch them. What about Daisy though? You worked so hard to keep her home. You said it was best for her."

Ian's grin faltered. His gaze held hers, honest, solemn.

"Not anymore. Something Vince said made me see that it was time. Said he'd bring the whole Moreno family to take care of her when the baby came. It was no exaggeration. She needs more than just me and Annabelle.''

''I offered—''

''I know you did.'' He glanced sideways at her, his tone serious. ''But I couldn't sacrifice your safety, or the baby's, to make things easier on me.''

Violet blinked to clear the moisture distorting her view. ''You shouldn't have to choose. I wish there were another way.''

''Look, Vi, I've never lied to you and I'm not going to start now. I had some doubts about whether it was the right time. If I didn't have you in my life, I probably would have been bullheaded enough to keep trying.''

Violet's heart sank with sadness. It was what she'd wished for, in a small secret little place in her heart. Wanted him to commit, completely, to building a life with her and their child. But there was another part, the part that loved Daisy like a mother and mourned for her.

Ian put his arm around her shoulders and pulled her close.

''But it wouldn't have been best,'' he whispered. ''Not even for Daisy.''

''She seems happy enough…I guess. You said Zee helped you find this place? What in the world did she have to do with it?''

He didn't answer. Just fingered a strand of her hair and let his gaze wander over her face. It stopped at her lips, and he leaned over and nibbled at her lower lip, then placed a soft, solemn kiss there.

''That's the funny part. After the ultrasound, remember I went to the lobby to wait for you to dress or…whatever?"

"Yes."

"Well, I really kinda went to apologize."

"Apologize? Whatever for?"

His neck flushed, his ears turned red. He rubbed the back of his neck and smiled sheepishly. "I was kinda, well, short with the receptionist. So I went to apologize. Zee was there, and I told 'em a little about why I was so late, why I looked like something the cat dragged in, why I pretty much lost it."

"You? Lost it? You were cool as a cucumber when I saw you."

He chuckled. "Vi, I could have painted my face green and purple and you wouldn't have noticed. You were too busy trying not to explode, remember?"

Violet looked away. "Yes, I remember. That's the deal with this whole pregnancy thing—it's just one humiliating examination or test after another. And the movies…wait till you see the childbirth movies. No dignity at all."

"Hey, we'll get through it together. I'm here now, ready, willing and able."

"Ha. Easy for you to say. So what about Zee?"

"She explained to me about Marge's setup for Alzheimer's patients. Gave me her card. I didn't take it too seriously. Until I got to thinking about what Vince said. About Mom needing a big family. That's kinda what it's like here…a big family."

"Doesn't she…miss you? Her house?"

Ian hesitated. "She has no idea who I am. Sometimes she thinks I'm my dad. Other times, I'm her friend. And the only home she wants is the one we lived in when I was twelve.''

Violet didn't know what to say. His loss was so profound, it was almost like a death. And she knew it must have seemed that way to him.

Squeezing his arm, she said, ''I know it hurts. I know the decision you made wasn't an easy one. But it was a decision made with love.''

Ian looked away, but not before she saw the grief reflected in his eyes. ''It was the hardest thing I've ever had to do. Getting her ready to move, packing up the stuff she needed, I just about died. Then leaving her here, alone, with strangers. I got two blocks away and pulled a U-turn. But then I realized it wouldn't do any good—I'd just prolong the pain.''

''I wish I could have been there for you.''

Ian's arm tightened around her shoulders. His voice was husky. ''I know. But it was something I had to do on my own. I wasn't one hundred percent sure I was doing the right thing. I needed to work through it myself. Marge told me not to come back for two days—it'd help the transition for Daisy. But I think it was really me she thought needed the time to adjust. Then I slept, that afternoon, all night long and until five the next day. It was one of those times when you wake up every once in a while and can't move a muscle, not even to roll over.''

''Oh, Ian, why didn't you tell me? I knew you were exhausted, but I told myself you could get caught up on your sleep when Daisy was at the center.''

''They quit taking her a month ago.''

Violet pulled away to see his face.

"You told me you'd never lie to me. But you did. About the center."

His face flushed, but his gaze was level. "A white lie. I didn't want to worry you. It's not good for you or the baby. If something happened to either of you, I couldn't handle it."

"I'm your wife. It's my job to worry about you. And I can't make good decisions if I'm afraid you're keeping something from me."

Anger vibrated through every cell in her body. "Don't *ever* shut me out again. For any reason."

Ian ran a hand through his hair. "I didn't look at it that way. I guess I've gotten used to doing things myself."

"Maybe. Or maybe you thought you had to be St. Ian one more time. That's not the way a marriage should work."

"Violet, you've gotta believe me, I want our marriage to work more than I've ever wanted anything. I'm willing to learn to be the kind of husband you need."

"I need a husband who will share his life with me and hold nothing back. And know our love is strong enough that we can handle any problem together. Can you tell me you're willing to do that, Ian?"

"I think I can. If you can cut me some slack if I slip up and get all protective once in a while. Can you do that?"

"Maybe," she murmured.

His breath was warm on her face. "Only maybe?"

"Ian, I love you so much it hurts. But I'm almost afraid to believe in us again. Because I don't think I can get through another loss like the last few months without you.''

He cupped her cheek.

She leaned into the warmth of his palm and closed her eyes, afraid of what she might see in his eyes.

''You're stuck with me. And that's a promise.''

Ian's mouth was warm, loving and persuasive as he kissed away all the doubts and insecurities of the past few months.

Violet smiled against his lips. He was hers completely, this man who didn't shy away from tough promises.

EPILOGUE

IAN WATCHED the two stroll barefoot in the orchard, hand in hand.

Violet reached up and snagged a ripe peach. She dusted it off against her shirt and handed it to the little girl with the golden curls.

A chubby, dimpled hand accepted the treat.

Ian's nose tickled, his knees felt weak.

Darn allergies.

He sank to the comfort of the bench, and the fluffy down cushion took the sting out of the drop.

Minutes later, a pudgy hand, juice running past the dimpled wrist, offered him a bite of peach.

"Delicious," he pronounced, as he chewed. Then he made great monster noises and gnawed at the sweet little arm.

His daughter's giggles lit his soul.

He picked her up and deposited her on the cushion next to him. Her big hazel eyes searched his face. "Gramma's bench," she announced.

"It sure is, sweetie."

The little fingers traced the wrought iron filigree, a twin to the floral print cushion—daisies and violets intertwined with big cabbage roses.

"There's Grandma's name." He pointed to the

small, bronze memorial plaque. ''She was a great lady. And she loved you very much.''

''Mmm. Cookies.''

''Yeah. She shared her cookies with you. Your first solid food.''

''Belle?''

''Annabelle was Grandma's dog.'' Ian recited the much-loved story. ''But when Grandma went to be with Jesus, she left Annabelle with us, so we wouldn't be so sad.''

His daughter patted his knee. So in tune with his moods. And his allergies.

She watched her mommy walk toward them, her eyes never leaving Violet's face. Under her breath, she hummed a little tune….

Violet picked up the tune, singing ''I'll bring you a daisy a day, dear….'' She picked up their daughter and twirled her around. The spring sunshine lit their matching smiles. His two flower women.

''SEE YOU NEXT TUESDAY,'' Violet told Marge as she snatched a ginger cookie from the plate.

She lifted Rose from the counter, where she'd been helping Marge count cookies. A daunting task since hands appeared from everywhere to snatch a treat— young ones, wrinkled ones, paint-spattered ones. Even Ian's big paw.

''You be sure to bring Rose with you next time, too. I need some flower women around to keep me on my toes. Zinnia says so.''

Violet's heart squeezed as she gazed at her beautiful little girl. So young, yet so adept at bringing the older folks out of their shells. She had Daisy's sparkle, no doubt about it.

"Thanks, Marge. They did great today. Mabel even dipped her toes in the paint this time. I think she's coming around."

"They look forward to their painting day with Daisy's friend. And those exhibits pay for lots of cookies. I can't thank you enough."

"No need to thank me. I love it. Besides, my paintings are starting to pay for some treats around our place, too. Combined with Ian's new book contract, we need to spread some cookies around."

"That boy's proud as a peacock. So am I. Every time I see his book on the bestseller rack. I tell everyone I know."

"Me, too." Violet smiled as she hoisted Rose on her hip. Two sturdy arms locked around the back of her neck.

"I know one flower girl who needs a bath."

"No. No. No."

"You know you're just like your Grandma Daisy. She hated baths, too." She headed out the door. Rose could probably tell the story as well as she could, she'd heard it so many times.

Violet's heart skipped a beat when she saw Ian leaning against the van. His left shoulder almost touched the bright, blue lettering.

A Daisy A Day Mobile Art Studio.

The scent of orange blossoms tickled her nose as the breeze carried Ian's whistled tune to her ears.

"I'll bring you a daisy a day, dear...."